WHEN THE PONGS GO PING

WHEN THE PONGS GO PING

A gallimaufry of delights

JOHN BOBIN

By the same author

Bark Staving Ronkers (2006)
The Royal Worms (2015)

This book is a work of fiction. In some cases, true-life figures and places are mentioned, but this is for literary purposes only. All other names, characters, places and incidents are products of the writer's imagination or have been used fictitiously and are not to be construed as real. Any resemblance to persons, living or dead, actual events, locales or organizations is entirely coincidental.

ISBN: 1534959998
ISBN 13: 9781534959996

CONTENTS

Chapter 1 The beauties of a rose 1
Man with angry face 2
Chapter 2 The whine seller 9
Try me once 10
Chapter 3 The Lady of the Mourning 16
The last hymn 17
Chapter 4 When the pongs go ping 20
The day of the wreck a Ning 21
Chapter 5 An angel's kiss 30
An angel always lifts the mood 31
Chapter 6 His altar ego 34
Pulpit limelight 35
Chapter 7 High spirits 40
Carousing in the midnight hour 41
Chapter 8 I hate my job 45
Day to day boredom 46
Chapter 9 I think I am a dog 50
Meat and kibble 51
Chapter 10 Dotage doubt age 59
A curry, books and beer 60

Chapter 11	Nosey parker	64
	My eyesight's going rather dim	65
Chapter 12	Senor Momentz	68
	I forget the next line	69
Chapter 13	Light humour	72
	I'm like morse, dot, dot, dashing	73
Chapter 14	Crumpet voluntary	75
	A friendly, happy tart.	76
Chapter 15	Once I was Elvis	84
	I call myself - Big Jed	85
Chapter 16	Inn consequential	93
	A pint, some nuts, a game of darts	94
Chapter 17	Moustache	99
	A touch of grace	100
Chapter 18	The princess and the pee	108
	The servant came	109
Chapter 19	Stinker the drinker	114
	The whole room whirls	115
Chapter 20	Total eclipse of the tune	120
	A million, trillion quavers	121
Chapter 21	Lend me a tenner	128
	Faulty blunderhood	129
Chapter 22	The annals of crime	136
	The search was long and painful	137
Chapter 23	Floyd, flawed and floored	144
	A pugilist like a pugilisn't	145
Chapter 24	The giddy goat	151
	I am a silly, wayward billy	152
Chapter 25	Dial Emma	155
	The right decisions	156
Chapter 26	Gnat King Cole	164
	Nightly jaunts and flits	165

Chapter 27 Al Most-Human 171
I'm tattooed, dyed and pierced 172
Chapter 28 A good egg, no yolk 178
The white stuff isn't quite the same 179
Chapter 29 Old wives' tails 185
Our neck skin sags 186
Chapter 30 Moaning acid 193
I'm serene and quiet and more 194
Chapter 31 Bonkette 199
A squalid place of pleasure 200
Chapter 32 Reigning cats and dogs 206
Dogs are faithful servants 207
Chapter 33 My true love 212
A scent, a touch, a letter 213
Chapter 34 The memory still lingers 218
His coal black pair of eyes 219
Chapter 35 Flim flam 223
Nowt in the attic 224
Chapter 36 Mr. Alucard 231
A red allergy 232
Chapter 37 Is it a poem? 238
They resemble woolly mammoths 239
Chapter 38 Two so-called sisters 245
We love each other well 246
Chapter 39 Delicate Essen 250
She was a dainty lass 251
Chapter 40 No fix, no mend 256
Just like Norman 257
Chapter 41 Eddie de Snake Oil 261
All manner of notions 262
Chapter 42 Quarrelling 267
The onset of a tiff 268

Chapter 43 Des tiny · · · · · 274
No easy ride · · · · · 275
Chapter 44 Word buds · · · · · 279
Phrases fine and sound · · · · · 280
Chapter 45 The door to happiness · · · · · 290
The air is clean, warm is the sun · · · · · 291
Chapter 46 Juan Summer · · · · · 297
It will shine a very special light · · · · · 298
Chapter 47 Olde time dancing · · · · · 306
Latino dances for lovers · · · · · 307
Chapter 48 On tender hooks · · · · · 312
I do want (for me) · · · · · 313
Chapter 49 Bare bear display · · · · · 319
Quite furry 'nuff · · · · · 320
Chapter 50 Fido fidelity · · · · · 324
I am a dog, not a mere cat · · · · · 325

About the author · · · · · 329

DEDICATIONS AND EXPLANATIONS

My two previous offerings were unlike this latest publication. *Bark Staving Ronkers* was published in 2006. The book explored and elaborated upon the first twelve years of my musical experience as a bass guitarist. *The Royal Worms* was unveiled in 2015, and it was a fictional adventure, with elements of fantasy, plenty of jokes and a sprinkling of sex.

I have never written any poetry (except for the first part of this latest tome, which was a juvenile attempt to describe a rose.) I know nothing about the rules of poetry, nor do I intend to try to understand how poetry works. Therefore, each chapter contains an *almost poem,* followed by a loosely related short story.

I dedicate this opuscule to my darling, long-suffering wife, Pauline. She is an absolute gem. I love her dearly, and she supports me in all that I do. I would also like to dedicate *When the pongs go ping* to my late and marvellous mother, my wonderful children, my lovely grandchildren and my beautiful dogs. They have all added immeasurably to life's rich tapestry.

Any money which I make from this book will be donated to Greek Animal Rescue. This is a worthy charity which aims to help the abused, neglected, stray and injured animals of Greece.

Finally, I have to thank a special, dog-walking friend, Bradles, for his awesome cover painting of pongs pinging. It would have been so much harder to visualise if it were pings that were ponging! However, he is a very talented (but modest), artist, and I feel sure he could have painted that if necessary.

Chapter 1

THE BEAUTIES OF A ROSE

The beauties of a rose shine out,
while man with angry face doth pout.
The beauties of the living plant
will soon calm tempers and enchant,
this world of sin and death's too real.
Rabbits scurry from farmers' guns.
And soon all men will see the sun.
In a world of peace and righteousness.

(This fatuous nonsense was written when I was about 11 or so. I seem to run out of steam towards the end of this momentous piece of writing.)

MAN WITH ANGRY FACE

Daisy had never been given flowers before. When you are only just sixteen and are given red roses, you just don't know how to respond. Lionel had paid courteous attention to her whilst they were at St Michael's School, and she had only gradually realised that his polite friendship was an early overture to how their real-life opera would eventually blossom.

Lionel was besotted by Daisy, the ethereal and elegant, young girl who had captured his heart. One look at her pretty face, her dark eyes and her upswept, chestnut hair was enough to have him in love-struck ruins. To be fair, he was quite a catch too. He was athletic and had the lean grace of a muscular tiger. He was also a handsome, young lad, and there was a saturnine darkness about him, which masked his dry sense of humour. The roses came as a complete surprise to Daisy. She was flattered, of course, but still wary about his intentions. Her father had long since laid down the law about the perils of teenage, sexual experimentation.

"I don't want my lovely daughter to be sullied by any macho ape, who thinks she is fair game," she had overheard him saying to her mother.

"But Adam, don't you remember what you were like when we were first together? You just wouldn't say no."

Daisy heard a slap, a scream and stifled sobbing. She knew that her parents no longer saw eye to eye and hoped that this was not an omen for her future with Lionel.

When he came to collect her that evening, she left the house in a hurry, before her father could inspect her face for too much make-up, and her legs for a skirt that was far too short. She had already told Lionel all about the regular fights her parents had, which she had been privy to only by eavesdropping. They acted out their perfect parts in front of her and her younger brother, Will, and nobody who saw them in these roles would ever have suspected the real truth.

However, Daisy knew that her father, Aubrey, was a bully and an aggressive scoundrel who poked, prodded and hit poor Ethel. To make matters worse, he only did so in his cowardly way, behind closed doors. Aubrey had always tried to be the best runner, the best footballer and the best fighter. He had long since ditched his real name, which he thought was too weak, and adopted the nickname Butch.

Occasionally, Daisy's mother would come downstairs in the morning, sporting red eyes and hastily applied concealer. The sketchy foundation cream didn't even begin to conceal her bruises. Daisy hated her dad with a venom that surprised even herself. Lionel, being a gentle and amiable boy and only a few months older than Daisy, had been astounded to learn how bad the situation had become between her parents.

When Daisy returned home a little later, on the very day she had been presented with her first bouquet, she found the house in darkness. Her mum was weeping in the lounge, but she quickly pulled herself together. She was relieved that her son was staying with one of his school friends.

"Is that you, Daisy? Come here immediately," roared her father.

"In a minute, Dad."

"I said now!"

"I won't be long."

"If you know what's good for you, you'll do as you're told."

Daisy traipsed upstairs, in some trepidation. She found her father, waxen-faced and hicupping, in his study. He was slumped on an old sofa. He was in his shirt-sleeves, and his pale green shirt was hanging out of his tweed trousers at the back.

"Give your old dad a kiss."

"Father, I think you've been drinking."

"Too bloody true. That bitch downstairs is enough to drive anybody to drink. She is a frigid, old cow, who wouldn't know real love if she stumbled over it."

"Mind your language, Dad. I don't want to know the sordid details of your love-life, nor do I want to be any part of your rows. She's my lovely mum, and you should treat her with more respect."

Butch staggered to his feet, reeking of alcohol, and he belched ferociously.

"That's better!"

He grabbed Daisy's shoulders roughly and forced her onto the sofa. He took a grubby handkerchief from his pocket, and before she could protest, he had rolled it up and pushed it into her mouth. He took his belt off and lashed her legs, her back and her sides with the heavy, metal buckle. Daisy was crying and frightened.

Butch tied her hands behind her back, with his belt. He leaned over her and breathed whiskey fumes into her face. She was petrified and tried to leave the room. However, her father was several stones heavier than she was, and he easily overpowered poor Daisy. Worse was to come. He undid his flies, pulled down her flimsy panties with force, and he did the unforgivable, that thing no father should ever do to his daughter.

After he had finished, he slumped sideways on the sofa and started snoring. Daisy heard someone coming up the stairs. Lionel stepped into the room and took in the situation without delay. Her mum followed him, and she started sobbing again. Luckily, Lionel took command. As usual, he seemed calm and unflustered, as he stood there in his immaculate, dark blue suit and white shirt.

"Untie Daisy, Mrs. Johnson. I have a job to do."

Ethel removed the belt, which was round Daisy's hands, and took the hankie from her mouth. Daisy and her mother clung to each other in fright. Lionel embraced Daisy tenderly and kissed her on both cheeks.

"Go now. Leave the house and stay in a restaurant in town for at least two hours."

"But Lionel, what are you going to do?" asked Ethel.

"It's best if you don't know."

Ethel looked as if she was going to say something else, but she nodded, took Daisy by the hand, and they left the room together.

Lionel opened Butch's tool box and selected a heavy, claw hammer. After he heard Daisy and her mum go out of the front door, he rained several vicious blows down on Mr. Johnson's head. The resultant blood and gore were contained by the throw which Lionel had removed from the sofa, upon which Daisy had been deflowered by her father. Poetic justice, thought Lionel.

He opened the drawers in the desk, at the bay window, and strewed the contents all over the floor. He also put to one side anything of value. Lionel shoved those items into a rucksack, which he had brought with him when Daisy's mother had phoned him for help, after becoming worried by the sounds coming from her husband's study. She had been much too scared to tackle Aubrey by herself, and she had turned to Lionel for protection. (He had promised to come straight away.)

Lionel moved through the house, doing his best to create visual "proof" that burglars had been at work, but he was doing so quietly and thoroughly. After he had finished his task, he realised that he had been at work for an hour and three quarters. He left the bloodstained hammer in situ, but he dragged the corpse to the top of the stairs and kicked it to the bottom. He made certain he had no blood on his clothes before going downstairs.

Pausing only to shove the body right up to the front door, he did a quick job of opening cupboards and drawers in all the rooms on the ground floor, again only taking away valuable items, which he dropped into the rucksack containing the other items from upstairs. Before leaving the house, he went to the back garden, using the side alley, and he threw the rucksack onto a flower bed by the back door. He smashed a pane of glass in the door, after covering it with his gloves. Lionel reached in and opened the door (which was locked on the inside), and took the key from the lock. He re-inserted the key in the lock, this time on the outside of the door.

Moving quietly and with some speed, he walked along the road and rounded the corner. He circled the block and went back up towards Daisy's home, singing noisily. As he neared the house, he was pleased to see a front door being opened. It was Mrs. Salisbury, Daisy's next door neighbour, who emerged. She pulled her floral housecoat round her withered body, and she huffed.

"Oh it's you, Lionel. You were making such a din!"

"Hey, look Mrs. Salisbury, what's that up against the front door?"

The short-sighted, old lady peered through the glass.

"Oh no! It looks as if Mr. Johnson has fallen downstairs."

"We can't open the door with him up against it. I hope he hasn't hurt himself. Let's try the back door."

They walked round to the back garden and Mrs. Salisbury asked Lionel, "Why is that rucksack on the flower bed?"

Lionel ignored the question and let out a gasp.

"Look, the window in the back door has been smashed from the outside. There's glass all over the kitchen floor. Why is the key on the outside?"

They both went into the house, with Lionel in the lead. He was so grateful for Mrs. Salisbury's innate nosiness. They looked down on Butch Johnson's body with horror, she with real fright, whilst he simulated terror. Butch's head was badly wounded, and a hammer shaft was sticking out of the shattered bone, with the hammer-head still inside his broken skull.

"Oh Lionel, thank goodness you came. But where are Daisy and Ethel?"

"I think Daisy said something about going for a meal in town with her mum. Let's look around quickly, before I ring the police."

Lionel went upstairs, with the inquisitive octogenarian behind him. They looked into the office. Mrs Salisbury said, "All the drawers are open. I bet they took the jewellery and scarpered."

Lionel had taken his mobile phone from his pocket and was ringing the emergency services number.

"Police, please."

"Connecting you now..."

Lionel heard clicks and buzzes.

"Police, how can I help you?"

"There's been a burglary at 34 Sycamore Close, Maundesley. I'm the boyfriend of the girl who lives here. My name is Lionel Collins. I'm here with the lady from next door, and we discovered the situation together. Worse than that, it looks as if Mr. Johnson, my girlfriend's father, is dead. He must have interrupted the burglars."

Lionel closed the call smartly, and he rang Daisy.

"Daisy - Don't say anything, as I have really bad news for you. I'd been out for a jog and decided to take a shortcut home through your street. As I came up the street, Mrs. Salisbury opened her door, and we had a chat. We then noticed that there was something against the front door. Mrs. Salisbury was really helpful," (the old girl nodded), "and she thought your dad might have fallen down the stairs.

"We went round the back, and the glass in the door had been smashed. It looked as if burglars had taken the key out and used it to get into the house. We went inside, and I'm afraid I have to tell you that your dad is dead.

"He's been attacked with a hammer, presumably by a burglar. It seems he (or maybe they), searched for anything worth selling and were interrupted by your dad in his office. He must have tried to follow them, but it looks as if he fell downstairs.

"I've already phoned the police. The burglars have ditched a rucksack in the back garden. Go to my mother's place, and when the police arrive, I'll tell them where you are."

"Oh no! We'll be with your mum."

Luckily, Daisy had heeded Lionel's instruction not to talk, even though her heart was pounding, and she was petrified. She told her mother what Lionel had said, and they left the restaurant shortly thereafter. The waiter grumbled.

"They weren't hungry. Ladies only pick at their food these days."

Lionel's mum was like an old mother hen. She sat them down, made tea and listened to their terrible story, or at least the one which Lionel had made up.

"Daisy, I'm so pleased Lionel showed up by accident."

"Yes, Mrs. Brown, I don't know what we would have done without him."

Chapter 2

THE WHINE SELLER

Come here sonny, let me sell you a moan,
if you need some trouble and strife.
You need me if you're feeling prone,
to happiness and glee or joy.
One for the sorrow, two for the pain,
three for the lost little boy.
Try me once, and you'll need me again.
It's addictive, again and again.

TRY ME ONCE

Stan Williams was a professional whinger. No, that isn't right. He wasn't paid to whinge, but he seemed to enjoy doing so. He complained about everything, almost incessantly. If it wasn't the weather, it was a late bus, an arduous task at work, or some trifling misdeed committed by his patient wife, Muriel.

He was a fastidious man and always wore a black blazer, with a pale blue shirt and a sedate tie. If there were any small stains on his clothes, he discarded them immediately when he came home, and he nagged his wife about any failure of hers to keep his garments spick and span. He kept his hair brutally short, and the stubbly, white hairstyle made him resemble a human, tennis ball.

His features were small, and they were crowded into the middle of his podgy face. His children, colleagues at work and friends, all knew better than to ask him how he was. If they did so, they risked getting a long list of aches and pains, medical symptoms and detailed criticism of the N.H.S.

He played bowls every Tuesday and always said he hated the game. He went to the same pub with Horace Smedley (his oldest friend), every Wednesday. He grumbled about Horace being boring. He also thought the pub was awful and had written to the brewery to complain about the new décor, and he told them that he hated the "deafening" sound system. He particularly loathed the awful, modern music, which blared out from large speakers mounted on each wall in the long bar.

Horace, his carefree pal, liked the pub. He thought the music was fresh and invigorating. He was also pleased that the owners had tarted the place up, and he loved the lilac and green, striped wallpaper, but his pal Stan said it gave him a raging headache. Horace was the antithesis of his moaning mate. He was a happily married man, with wonderful children, beautiful grand-children and a faithful and energetic Border

Collie, which never left his side. He was always jolly, and he even looked like a particularly genial, but slightly younger, Father Christmas.

"That smelly mutt of yours is polluting the atmosphere, Horace."

"Come on Stan, he's just a dog. He's entitled to smell like a dog."

"He leaves black and white hairs all over the place."

"It would be pretty clever if he left red and green hairs on the chairs, wouldn't it?"

Horace laughed. He always looked on the bright side of life. He just couldn't understand why his old chum was such a pessimist.

"The Legion are arranging a trip to St. Malo next month, Stan. Let's go on the coach and have a lovely day out."

"I'd only be seasick, and I bet the coach would break down. The food would be terrible, French muck, and we'd get back after my normal bed time."

Horace shook his head in dismay. They both finished their drinks, said goodbye to the cheerful, young and punky barmaid, and they walked to the street in which they both lived. Horace gave a mock salute to Stan, and he whistled to his dog before taking his leave of his miserable pal.

When Stan entered his house, he could hear the T.V. and recognised one of those dreadful, reality programmes. He shouted to Muriel that he was going up for an early night. Horace, on the other hand, sat with his wife, and they had a convivial discussion about the programme which Stan had deliberately avoided. Horace made some of their favourite drinking chocolate, and after he and his wife had drained the last vestiges from their china mugs (with dogs on the front and back), they mounted the stairs. Muriel asked him how his drink had been with Stan.

"Oh well, you know how he is. Nothing's ever right. Tonight, he pontificated about the usual subjects, plus how he would run the government and why ladies should never have tattoos."

"I don't know why you bother with him. He will wear you down eventually."

She kissed her spouse and rolled over. He put his arm round her, and they assumed their traditional, spoon positions. Before too long there was a loud, yet delightful and harmonious, evidence of their deep sleep. At about four in the morning, there was a sharp knock on the front door. Horace looked over at his wife and saw that she was still fast asleep. He edged out of the covers, and he put his checked slippers on and his soft, warm dressing gown, which had been a present from his eldest daughter, Patsy.

By the time he reached the door, he was beginning to wonder if he had imagined the curt summons. He turned the handle and inched the door open. Outside in the open porch, there was a tall and stately man, with steel-grey hair, wearing a light-beige, Humphrey Bogart type trench-coat. He was clutching a leather, attaché case.

"Mr. Smedley? I'm so sorry to bother you, but I must speak to you on a matter of the utmost importance. It's been reported to the people for whom I work, that you are much too happy. I need to explain the problems this might cause, and I want to offer you an ideal path to what we believe is a more balanced view of life."

Horace was taken aback. Normally, he would never let any salesmen enter his house without an appointment, but this gentleman seemed to be polite and genuine. The caller produced an embossed, photo ID card proving that he, Donald McAbre, worked for the Ministry of Doom and Gloom. Much against Horace's better judgement, he let Mr. McAbre in, and he took him to the front room.

"Would you like a cup of tea?"

"Oh, no thanks. That would make me far too relaxed."

The distinguished looking fellow opened his attaché case and removed a pack of glossy pamphlets. Horace could see the titles of a few of them:

You need some trouble and strife.
Too much glee.
Moaning is addictive.

"It's come to our notice that you never, ever moan and that you are always cheerful. Do you realise that this places an incredible strain on the area of your brain which handles normal reactions to happiness?"

"I've never heard of that. I always thought that a cheerful disposition was good for you."

"Our research boffins have discovered that there is a small part of the brain called the Nonecstatimus. This helps to regulate pleasurable sensations. Over stimulation caused by happy events (and even pleasant, relaxed situations), can wear this part of the brain out. If that happens the brain then fails to recognise the very stimuli which have caused the melt-down, and the end result could be to render the patient insensible to any normal emotions."

"So, why did you come to me at this unearthly hour?"

"This is about the time that the Nonecstatimus rests and recharges itself, and it readies itself for another day of intense glee."

"What are you proposing Mr. McAbre? Do you have any concrete suggestions?"

"Oh yes, we run counselling groups every Wednesday at the Town Hall - in Room 15, which is on the second floor. We'd very much like to see you at the meeting next week at 10:00 am."

"I'm not at all certain I'd benefit from this kind of group. What do you have to do?"

"At first, you just listen to the experiences being recounted by the other members of the group. You can have a cup of tea and a biscuit, whilst you hear what they have to say. If at the end of all that, you wish to share your problems with them, you just stand up and say, "I'm Horace, and I am prone to happiness and glee and joy."

"You can share with them the way that you are thinking, and they will discuss it with you. There are twelve steps in the Doom and Gloom programme, and the first is to admit that you are powerless over happiness."

"But that sounds like the A.A. Twelve Step programme."

"That's right. It's been so successful for them, that we at D. and G. (sorry - Doom and Gloom), have adopted their philosophy for our re-training. Please read the papers I gave you and come along for a chat."

Mr. McAbre picked up his case, stood up swiftly and nodded to Horace.

After the caller had left, Horace went back to bed quietly, so as not to disturb his wife. In the morning, he told Muriel about his visitor, and he explained the proposal which he had made to him, about attending the group therapy session. To his surprise, his wife said, "I think that's a good idea. I do love you, but your incessant, good humour can be really wearing. Maybe you should learn how to tone down all that jollity."

All day long, Horace mulled this problem over. In the end, he decided that it couldn't hurt to attend just one session. Consequently, he turned up at the Town Hall the following Wednesday morning, as suggested by the man from "D. and G."

He found the room after searching carefully. He had expected a largish, meeting room, but the door opened onto a tiny annexe, with an old, metal filing cabinet, and he saw a dusty desk pushed against one of the walls. On the desk there was a long, slim envelope addressed to *Horace Smedley Esquire*. He opened it warily. Inside there was a two-page document. The first page started:

To the party of the first part, Horace Smedley, and on behalf of the party of the second part, Donald McAbre, an offer is hereby made for the party of the first part to attend rehabilitation counselling sessions, in order to retrain his Nonecstatimus, for the purpose of exacerbating the deliverance of a levelling flow of sensations, made up in equal parts of those feelings in relation to happiness and joy, and those pertaining to doom, gloom and despair.

There was much more of this verbosity than it is necessary to quote in full, but by now you will understand that this looked, to all intents and purposes, like an official offer. Reaching the end of the first page, Horace looked at the next page, and this is what he saw written on page two.

The party of the second part would now like to reassure the party of the first part that this legal offer is made purely in the spirit which is appropriate for the date upon which it has been delivered – April Fool.

Horace looked at the date on his watch, and – yes, it was 1st April. There was a knock at the door, and Stan and Muriel peeped round at their friend and husband respectively. They both started laughing, and Horace shouted at them, "You've made me look a proper fool."

He suddenly realised that this was the first time he had been angry for many years.

"Be careful Horace. You might damage your Nonecstatimus!" said his giggling wife.

Chapter 3

THE LADY OF THE MOURNING

I'm fair and tall but gaunt and grim,
and I come when the end is near.
When they gather round and sing the last hymn,
I am present to ease your fear.
As you pass from this world to the next,
it is I, who holds your trembling hand.
From the woe and sorry, when you've been vexed,
to the far off Promised Land.

THE LAST HYMN

The congregation had been well behaved, and it was now time to say their last farewell to Doris Delaney. The vicar had read the eulogy with hardly any mistakes, which is apparently quite unusual. Doris had chosen her own music for the funeral service, and the organist struck up *Jerusalem,* in a suitably restrained way. With some shuffling and coughing, the attendees to the service started to sing, mutter or mime the words of the well-known piece of music

The Funeral Director came to the front of the chapel, and he faced the coffin (which was already placed on supporting rails, on its way to oblivion in the furnace), and he bowed politely in the direction of the polished, oak receptacle for Mrs. Delaney's remains.

Unbeknown to him, Doris stood right next to the undertaker. She had been pleased to find that she no longer had to choose what to wear, after her death. The long, white gown which was now her customary garb, was beautifully cut, and she felt quite happy, even though she was definitely as dead as a dodo.

Whoever had decided how her hair should be dressed, was a master at après-death, tonsorial arrangements. Her stylish, ash-blonde chignon complemented her well-cut gown, and the understated make-up had been applied perfectly. She tried to tickle the undertaker, but every time she put her hand near him it went straight through his body and out the other side.

She had been trying to communicate with her friends and relatives ever since she had died, but they had not been able to hear her, nor could they see her. Her dog had recognised her immediately, and he had sat next to his mistress on her aged sofa, every night for the last fourteen nights. Doris had been introduced to several other people who were waiting to go to the Promised Land, but none of them could tell her what might happen next, nor when she might be allowed to travel to her ultimate destination.

"Ashes to ashes," she croaked, "might just as well be sausages to sausages."

She was startled to find a tall and beautiful lady standing next to her.

"I know this is frustrating, dear, but the mourners like all that kind of thing. It makes them feel better."

Doris studied her companion more closely. She was a little on the grim side, but she was graceful and tall, and she looked like an elderly, but still lovely, ballet-dancer.

"And who might you be?"

"I am The Lady of the Mourning. You may be frightened, and it's my task to reassure you and to hold you steady, as you go to your maker."

"Is this really the end then?"

"Oh no, this is just the beginning. You will find that your days here have been as nothing, compared to the next place in which you will find yourself."

Doris spoke again, and she was surprised to find that her croaking had been transmuted into a melodious tone, which would not have been out of place for a young mezzo-soprano. She turned and faced the window behind the vicar, and he seemed totally unaware that she was near him. Moreover, she could only see a pretty, young girl reflected in the window, and her guide was not reflected in the glass at all.

"Who's that lovely girl, and why are we not reflected in the glass?"

"My dear, the young lady is you. I no longer have a reflection. Actually, neither do you, but we wanted to show you how you might look to the spiritual denizens, on the other side."

"Oh gosh! I'm frightened now. Will our journey be long?"

"My dear, you must take my hand and walk towards the crucifix."

"But what will happen then?"

"You'll soon find out. Walk slowly and quietly."

It is not known what happened next and never will be, until you are ready to make the same journey. Even then, you will not be able to forewarn your friends and relatives about their own post-demise travel.

Doris tried to reassure her daughter, and she talked to her for hours. However, Sheila couldn't hear her mother speaking and was oblivious to her presence. Doris made do with changing the T.V. channel repeatedly, and she did so with no obvious rhyme nor reason.

"We must get this fixed. Mum would have been furious if she missed her favourite programmes."

Sheila fondly imagined she could hear her mum laughing

Chapter 4

WHEN THE PONGS GO PING

"Be careful today," said Thomas Ning,
"You're in danger, so be very wary.
If you're scared, try a smile and a bit of a song - sing!
You must be very chairy.
Today is a day when the pongs go ping,
and the world goes from verse to worse.
Or just go to bed, ring a bell - ding a ling
Come the day of the wreck a Ning."

THE DAY OF THE WRECK A NING

Thomas Ning was a lovely man, with a gentle nature and an engagingly absent-minded approach to his appearance. He often appeared in outfits which looked as if they had been personally selected by Helena Bonham Carter, with her joyous disregard for colour matching, and her outlandish talent for wearing different articles of apparel which definitely don't match.

He had eyebrows like dark, woolly caterpillars and an impressive amount of brown hair, resembling a super toupée which perched precariously on his head. He was rather prone to wrinkles, but he often said that he would be the supreme, world champion in any Laughter Lines contest.

He prided himself on being a protective, loving and kindly father. His family had grown at an alarming rate, and his friends all joked that he might one day discover what was causing his burgeoning brood. They thought that might stop him adding a new Ninglet to the family every year. At the last count, he had twelve offspring - three boys and nine girls. They were all sweet and friendly and had inherited their father's lenient and easy-going nature. That was just as well, because their mother was a bitter harridan.

She nagged poor Thomas morning, noon and night. It's a well-known fact that women who complain all the time, end up with a face resembling a smacked arse, and she was surely no exception. She spent her life looking at things which, to her mind, were a complete disgrace, and she often pursed her puckered lips, ready to explain observed deficiencies in long and vituperative detail. Being the kind of chap that he was, he let all of this bitter recrimination and vociferous criticism go in one ear and out of the other.

He usually went into another room when the tirade started and picked up a guitar. He sat strumming his beloved, old, acoustic instrument and composed wistful ditties, which he never played anywhere else other than in his tiny den. His prized possessions were all in this small room. His awful wife, a leaden and lumbering beast, called Mildred, never entered his inner sanctum.

She hated his framed pictures of bygone, movie and musical stars, his classical books and his small collection of amber pieces from the beach at Southwold, which he fondly imagined looked like cats and dogs. (He was wrong.)

One day, in the spring of 1967, Thomas wrote a simple but humorous effort called *When the pongs go ping*. He sang it to himself and laughed. It didn't take much to amuse him, and he decided, apart from being lumbered with his hateful but productive wife, life was good. He had tried to name his children in alphabetical order, so he could remember their names and respective ages. He often recited these details to himself:

Alice – girl
Bertie – boy
Clarissa – girl
David – boy
Ellis – boy
Francesca – girl
Grace – girl
Helena – girl
Iona – girl
Jessica – girl
Kim – girl
Lucille – girl

He always added the gender to help him remember what they looked like. He knew that fathers are not supposed to have favourites, but Alice was the one whom he loved the most. She was always sunny and amiable and had a natural grace that his fourth daughter, actually called Grace, did not possess.

The Nings lived in an old and dingy, Edwardian manse, which had gone to rack and ruin. Thomas was an unambitious sales rep. It has to be admitted that he was not a successful commercial traveller. His territory was much too large, comprising all of the Home Counties. Thomas sold paper, cardboard and general office supplies, working for a small company, which was struggling to make ends meet. He was often away for days on end, staying in tatty, bed and breakfast establishments, or he sometimes slept in his car. He had to do this when he was especially devoid of funds.

One morning, at the tail end of 1979, he packed his samples in his dilapidated estate-car, toted his case out to the front garden, and he lined up all of his progeniture for a farewell kiss, followed by a paternal hug.

He waved at them as he left his house in Upper Wissenden, in order to try to sell more products. He had been told by his boss, the previous week, that if his performance did not improve, the firm would be forced to dispense with his services.

He looked at his reflection in the rear view mirror, before he switched on the car engine. He had bags under his eyes - and yet more bags under those. He had dark rings all round said peepers, and his face was riven with deep wrinkles. He always maintained that he was proud of those lines; he believed they showed how often he smiled and laughed. In truth he was no oil painting, but he still had that shock of hair which many a younger man would be proud of. Thomas was fifty-five (or forty-fifteen, as he liked to say.)

His wife never came out to say goodbye. The only things which she liked about Thomas were his ability to satisfy her sexually, and the closely related way in which he could help her to produce more and more Ninglets.

Mildred was younger than Thomas, at forty-one, but she was a raddled wreck. Her septic character had made her look as bitter as she sounded. Her hair was frizzy and thin. Her eyes were bleak and glassy. Her constant harping on about Thomas' faults (and those of all who knew her), had gradually worn out all of her friends and relatives, and her social circle was correspondingly tiny, and dwindling. With each falling out with her chums, family members and shop assistants, she found another example of how everything that went wrong was somebody else's fault.

Her children had learned never to disagree with her, but they all knew that their sainted father had to put up with long lists of his misdeeds, or deeds which should have been done, but which he had not completed or in some cases, not even started. Alice had tried to make the peace, bless her. This hadn't worked, and her father had advised her just to continue in mock agreement with everything Mildred said.

Thomas was thinking this over, as he drove over a hundred miles, to his first appointment. When he walked into Frederick Walker and Son's office in Little Staunton, he stopped and stared at the lady who was sitting behind the reception desk. She was a handsome woman indeed. She had dark brown, glossy hair, large and luminous, golden eyes and a wide smile which showed her warm personality.

There was an immediate frisson of animal magnetism between them, and Thomas was astounded. In all of his married life, he had never paid attention to any other woman but Mildred. In spite of this, he had now decided that if he was given the slightest encouragement by the receptionist, he would definitely throw caution to the winds. He had to have this woman, and it looked as if she wanted to encourage him.

"Good morning, Mr. Ning," she said, after looking at his business card. "I'm afraid that Mr. Walker and his son have both been called out for urgent appointments, at the golf club. They said thanks for coming, but they have decided to close your account."

Thomas sat down, all of a sudden. This would be the last nail in his coffin for his employment at his firm, Quality Stationery Essentials. He feared that he would be for the high jump when he returned, even if he had more success with other calls. The Walker account was his largest, in a small and ever decreasing portfolio, and it was the source of almost seventy-five per cent of his generated revenue. He hoped he wouldn't cry, but he had to wipe away several large tear drops.

The lady behind the counter was quickly in front of it, and she cradled Thomas' head in her capacious bosom. Thomas felt her arms encircling him, and he could smell her delicate fragrance - Lily of the Valley. He happily kept his head where it was for five, comfortable and blissfully reassuring minutes. As he extricated himself reluctantly from her warm embrace, he said, "You're so kind. I'm really not used to attractive ladies being so friendly with me."

"Thomas - if I may call you that, my predecessor has told me all about you - how kind and thoughtful you are, and how you have a large and lovely family."

Without even thinking, Thomas started to tell her about Mildred and the way that she spoke to him. He also found himself trying to make excuses for his horrid spouse, but these were not convincing. The receptionist interjected.

"Thomas, my name is Eleanor, and I was just going to shut up shop. I intended to play hookey this afternoon, as the big boss and little boss are probably at the nineteenth hole by now. Once they do that, they never come back. Why not come to my flat, and I'll make you a light lunch. Do you like omelettes? Or, we could go to a pub."

"Eleanor, I think I would like slugs on toast if they were made by you."

Eleanor laughed - a sound like delicate, crystal chandeliers blowing in a slight breeze. She shrugged on a red, patterned coat, asked him to follow her out and pulled the door shut on its Yale lock. She double-locked the door, took his arm and led him onto the main street of the town.

"Your choice - pub or flat?"

"Flat – definitely," said Thomas.

The flat was small but immaculately clean. Everything was in its proper place, just like its owner. The furniture was tatty, but comfortable, and her home was welcoming. Eleanor produced a light and fluffy omelette, which they shared, and it was accompanied by a mixed salad and chilled, white wine.

After the meal, she sat very close to him on the sagging settee, and then she moved even closer. Thomas didn't know what to do, nor quite what was expected of him.

"I think I'm a little sozzled," said Eleanor.

"Me too. Perhaps I should be going."

Eleanor pulled Thomas' head closer, and he felt her soft, luscious lips parting beneath his. He hoped he would be what she was expecting. They kissed and cuddled for some time, and finally she stood up and pulled him into another room. Thomas looked around, and he was pleased to find himself in her bedroom. However, he was shaking and just a little frightened.

She soon made him feel at home, and as one thing led to another, they became more abandoned. Finally, the sumptuous adventure was over. Thomas held Eleanor tight, and he wondered what to say. Eleanor held Thomas tight too, and she had similar thoughts.

Thomas said, "Eleanor, you are so perfect. But what happens now?"

"That depends entirely on you. You made no promises, and I did lead you on. I've never done anything like that before. I was married once, but we decided to part on good terms, before things got worse. We went our separate ways, four years ago, and I haven't had any relationships with other men since then. The minute I saw you though, I knew that if you wanted me, you were the one."

"Darling Eleanor, I need you now and forever, even though we have only just met. I just know that every time I see you, that fire will burn even brighter."

Eleanor silenced him by reaching for his hand, which she placed on one of her perfect breasts.

"Can you feel my heart beating?"

The afternoon passed quickly, and Thomas surprised himself with his renewed stamina and inventiveness. He used her phone to call his boss, and he explained about the cancelled account.

"Where have you been, since just before lunchtime? You are an incompetent nincompoop."

"I've been studying my portfolio, in order to decide how to make up for the reduced income."

"I want you here at nine o'clock sharp on Monday, so we can discuss your future."

Thomas put the phone down, none too gently.

He and Eleanor spent the whole of the weekend in bed. They had occasional breaks for tea, accompanied by peanut butter on toast, and their love-making became even more joyous, during an extremely passionate Saturday and Sunday. Thomas phoned his home, on the Saturday morning, and he made weak excuses to Mildred, about scouting for new business, to explain why he had not returned.

She wasn't surprised he had lost yet another account, and what about his promise to clean the rabbit out, and wasn't he a useless provider, with cotton wool for brains, and don't bother coming back until you've got some more customers, and what about me and your poor, destitute children...Thomas hung up on her. It felt mighty good, too.

He got up early on the Monday. He shaved, showered and breakfasted and made his weary way straight back to his employer's office. Mr.

Wilberforce glowered at him over his large, metal desk and asked for an explanation.

"Well, my explanation is this. I've always done my best for the firm. You gave me poor leads, and you assigned accounts which were already in a terrible state (often with clients who were on the brink of bankruptcy.) If I had done something wrong I would have admitted it, but I haven't."

Wilberforce was going red in the face. He could no longer contain his rage.

"Get out! I never want to see you again. Take all of your belongings from your desk, and be assured that you'll never work for us, nor for any other similar firm in the future."

Thomas felt an unbelievable calm coming over him.

"Thank you so much, sir. It would be awful to have to continue to work for you for one minute longer. Also, any company which listened to a malicious warning-off from a horrible person like you, would be a company for which I would not wish to work. Good day to you."

Thomas stood up, nodded at the astounded man, and he went out of the door, before he said anything worse. He got back in his rusty car and drove home. When he reached the door he found a policeman standing in the porch.

"Mr. Ning?"

"That is I," said Thomas, very correctly.

"I have some bad news for you. Your wife was found dead, early on Sunday morning. She was in her bed. The cause of death is still unknown, although it is likely that she had a fit brought on by an argument with one of your daughters."

He consulted his notebook and continued before Thomas had a chance to say anything.

"Your daughter, Alice, says she had to give your wife the bad news on Saturday evening, that she is pregnant. The father is a man called Laurence Stone, who may be known to you."

"Yes, of course I know him. He's Alice's fiancée, and a fine young man. He's honest and hardworking and has a good job. They're getting married in the spring."

"Well, it appears that Alice told your wife, that they would now be bringing the marriage forward and that a simple registry office wedding would be planned, to take place shortly. Mrs. Ning was not best pleased and started to rant and rave. (That's how Alice put it.)

"Your daughter tried to pacify her, but she became incandescent with rage, and threatened Alice with physical violence. After a while, she decided to leave your wife to it, and Mildred went upstairs to bed. It was only in the morning that Alice found her, ahem, stone cold and beyond help."

Thomas now saw Alice behind the police officer. She was standing at the end of the hall. He rushed past the P.C. and embraced his favourite daughter.

"The others are next door. I thought that would be best. Oh, Daddy, what have I done?"

"Alice, my little angel, none of this was your fault. Your mum was always heading for disaster. She was angry and het up all of the time."

Alice squeezed her father's hand.

"We tried to reach you, but we had no success. Even early this morning, there was no answer at your firm's office."

Thomas passed a weary hand over his eyes. This would take a good deal of explaining.

Chapter 5

AN ANGEL'S KISS

Today, an angel kissed my cheek.
I felt her butterfly caress.
It was nothing that I sought, or seek,
but I loved her, nonetheless.
Her breath felt warm,
like a small puppy's skin.
With the power to save and soothe.
No matter what, the state you're in,
an angel always lifts the mood.

AN ANGEL ALWAYS LIFTS THE MOOD

Derek could never remember quite when it was, that his personal angel first made herself known to him. For some time before that, he had been hearing musical laughter and tiny footsteps throughout his house, which was an ordinary, pebble-dashed, two up, two down, terraced home, in a small back street of Fosbury-on-Sea.

His hearing had been on the wane for a long time, due to his playing in a heavy rock band. They called themselves The Fosbury Giants of Rock. The doctor and the audiologist at the hospital had both blamed his loss of high-frequencies on loud guitars, or possibly the bells of cymbals. He also had tinnitus, and at first he ascribed the laughter and footsteps to the ringing in his ears. If that was the case, he thought - bring it on.

He was getting ready for one of their rehearsals, at a damp and poorly decorated studio, when he heard the footsteps again and thought he saw something out of the corner of his eye. He turned round quickly, and was flabbergasted to see a small, fairylike figure, perched on the worktop in his kitchen. The figure seemed to be a tiny lady, of no more than eighteen inches in height.

She was absolutely delightful, with long, blonde ringlets and pale blue eyes, with a dark blue ring around each of her irises. She was clothed in what looked like a muslin dress, and she had pointed, open-toed sandals on her perfectly formed feet. As Derek looked at her, she unfolded a pair of large, feathery wings, and she waggled them backwards and forwards.

"That's better. They sometimes stick together if they're not unfolded regularly. I didn't mean to let you see me, but who cares? You look like a nice man. I'm Elise, and I'm your personal angel."

Derek closed his eyes, and opened them again. Elise was still there. He couldn't believe what he was seeing.

"What do you mean, my personal angel?"

"Everybody has one. Sometimes they appear like this, and at other times as an animal - perhaps a Labrador. Haven't you ever wondered why people have instantaneous connections with young puppies? They are often trainee angels."

"Is someone having a laugh at my expense?"

"No. Just try to pick me up and see what happens."

Derek reached over obediently. He put his hand out, and he couldn't feel Elise's wings, even though his hand was now touching the wall behind her.

She laughed prettily and said, "There you are. I am here in vision, but I'm elsewhere physically."

"Are angels physical?"

"Of course. I'm physical somewhere else, too. There, they can feel me as well as seeing me. And don't forget those puppies. They can be felt. Not all puppies are like me, but the ones that are angels can be felt and seen here, as a special dispensation from Algernon, who is the chief angel."

"Why have you come to see me?"

"We know about your oncoming deafness and your tinnitus. I needed to help you through, what must sometimes seem, a worrying and dark time to sufferers."

"Elise, the main thing that worries me is that I may have to give up playing my beautiful Fender Stratocaster."

"Derek, remember that it's just a guitar. There are lots of guitars and not everybody even likes that make. Some people like Gibsons better."

"How does an angel know about guitars?"

"We know everything. Right now, you think you must be seeing things, and I bet you're still not certain I'm really here. Try me out. Think of something that I couldn't possibly predict, and I will tell you what it is."

Derek decided to think about a cat, a dog and a pig playing darts.

"Are you ready?" said Elise "I see a black cat, a poodle and a fat, pink pig all playing darts in, what I believe, is called a tavern."

Derek was amazed. Elise had told him exactly what he had imagined.

"So, what happens now, Elise? How can you reassure me about my hearing?"

Elise took off from the worktop, hovered in mid-air and placed a hand on his forehead. Derek was surprised he was able to feel her cool, little fingers on his brow, but he made no attempt to grab her. She leaned towards him and kissed his cheek.

As she did so, he realised that he could still play guitar, that he had friends with whom he loved to joke and laugh, and he knew that all was not lost. He also had a strange desire to paint a picture.

He was just about to mention this to Elise, but she disappeared, fading little by little, tinkling with laughter as she did so. Derek went to an art shop, that afternoon. He bought some paper, watercolours and brushes. He rushed home and painted his first offering, *An Angel's Kiss*.

Over the years, he was to become a famous and proficient painter. He was popular and sold many of his works, although some said his best effort by far, was his first painting.

Chapter 6

HIS ALTAR EGO

Our new vicar, he's a card.
He loves his pulpit limelight.
He finds the speaking not so hard.
His sermons are his highlight.
He loves his stardom up on high.
Drones on and on, forever.
The curate never gets to try.
His cap's without a feather.

PULPIT LIMELIGHT

The new vicar was depressingly Tiggerish. He was bright, bouncy and affable, and on a scale of rumbustiousness of one to ten, he was a definite twelve. He was good looking, well-spoken, charming and eloquent. Even his name was respectable, David Squires.

He had been to university in Oxford; then he had worked as an English teacher in Staffordshire for seven years. After that, he had been to a theological college in Worcester, before being ordained as a vicar in the almighty Church of England. His curate hated him on sight, but immediately felt guilty. He made his mind up to forgive himself, as his first act of penance that week.

Jeremy Wibble was not a confident man. Who could be confident, with a name like Jeremy Wibble? The members of the choir all called him Wobbly Wibbley, and there was some justification for this unflattering nick-name. He was indeed wobbly. He changed his opinions according to whom he was speaking, and he was also wobbly because of a passion for jam doughnuts, coupled with a vehement dislike of exercise.

Furthermore, he had a certain wobbliness in the way he dressed, with his usual attire resembling a pile of clothes heaped on top of a shambling, human frame. He was a gingery kind of fellow, with hair, freckles and eyebrows to match, but in spite of this description, his appearance was likeable, and he was an all-round good egg.

Jeremy soon learned that David Squires was a skilled and fit rugby player, and he had been an Oxford blue oarsman. The ladies who looked after the flowers and refreshments after services, fluttered round him like thirsty bees seeking nectar from a new flower in the neighbourhood.

Wobbly Wibbley had held the fort during the twelve weeks between the cessation of tenure, due to the sudden death by a massive stroke, of the previous vicar, Lansdowne Fernley-Green, and the starting date for the new incumbent.

Old Fernley-Green was as uppity as his name might have led you to expect, but he had a certain dignity, and despite what he termed his "short sermons" being anything but brief, he had a reasonable following in St. Nicholas' the Less church. His unfortunate demise, (Is there ever a fortunate demise?), had created a vacancy for a fully qualified vicar, and David Squires had applied, been interviewed, and had taken the position quickly.

He qualified his availability, by explaining that he had already agreed to spend three months in Outer Mazutoland, in deepest, darkest Africa, helping to build wells for fresh water, having raised the bulk of the money by sky-diving, marathons and other praiseworthy, sponsored events.

Bishop Rook thought that there was no way that he could force the issue regarding an early start, and he had consoled himself by feeling that Jeremy could not do any real harm in the interim, even if his speaking style was bland and boring. Jeremy had been excited to undertake the duties offered to him, as a kind of stop-gap vicar.

He had desperately tried to compose interesting and witty sermons, with hard-hitting messages, but many of the parishioners fell asleep during his services. Obadiah Dobson, the small town's best butcher, had a deep and rumbling, nay stentorian, basso profundo way of announcing to the world, that he was snoozing. The ladies who later fluttered round the new vicar, made much sweeter, gentle, buzzing sounds, when they dozed during Jeremy's wandering sermons.

When he returned from Africa, David called a special meeting of the Church Council, and he set up a laptop with a large screen connected to it, so he could show boastful videos of his heroic work in Outer Mazutoland. He bounced in and immediately started to throw out inspirational and evangelical comments.

He made Jeremy's head ache, with his buzzword-loaded, linguistically challenging, verbal torrents. However, there were many nods and smiles, and when he directly addressed Mrs. Pinkney, she of the Parma Violets and lavender scented everything, the good lady pinkneyed up nicely, under the warmth of his gushing and infra-red style.

The videos showed David, working with the villagers, teaching them basic English, digging wells and planning everything perfectly. He even took the time and effort to thank Jeremy Wobble for looking after things "so admirably," pending his arrival. (Yes - he said Wobble. Who knows? This may have been a mistake.) When he did so, there was one of those famous, muffled titters, which we used to read about frequently, but which now seem to be almost extinct.

Over the next few weeks he proved himself to be (if not quite the saviour of the human race), a good supporter of He who has a much better claim to that soubriquet. The services became well attended. Meetings of the scouts, cubs, guides and brownies were full to the brim, and all of the other activities run by the church (whether already in place, or introduced by the incoming vicar), were a terrific success.

Offerings collected after services (and other donations), increased, and the bishop made several visits to gaze admiringly at David Squires, in the pulpit. When he did so, David sermonised in tribute to his boss, in a flattering style which was much more like that of said Bishop Rook, than his own. Things were getting just a touch too wonderful for Wobbly Wibbley.

One warm, July day, Jeremy was sitting on a bench in the churchyard. He noticed that a young, black girl, of about sixteen or seventeen, had disembarked from the bus which connected, sporadically and infrequently, with the railway station at Little Andoften. She looked around warily and noticed Mr. Wibble. Now Wibble was, and still is, a respectable looking cove, and therefore she made her way to him.

"Good day, sir," she said in a charmingly correct, but old-fashioned manner.

"Hallo, young lady. What can I do for you?"

"I am looking for the Reverend David Squires. I met him at my own township, in Outer Mazutoland. He taught me at school and helped us to build wells."

"My goodness, he'll be delighted to see you. What's your name, and how do you come to be here?"

"I am Jalimba Motingo, and I have been offered the chance to work as a maid, in Great Andoften. This happened out of the purple (Wibble forgave her tiny, but beguiling, mistake), when a missionary visited us. He knows Lady Grosvenor of Grosvenor Towers, which I have been told is just outside Great Andoften.

"Lady Grosvenor had mentioned to the missionary, a little while before he came to see us, that it would be good to take on a villager from Africa if she was prepared to learn how to be a courteous, lady's maid.

"To break a long story short (Another lovely turn of phrase, thought Wibble), here I am after a long and tiring journey."

Jeremy stood up, shook her by the hand, and he ushered her onto the path that led to the vicarage. When he reached Squires' front door, he rang the bell and waited with her. The vicar opened the door, and he blanched noticeably when he saw Jalimba at the door.

"How wonderful to see you, Jalimba. Have you interrupted your journey specially to see us?"

"Oh no, Mr. Squires, I will be living at Grosvenor Towers, so you will see a lot of me!"

"That's really good news, Jalimba," said the vicar, but his enthusiasm was not exactly convincing.

Jeremy, doffed his panama to Jalimba, whom he had to admit was a perfect specimen of young ladyship. She was lovely to be with, pleasant, polite and friendly. He walked back down the path, and as he went past the vicar's study window he caught a snatch of conversation.

He tried to pretend to himself that he had not done that deliberately, but this was to no avail. The vicar was speaking very quietly, but he said something like, "…pregnant? Who is the father? ...are you sure? …surely you cannot be serious? ….we hardly know each other and…"

At this promising juncture, the window to the study was slammed shut. Oh yes, thought Wibble. What a result! David Squires has been caught with his sanctimonious breeches down. He went back to his humble flat, over the greengrocer's shop, and he started to dial Bishop Rook's private number, which he had given to Wibble, just in case he needed advice whilst looking after the church, until the new vicar arrived.

"Good afternoon, Bishop Rook. I have a delicate matter which I need to raise with you."

Chapter 7

HIGH SPIRITS

Drunken ghosts are not much fun,
carousing in the midnight hour.
Just one more, oh yes just the one,
a brandy seems to give them power.
A little dash of whisky, never does no wrong,
although the measure of a tot is larger.
They do like their cocktails so very strong.
Tales once brief, they're now all sagas.

CAROUSING IN THE MIDNIGHT HOUR

Phil Spectre was depressed. He had been a ghost for ages, but he had never been promoted from his lowly role, as a mere apprentice phantom. His Spirit Guide, Dr Spook, said that it was his own fault because he would not study the ancient and hallowed, haunting manuals.

Furthermore, he found it difficult to communicate solemnly with human beings, because his natural gaiety overcame the serious process of chanting and whoo-hooing, which should always precede a manifestation of a dearly departed before their earthly relatives, colleagues or friends.

The business of haunting complete strangers was even more difficult. Phil behaved badly when he was asked to appear before somebody whom he did not know, sometimes to the extent of whistling a song about *Strangers in the Night*, which slightly undecked the necessary decorum, for such an important duty.

He had spent many nights in The Headless Man, his favoured alehouse in the spirit realm, and he loved their Unhappy Hours, which helped him to while away the time which he should have spent on the homework set for him by Professor Liking, who was his special, ghostly tutor. The professor had been assigned the hapless task of bringing Phil into line.

After a while, Phil had a regular crowd of cronies who all met for convivial evenings at The Headless Man. They were, Rafael McIntosh, Kenny Getta-Witness and Mark Mywords.

Rafael was a complex character, as any Spanish and Scottish mixture might imply. He loved being a wraith but wished his body was more solid. It unnerved him to see beer, brandy and whiskey mysteriously gurgling away into his filmy, lower parts. However, that did not stop him from making up drinking games, which frequently ended up in poltergeist games of dare. He had once suggested, that Phil should throw things around, before materialising in the cab of the engine-driver on the 17:10 from King's Cross, but even Phil could see that this was not a good proposition.

Kenny originally had a more prosaic surname, which was Dunton. He was a voluble speaker. In order to emphasise the wilder and more improbable parts of his long and convoluted stories he often said: "As God is my witness..."

Mark was a pleasant enough vision, but he competed with Kenny in the telling of tall tales and the warnings of doom to come, which were usually prefaced by, "Just mark my words."

One evening in the tavern, Phil suggested a drinking game. He asked the barman, Wilson, to line up shots of spirits. (Alcohol that is, not photographs of phantasms.) He also asked Wilson to pass his own choice of high-octane ambrosia, to each of them in turn.

Their task would be to drink everything which was passed to them, until the midnight hour. Kenny asked if they could choose their own first drink. Phil was adamant that they should let Wilson pick it. After three or four hours of this tricky game, Phil was the only one left standing.

Rafael was trying to seduce the cuddly barmaid. He seemed to have forgotten that he had said Gloria looked like a horse, earlier that day. His eyes could hardly focus, and he was muttering, "Stand still, my dearest little shade. I must drink in your loveliness."

She was a truly a jovial lass (or she had been, before being run over by a tractor, on her father's farm.) She liked Phil and his chums, even though they were all ne'er-do-wells. Gloria took Wilson to one side, and together they plotted a little sequence of events, which they thought might teach Phil and the others a lesson.

She went to her room, and she wrapped a long, linen dress round her stout, but comfortable, frame. After that, she placed a ruff made from cardboard, round her head. She looked in the mirror, through the eyeholes she had cut in the ruff. She was pleased with her appearance, as an apparently headless lady.

When she went down the stairs, Wilson came out of the kitchen with a pig's head. It had belonged to a previous customer, who had been a pig in one of his lives, but he was being punished by The Lord of the Ghosts. He had been told that he had to stay in limbo, until he could get a beautiful lady to kiss his snout. Gloria had accepted the task with grace, and the pig ghost was so surprised, that when he moved on, he left his old head on the bar. (I said on the bar, not on the boar – Oh, please yourselves!)

Being a spirit head, it had not deteriorated and was still a fine-looking, bristly noggin. Wilson started to bang trays, to rustle paper and to pull objects along the bar. (He had tied these things together with twine.) The barman placed an old record on his gramophone and waited for ghostly music to be played. These plinking, plonking melodies preceded the terrifying sight of a headless pig-lady, who moaned and wailed, whilst approaching the half-slumbering and over-oiled chums.

Gloria placed a hairy snout (the pig's, not her own), against Phil's open lips and shouted, "Kiss me, my darling. I know that you have been waiting for a true love, and here I am. I am your special, true spirit."

Phil woke up with a jerk. (It was Rafael.) He was beside himself. He was also beside his two other friends, as they ran out of The Headless Man, screaming in terror. From that day forth (or it may have been the fifth day), he was a reformed character.

He listened to everything that Dr. Spook and Professor Liking had to say. He asked their advice regarding haunting practices, and he took his exams to become a fully-fledged ghost, which he passed with flying colours. Rafael, Kenny and Mark were already accredited spirits, and they enrolled in an advanced course showing how to terrify from afar.

The moral of this story is: if you ever see a phantom which looks like a headless ghost, and which carries a pig's head, it is probably only Gloria from The Headless Man. It might not be Gloria. It could be a headless ghost which carries a pig's head. On second thoughts, maybe you should just run.

Chapter 8

I HATE MY JOB

The day to day boredom, is all very well.
I loathe the work I do, with a passion.
Rolling and a-swaying 'cross the ocean's swell,
there's a rhythm to it, after a fashion.
We are slaves in a galley, upon the sea.
The whip on my back is a spur.
We are chained and confined, so we cannot flee,
and I pull on my oar with a frown.
The galley master tells me to call him, sir.
If I argue, he threatens I will drown.

DAY TO DAY BOREDOM

In theory I shouldn't even be on this galley. I'm not a free man though, and I don't have any choice. In times of desperation our Roman masters press-gang rowers, and I was picked up early one morning, after a drunken night out at a local taphouse, in a tiny village near the coast - way down south near Cercantia.

I was taken to the galley, seated and chained and drilled with deadly precision, until I could have done my job with my eyes closed. I was only too much aware, that if I missed a beat, it would upset the whole rhythm of the rowers, on my side of the boat. I had also been told that such an error may even have led to the galley spinning out of control.

After a while, I found that I was almost proud of my newfound skill, but the sores on my backside were red and raw, and although my arse was like tough, old leather in the end (and on the end), the first few months were sorely trying.

I've never had a more boring job. Day after day, we bend forward and pull backwards, hundreds if not thousands of times. The view is limited. I have been looking at Aelius' thick neck, for over three years now. He's always just in front of me. I've spoken to him from time to time, but our conversations have been tedious. He's told me about his wife and the argument which they had, which led to him being tried for manslaughter.

They'd been drinking mulsum, and the sweet, sugared wine had led them into thinking that they were drinking less than they actually were. They both became maudlin, and they'd talked about the early love and the affection which they both had for each other, until they grew too accustomed to their marriage.

Aelius had made the mistake of referring to a cute serving-wench, called Antonina, who worked at the nearby grog shop. (He had admitted to himself privately, many months before the argument, that if

Antonina had responded to his clumsy flirting, he would have happily enjoyed the whole process.)

On the night in question, Aelius had told his spouse, Domitia, that if she looked like "that girl in the inn," they would be having sex now, rather than just talking about how great things used to be, when they were first wed. One thing led to another. Many severe criticisms were levelled at each other, and finally Domitia huffed off upstairs to her bed.

Aelius followed her shortly afterwards, and they had a brief, verbal and physical tussle. Sadly, this took place at the top of the rickety stairway. His wife had heard him coming, and she had tried to bar his way into the bedroom. Domitia lost her footing, fell down the stairs and broke her neck.

Her husband was desolated. He had loved her, even if she was in no way as attractive as that little teaser, Antonina. The Roman army officers who acted as police, came quickly. (Aelius' neighbours had alerted them to the disturbance in the unhappy household.)

Aelius was tried for murder. However, he eventually pleaded guilty to manslaughter. He was sentenced to spend fifteen years, as a galley slave. The first time he told his story, it was interesting. With each retelling it became less so. The galley master, Jovian, kept telling Aelius to shut his mouth. He said he felt sorry for Aelius' poor, dead wife.

"I bet you were an incredibly boring husband. I expect you repeated everything at home, as much as you do on board this vessel. The next time you mention Domitia, you're going over the side."

"But Jovian, sir – I loved her and wouldn't have done anything to harm her willingly. We were drunk and stupid. She just fell, and here I am now - with another twelve years to go on this long ship."

Luckily, Aelius had not said the name of his deceased spouse again. I felt certain that Jovian was serious about ditching Aelius in the sea if he did so.

Our food is sparse and uninteresting. We often have dry bread and rough, wheat pancakes. Back at home, we might have had dates and honey with those pancakes. Here we have pancakes with pancakes, but we don't even have many of those. We're fed just well enough to enable us to row for hours on end. We don't have any wine, and the water we have is rationed strictly, and it's green and foul.

I've asked Jovian when I might be released. He said it really depends on how desperate the need is for extra rowers. This morning I woke up and stretched as far as I could. They keep us chained loosely, even when we are at anchor. I could see that Aelius was awake too, and I grunted a reasonably friendly, "Good morning, fellow slave."

He responded, in kind, to my salutation, and I'm blessed if he didn't start going on about Domitia. Jovian rushed down the aisle of the galley. He took out his huge bunch of keys and leaned over to unchain Aelius.

"That's it. You're going into the drink. Up you get, now!"

Aelius protested and tried to placate Jovian.

"Follow me. We need to be at a convenient part of the ship to toss you over the side."

Aelius was grabbed by two of Jovian's burly helpers, and they all made their way to the stern, where the side of the ship is raised. Jovian pushed him off the side. I waited to hear a splash, but there was only a dull thud. When Jovian returned with a replacement for Aelius, I asked him what had happened to my rowing friend.

"Like I said - if you don't do what I tell you, you go for a long, final swim."

The discipline on the boat was much stricter for several weeks. One fine morning however, Jovian let slip that Aelius had been released early. New evidence received by the court officials had suggested that he had tried to prevent his wife from falling. His neighbours had now remembered, that they had heard him saying: "Take my hand quickly. Please don't struggle."

Domitia had spat at him and said, "I would rather you went to see, darling Antonina."

She had pulled her hands away from Aelius, and the backward thrust had caused her to over-balance, and she had toppled down the stairs. Jovian stuck his brawny face up to mine, and he said, "If you tell any of the other rowers that Aelius was released, I will feed you to the fishes!"

Chapter 9

I THINK I AM A DOG

I think I am a dog.
They often only mutter.
They might have said a cog,
They shout, and they stutter.
I could be Smelly.
They said some words to me.
"Look at your soft warm belly."
Perhaps my name is Flea?
Alpha male, I love him too.
He feeds me meat and kibble.
I'm his idol; that is true.
He loves me, though I dribble.

MEAT AND KIBBLE

I was living in Greece, with an alpha male who was not the ideal lord, nor a suitable role model for me. He chained me to a barrel to protect his small and shabby, rubbish-strewn yard, and he often forgot to give me any food or water, sometimes for days on end.

He had several names for me, but they all sounded harsh and bitter, and he seemed to make up different names up each day. The way he used to speak to me was loud, and it hurt my ears. He sounded like he was swearing and cursing, but I didn't know what I had done wrong.

The other day, I ran up to him, as I wanted greet him when he came near to me, but the chain from the barrel was too short, and he had wrapped it tightly round my left hind leg. When I reached the end of the chain, the steel links bit into my flesh, as I was pulled up short.

I barked at him, just to let him know that I forgave him, and I even tried to lick his sweaty and dirty hand, but he just cuffed me round the head and kicked me in the side. That hurt. I felt physical pain and was also upset by his hatred.

Dimitri looked as if he was a gentle man. He had dark hair, with curls at the sides and big, brown, dog-like eyes. He always wore a T-shirt with a smiley face on it and dark blue jeans. He didn't look nasty at all, but I knew better.

I used to try to understand, what I might have done wrong. When I was a small puppy (not that long ago), I did chew some things, and that seemed like fun, but my master was so angry, he threw an old house brick at me. He had taken my mum, brothers and sisters away, and they didn't come back.

I waited for days on end, hoping that they would return, but after a while I realised that they must have moved away. I decided to prove to my man that I could be a good dog for him, and that I could guard his barrel and the little back-yard, so that he didn't have to worry about the other dogs who came by.

I heard him say that they were strays, but they looked like dogs to me. One of them came to see me frequently, and he gave me lots of good advice. Brown Dog (that was his name), told me never to look at Dimitri, when he seemed to be angry.

"Just avoid his eyes. If you see him glaring at you, remember that he's looking for someone, or something, to blame for his own faults. Never speak to him when he's been drinking that awful smelling liquid which they call Retsina, and if he has had a drink called Ouzo – watch out."

Brown Dog was chatting to me a little while ago, when Dimitri came out with a long stick under his arm. He yelled at Brown Dog and kicked out at him. Brown Dog ran away, out of his reach. Dimitri hit me on the side of my head, right where he had punched me a few days before. Some red stuff ran down my face.

Brown Dog was angry, and he jumped up at Dimitri. He tried to bite his throat. Dimitri pointed the funny-looking stick at Brown Dog, and it made a loud, banging noise. Brown Dog was thrown up in the air by this sound, and he fell at Dimitri's feet. He lay very still, and his head looked like it had changed shape. Half of it was hanging down at the side. I heard a lady, who was walking up the path to the yard, telling Dimitri off.

"Why did you do that? The poor dog was only trying to protect your barrel dog. If you don't want a dog, why do you have one? You're a total disgrace."

"Shut up! I don't talk to wretched foreigners, who think that these pests are proper animals. Worse than that - you stupid, English people treat these beasts as one of the family. If you're so wonderful, and he is so great, why don't you take him away?"

The lady was red in the face, and I could see that she was frightened. She asked Dimitri to unchain me, and after he did so, she did a strange thing. She put her hand on my head and rubbed it up and down. I growled because I thought she was going to hit me. She started making pleasant, soothing noises - and to my surprise she put her lips on my nose.

She looked nice. She had long, yellow hair tied up at the back, so it looked like a horse's tail, but it was in the wrong place for a wagger. Her eyes were light blue. She had a floaty top with butterflies on it, and she wore white jeans. When she kept putting her lips on me, I wondered if she was trying to eat my fleas.

She picked me up and walked out of the yard towards an old cart, which was making a grumbling sound. Dimitri had gone back inside, and I hoped he wouldn't come back with the thunder stick again.

There was another lady in the funny, white cart. She was a different colour; her hair was even more curly, and it stuck out all over. She had large, brown eyes and was shorter than lady number one. The darker lady wore a bright, red shirt and a pair of short trousers. Maybe she had borrowed them from a smaller person. Lady number two was sitting behind a small wheel, which was inside the cart.

I couldn't see a donkey or a horse. I wondered if they would have to push that cart along. The first lady had opened a metal thing inside the cart, and she placed me inside it gently. There was a soft piece of padded material in the metal thing, and she gave me some nice, chewy biscuits. I knew what they were because my friend, Brown Dog, had told me all about them. I couldn't believe that they were so delicious. Even after I ate them, there was a sort of sticky liquid coming out of my mouth.

Later that day, I was taken to a bright place, which had a bitter aroma and shiny, metal tables. A kind man with large glasses, who was wearing a white coat, mended my head. He used soothing cream and a needle with thin rope in it.

"There you are. That should be O.K. until he gets to his temporary home."

The second lady handed him a small, plastic card, and he poked it into a machine. She pressed some peculiar buttons, and he gave her the card back with some bits of paper. She put the papers into her breast. That was strange. I realised later that she had a secret compartment, made out of material, on the outside of her shirt.

Back in the cart, which still grumbled, we set off again, as if by magic. That night, I was handed over to another beautiful lady, with two clumps of ginger hair sticking out of the sides of her head, just like horns. She caressed me, like her friend had done. She lifted me into another metal thing, which I heard her call a cage, and she gave me delicious meat and more biscuits. Attached to the cage there was a little, open place, so I could go into my own back-yard.

There were lots of dogs there, and some only had three legs. Some had one eye, and others had strangely shaped legs or paws. One of them told me, that he had been thrown out of a window. I wasn't sure what that was, but he explained this to me. I asked him about thunder sticks, and he showed me some bumps in his ears, that he called bullet wounds.

The two ladies who'd brought me to this wonderful place, Beverley (the lady with yellow hair), and May (the other lady with black hair), came to see me twice more, and I heard them talking to the ginger-horned lady. They mentioned passports, jabs and other things, none of which I understood at all.

I spent some time there. I can't tell you how long it was. It was longer than the time between when the sun comes up and goes down. It was also longer that the gaps between when the big, metal carts came, and noisy men lifted round, metal objects, before tipping rubbish out of them and into the cart. I think it was probably eight or so of those gaps.

One day, I was ecstatic to see that Beverley and May had come back. They rushed up to my room and opened the door. I ran out and went lick, lick, lick all over them. I liked doing that. Dimitri wouldn't let me do it, but the ginger-horned lady, who I think was called Darling, loved it. She had a man friend who always called her Darling, so that must have been her name.

I was led to the white sort of cart and put inside the thing, which I had now overheard was really called a car. Darling leaned in and patted me. Some strange, wet objects ran down each side of her nose. She kissed me, and kissed me again - many times, and I got quite wet from the water running from her eyes.

I knew that this lip caress was called a kiss by now, as I had heard her ask her friend, Bert, to kiss her, and that's what he did. His kisses looked quite harsh, but Darling wasn't worried about that at all.

Off we went in the car thing, and after quite a while, it ran up a ramp onto a big, floating cart, on some sparkling water. We spent hours on this strange thing, which I heard a man call a fairy. At least I thought he had called it a fairy, but when I later heard other people talking about it, it sounded like a different name.

Finally, we went down another large ramp, and the car thing propelled itself through terrifying, noisy places. In between these awful places, there were long stretches of special paths, on which many cars were speeding along, even without horses or donkeys to pull them.

Every now and then, we would pull off the frightening paths, for something to eat and drink, and the ladies always gave me something too. Dimitri only fed me when he had to, but they seemed to like giving me food.

Sometimes, we were stopped at barriers, so Beverley could show bits of paper to men in smart, dark uniforms. They looked at the pieces of paper, as if they were boring, and then wrote things in fat books. They often plonked a rubbery thing onto some of the papers, which made a mess of the lovely, empty, white space and left black patterns all over it.

We eventually reached a large area of smooth rock, where many cars (and larger things like cars but longer), were waiting for something to happen, all gathered in wiggly lines. May let me out to do a wee and a poo, and she also let out some other dogs who'd been in other cages inside the car, with me.

I didn't mention them before because I had so much else to tell you. They were a funny bunch. One was called Fleabag. Another said his name was Get Out of Here, and the last one was Look at Him. May and Beverley called them different names. To them, they were known as Rex, Charley and Adonis.

I liked those names better, as the ladies said them in soft, warm tones. The other dogs said that their original names had to be spat out harshly, accompanied by human curses.

Once we were on this different and larger water cart, I heard May say that she was glad we were on the ferry. Yes - I must have been wrong when I thought it was called a fairy. This ferry was a bit like the other one, but it was much bigger. We spent three sun up/sun down periods, on the ferry.

When we had stopped moving on the water, we went back down an enormous, metal ramp, to a place on land, whose name I have forgotten. May said it to Beverley, but I can't remember what she said. Off we went, and after many adventures we arrived at a place called Oxford. May came to let me out, and I said goodbye to Rex, Charley and Adonis.

"Here we are Peter. This is where you will be fostered, until we can find you a forever home," said May.

She had been calling me Peter for a few days. I didn't know that this was my new name, until she kissed me and said, "Peter – that's your name now. Good Boy."

I had thought that Good Boy was my name, but I didn't mind being called Peter if that was what she really wanted. They left me in what they called a house, with a man called Fred. He smelt of smoke and beer. There was also a smiling lady, called Margaret.

Fred was big and fat, and I was surprised that they could find clothes large enough for him. He wore a checked shirt, with green and white squares on it, and he had trousers with ridges going up and down, even though the material felt soft.

Margaret was small, and her skin smelt like flowers. Her clothes were smarter than Fred's, and were white (or very pale), every day. They looked after me well, and I began to think I was going to stay there forever. Some friendly people came to see me, but either they didn't want me, or Fred and Margaret didn't like them.

Finally, I met the people who were apparently going to be my new mum and dad. She was called Penny, and he was called Tom. Penny was tall and slim, with brown hair, and she laughed a lot. She wore bright, colourful clothes, and she had some funny, dangling things attached to her ears.

Tom was dark and small, and he wore a jacket with a hairy texture and blue trousers, with thin, white stripes. He always grinned when Penny looked at him. I think he liked her a lot. I did too, as she was fun. She was noisy in a jolly way, not at all like Dimitri.

They made a big fuss of me, and they waved pieces of paper at Fred, which must have shown that they were good people. I was allowed to get into Tom's horseless car, you know, the kind of thing that confused me at first, when I thought it was a cart, even though it had no donkey or horse to pull it.

Penny put me in the back on a soft, squashy bed, with some squeaky toys and some treat things, just like the ones Margaret had given me. I licked Fred and Margaret, and she too produced some of those wet, round things from her eyes. Fred also had some, but he pretended that he didn't notice them.

"I wonder what Peter will think of Essex? I bet it will be entirely different from Skiathos!"

"Oh Tom, he's so gorgeous. I love him to bits already."

We went off, in Tom's thing called a car. I was a bit confused, as they said it was a ford. I thought a ford was a dip in the road with water in it. After a long drive (still without a horse or a donkey), we drew up outside a house, and Tom pulled a lever up, with a clicking and clacking noise. He got out, opened the door of the car and lifted me out.

"Peter, this is your forever home."

I couldn't believe my eyes. The inside of the house was quite like Fred and Margaret's place, with soft, warm things on the ground and hot, metal things on the walls. The outside was like a doggy, fairy garden.

By now, I knew what a fairy was, as Penny had a sort of toy pinned to her top. This was a small lady with wings, which Tom had given to her on the way back. He said it was a fairy for his beloved. It didn't look anything like a ferry at all.

The garden was green and large, and there were dog toys all over the place. Tom had settled me on the lawn (a word I had heard at the foster home), and he said, "Well Peter – are you a happy boy?"

I wagged my tail and said, "You bet," but he just thought I was barking.

Chapter 10

DOTAGE DOUBT AGE

In my dotage I'm uncertain,
of the meaning in my life.
I note my little foibles.
My adviser is my wife.
I was young; I knew my place,
but I thought I was so special.
It's hard, a run-rat race,
Life is just an untamed wrestle.
Heading for the end, in fact,
it seems to be quite near.
I wonder if I need to pack,
a curry, books, and beer.

A CURRY, BOOKS AND BEER

Herbert had been elated, when he met the lady who was to become his third, best and last wife. There had been some problems within his previous marriages, which were not always entirely the fault of the ex-wives. He knew he could be a tad boring and had tried to be a more exciting man, but his heart wasn't in it.

Doreen was his new target, and, by golly, she was a real catch. She could cook, sew, decorate, paint water colours, and she was also terrific in bed. He was totally amazed, when she announced that she would give him permission to be the boss in their relationship. (I know - you don't have to tell me. He was obviously born yesterday.) As they grew older, their marriage suffered from those age-old bickeracious episodes, which often plague relationships, as they mature.

He knew he loved Doreen. She knew she loved him. However, they both took a hand in correcting one another's minor errors, and they criticised tiny foibles which each of them possessed, even though they knew, that these were originally thought of as endearing habits.

Herbert was a modest man and now realised that his small talents were enough to keep him happy, even though in his younger years his ambition had been more driving. He loved his banjo and his pet rat, Whitey. Whitey loved Herbert, but he didn't like the banjo, except when Herbert was not playing it - if that makes sense.

Every time Whitey heard his master open the case, and he heard those staccato and sharp sounds, he tried to bury his little, pink ears in his straw bedding. It was even worse when Herbert invited the other members of the Little Sneddingham Parish Banjo Society to rehearse in the front room of his house.

The most terrible rendition of a song which Whitey had ever heard, was their version of *My Boy Lollipop*, a song which he firmly believed was best heard by Millie. The society's banjo version was not only leaden and plodding, but it was also out of tune. Let's be honest. If even a pet rat can tell that the version is appalling – it really is!

Doreen made a point of going out when the club members were coming to see Herbert, and she didn't come back, until they had all gone. Unfortunately, Herbert had a wandering eye, and he was smitten by feelings of true adoration, when he sat next to young Sally Thompson, who was a member of the choir at his church.

She was at least twenty years too young for Herbert. He was sixty-eight, and she was a young forty. They had nothing in common except the awful banjo club. By that small phrase, I mean awful banjo - and also awful club. Twice as awful in fact. Herbert loved sitting next to Sally, and he could smell her enticing perfume, whenever he loomed over her. This was supplemented by another, more animal and musky scent, which drove him wild with desire, until he realised that she often had a pound of mince in her shopping bag.

One day, Sally turned up unannounced, with her banjo case over her shoulder.

"Mr. Jennings, I was taking my banjo to the music shop for a minor repair, but I decided that I'd like your advice about my playing. As I was near to your house, I thought I'd take the liberty of popping in, to get your help with my fingering."

Herbert's eyes nearly popped out, as he could have sworn that she was deliberately leading him on.

"Come in Sally, and please do call me Herbert."

He leered at her, unattractively. (Is it possible to leer attractively?) She had taken her glasses off and was polishing them, so she didn't see how pushy he was becoming. She sat down on the sofa, and was a little surprised when Herbert settled himself about three inches away from her, even though there were several other vacant seats in the room.

She and Herbert tuned their instruments of torture, and she showed him how she normally placed her small digits. Herbert placed his arms round her and helped her to hold her banjo in the correct way.

"This is the way to cradle your banjo, so that it's easier to play."

Sally was aware that he was breathing in a peculiar way in strange, husky snuffles. Whitey was also studying his pet human, and he couldn't understand why he was leaning over the young girl's chest in such a fascinated manner.

"Oh Sally, I do love your breasts. May I touch them?"

Although Herbert had asked for permission, he didn't wait for an answer. He made a sort of thrusting dive for her special temptations. As he was holding them, Doreen opened the front door.

"Cooee! I'm back early. Have you missed..."

She had entered the room just in time to see Herbert caressing Sally's chest in a frantic manner, and she could see that the poor girl was terrified. Doreen picked up Herbert's banjo and hit him, again and again, without mercy. Occasionally during this onslaught, snatches of accidental melody were heard. I know that some people think that banjo players always play tunes accidentally, but these little pieces of music really just happened, in an uncanny way. Herbert was by now in a bloody mess, in more ways than one.

"Mrs. Jennings, please believe me. I did nothing to encourage him. I feel sorry for him, but he brought this on himself."

"Sally, I think it would be best if you leave - right now!"

The young lady nodded her head meekly. She put her banjo into its case and almost ran out of the room. Herbert was just about able to speak.

"What a dreadful misunderstanding, Doreen."

"You're a stupid bugger. You're so pathetic. What on earth made you try it on with that young lass?"

"No, that isn't right. I was helping her with her fingering."

Doreen picked up a heavy paperweight from the shelf over the fireplace, and she brought it crashing down on Herbert's temple. Blood oozed out from a large gash in his head, and he started mumbling. Doreen leaned over and heard him say, "Goodbye. I leave you with three last requests. I want a curry, books and beer."

Doreen had noticed that Sally had left her shopping bag by the sofa, and she had smelt a beefy odour, emanating from its interior. She grabbed some mince from the bag and went into the kitchen. She placed the meat in a mixer, together with some curry powder, scotch bonnet chillies, half a glass of beer and several shredded pages from one of Herbert's books. With a grunt of satisfaction, she switched on the mixer and looked for a large funnel.

As she came back into the front room, Herbert was laying on his back with his mouth open. Doreen forced the funnel down his throat and emptied the revolting combination of his last requests into its opening.

"There, there, darling. I hope you'll be pleased that I gave you exactly what you wanted!"

Chapter 11

NOSEY PARKER

I like to poke, to prod and pry.
My eyesight's going dim.
Doing sewing and some daft I-Spy,
I'd like a nice cold Pimm's.
The attendant in the care home,
she's a bully and a toad.
I'd rather be in Rome,
dressed in clothes - all à la mode.

MY EYESIGHT'S GOING RATHER DIM

My son brought me to this horrible place, and I hate it. Everybody here is so old. They sit in a circle of scrawny flesh and bones, in the lounge, nodding and dribbling. The T.V. is always on, but we can never hear it because it's so quiet. The nurse says that's because we're all deaf, but what does she expect? We are all a million years old.

The meals are tepid, watery and bland. I want a scorching vindaloo, but they say it will upset me. I'm already bloody upset. I haven't had a decent bowel movement for three weeks. A fierce, hot vindaloo would soon sort me out. Oh yes! A volcanic, faecal explosion would do me the world of good.

The view from my window was interesting, when I was in my old room. I could see the car park and people coming and going. They were ordinary people, not worn out, ragged scarecrows, like the rest of the inmates (sorry - guests!) in the *Happy Times Retirement Home.* I wasn't happy when they moved me into another cell, at the back of the home.

My son came to see me every week at first, but he says he's busy now and can only come monthly. I expect he's tired out, poor boy, because of all that sexual jiggery-pokery with that fat, blonde tart. He's very taken with his new wife. I say blonde, but her roots are black, and she doesn't look too clean either. A scrub down with a heavy brush and carbolic soap would work wonders. She comes to see me, now and then, and she leans all over me with those massive, pendulous udders in my face. My bet is that they are full of silicone. How can he think it's fun to play with two sorbo mountains?

Jeff was always a little odd. At least I saved going a little gaga, until I reached a ripe, old age. I sometimes forget my son's name. I remember my eleventh birthday like it was yesterday, but I've found that recent things are more difficult to dredge up, out of my choc-a-bloc, little grey cells.

His wife's name is Maisiana-Jade. If you're going to make up ridiculous names, why not try for something imaginative, like the Red Indians used to do? They would have called her something sensible - like Big Lumpy Cow Who Comes Too Often.

The other bit of bad news, is that she's pregnant. Jeff says he's the father, but I wouldn't put my money on it. He met her at the casino, where he sometimes goes, to fritter away his dole money. She says it's going to be a little girl, but I reckon she'll give birth to a great pudding of a calf. M-J (I refuse to call her that stupid name invented by her parents) wants to call her baby, Aquarius-Darling. What a laugh!

I've invented a new way to keep myself occupied. I race (slowly) down the hall on my Zimmer frame every morning, after the post has been delivered and put into the correct pigeon holes.

If I work quickly, I can move the letters all round, and I can also pinch a couple of them, to read at my leisure. Mrs. Manderley is corresponding with a young man, who says he loves her mind and will always be with her. He tells her he is thirty-eight, but she is eighty-three if she's a day old. There is a wonderful reverse symmetry to their age pattern. He's asked her for the P.I.N. number to her bank account, so he can keep an eye on her balance.

She must be a mug if she gives it to him, always supposing she ever finds out about his request, as I burnt his letter. Poor Dolores Heap, she has interesting letters sent to her, but she can't read them and shouts at her daughter, as she thinks she's the tax man. I have to study these letters with a torch and a magnifying glass, as my peepers are not up to much anymore.

The attendants here are not too bad, except for that tight-mouthed, little bitch who has a ridiculous bun, with her hair all dragged back off her face. If I had a face like that, I'd have a straight-cut fringe about eight inches long, so nobody would have to see it. She's called Marjorie Gilbert. She takes every opportunity to stand on guests' feet. She also pinches them, under the covers. The last time she did that, I poked her with my dinner fork. She hollered, but I just said, "Oh Marjorie dear, I wondered where that fork was. Thanks so much for finding it for me."

This morning, I almost finished my jig-saw puzzle of Big Ben. I couldn't go the whole hog, as several pieces were missing. That encouraged me to mix up the pieces in all six of the tatty, boxed puzzles. The books in the library are not to my taste. They cover things like sickly romances and detective stories. There are also some dog-eared classics with teeny-weeny print, which even a keen-eyed youngster would find difficult to read.

My master plan is nearly ready to pull off. I've been saving as many pills as I can, and tomorrow - when the lights go down, I will swallow the whole lot. That'll teach them. I would like to be really sick, and I hope that when they find me, I'll be as stiff as a board, covered in reeking vomit. My final act of revenge was to make a new will, before I came in here. Those dogs and cats, at the rescue home, will make better use of my money than Jeff and M-J!

Chapter 12

SENOR MOMENTZ

My memory isn't what it was,
and neither is my body.
I like to think it's just because
I'm normal, not an oddy.
The aches and pains of senior age,
are not too hard to bear.
They're better than a terrible rage.
I'm happy, I don't care.
I used to be so furious.
There seems to be no point.
It's specious and it's spurious
I forget the next line.

I FORGET THE NEXT LINE

Ricky was always proud of the fact that he could remember the lyrics to all of the songs, which he performed with his band, The Forgotten Heroes. Together with Ralph (his bass guitarist), Dick on keyboards, Bertie on guitar and Terry on drums, he performed in pubs and clubs throughout Essex and had done so for over fifty years.

Bertie was the oldest member of the band, and he owed his nickname to Bert Weedon, who wrote the seminal, guitar-tutor book, *Play in a Day*. The promise was of course a ridiculous one, but at that time the Trades Descriptions Act hadn't been enacted. Bertie's real name was Clarence, and he was relieved that nobody ever called him that; who wouldn't be?

The band was a good, competent outfit, and they were usually re-booked quickly because they treated their punters well, and they were polite, even to people who insisted, over and over again, that they wanted them to play *Bohemian Rhapsody*. Ricky had frequently explained to punters, that Queen had used judicious over-dubs to achieve the famous, choral effect.

At one gig, a drunken hooray-henry came up to Terry eight times, asking for this song. On the last occasion, the toff had said, "I say old chap; you must know it. Everybody does. It's terrific. Why not just have a go at it?"

Terry stood up. He kind of unfolded himself from his drum stool, and he towered over the gentleman in question. He glared at him, and he said, "My dear fellow, please would you be a spiffingly good chap and do me a great favour?"

"Of course, old boy. What will it be?"

"Eff off."

"I've never been spoken to like that by an entertainer."

Terry told him there was always a first time. Tel was a gentle, giant of a man. He often helped Ralph to take his bass speaker cabinets upstairs if the function room was so situated. After a few months, he gave up doing it with Ralph, and he just put the cab on his shoulder, ran up the stairs, dumped it on stage and then went down for the other 4 x 12 cabinet.

Ricky was now finding it difficult to remember words for new songs. The fifties and sixties numbers, which they had played forever, were easy to remember, but new ones didn't seem to stick. He had begun to resort to having words on a music stand, but he wasn't happy about that. Bertie told him he should just remember, that even classical musicians (proper musicians, he called them), had music in front of them.

They also had problems with their current name. They'd been called The Forgotten Heroes for many years (having previously been The Almost Shadows, The Beat Sharers and Ricky and The Ricky-Tones, before settling on The Forgotten Heroes in the early seventies.) Another band with the same name, who played mostly in the North, had come across their website and had complained, as they said that they had been forgotten long before the Essex band had started to use the name.

Dick suggested that they should run a competition to choose a new name, with the help of the local rag. He asked them for assistance, and they must have had a dearth of decent news because they agreed to run a half-page spread, provided The Forgotten Heroes would appear gratis, at a gig in aid of a local charity.

Dick was happy to do this, and they posed for a photo, with their trademark Fenders and Ludwig drum kit, plus Dick's Roland keyboard - which could sound like anything. One of Dick's detractors had joked that it couldn't make him sound like a decent pianist. However, they were a pretty good band; although they were nothing to set the world on fire, they were always entertaining, and the dancers were on the floor from the get-go, to the end of every gig.

On the night of the fund-raising event, they looked at the huge flood of entries (six) and couldn't quite decide which of the three best suggestions should be chosen as their new moniker. Terry quite liked The Over the Hillbillies, but the others reckoned that would make them sound like a decrepit, bluegrass band. Finally, they just put all six names in a hat, and the winner was Senor Momentz.

Ever since then, Ray has been called Senor Momentz by the members of their audiences, and he tells anybody who is even vaguely interested, that his words on the music stand are just part of his act.

Chapter 13

LIGHT HUMOUR

I'm on, I'm off, or I'm flashing.
At times, I do all three.
I'm like morse, dot, dot, dashing.
It causes me great glee.
They think that they will fix me,
but I know, that they are wrong.
I still have tricks (Who me?)
They can't fool me, not for long.

I'M LIKE MORSE, DOT, DOT, DASHING

The Light Research Institute (L.R.I.) is an organisation based in Lucerne, Switzerland and has recently published a paper entitled, "Humour and Light Scintillation." According to the C.E.O. of the institute, Ray Ovsun, their detailed findings will be available in the Spring of 2021, but the paper mentioned above presents an overview, of their work to date.

Apparently, light emitting or light reflecting surfaces and devices, do have a sense of humour, and this has been borne out by a complex examination of inconsistent light failure and/or presence. Amongst other scenarios, this would also cover circumstances when all logical reasoning would insist that light should be absent - when a light emitting source is switched off, (or disconnected from its source of power), or should be present - when it is switched on (or connected to its source of power.)

"The study covers all manner of light reflecting surfaces," said Mr. Ovsun. "They do not consistently perform as we had expected them to, when they are shielded from light sources, or when they are exposed to them."

The Light Programme followed by L.R.I. revealed that electric, light bulbs are particularly prone to childish pranks, such as flickering in a front porch whilst the house owners are out for hours. Also, they may unaccountably switch themselves off, when the householder is searching for the right key to open the front door. Once the key is found (in the dark), the bulbs often turn themselves on again, but they tend to switch themselves off if the keys are dropped.

Dr. Yzit Mee, who compiled most of the statistics quoted in the initial paper, also noted that, at times, lights would switch themselves on and off for no good reason. He connected various bulbs to a diagnostic programme on the powerful computers operated by L.R.I., and the reports displayed by their system (Breaking Electricity Analytical

Moments – B.E.A.M.), showed that the intermittent presence of light demonstrated a remarkable similarity to Morse Code.

There was a particular repeated phrase, which baffled the scientists, until one of their associates, who comes from Bolakia, noticed that an ancient dialect from his home country, used words which corresponded with the phrase in question. The lights were saying: "I'm like morse, dot, dot, dashing."

Mr. Ovsun took great pains to insist that LRI's Light Programme is still ongoing, but he was unable to complete his statement, as the recording equipment which he was using started to go on and off, and the scientist from Bolakia said that the stops and starts were spelling out, "The joke's on you!"

Chapter 14

CRUMPET VOLUNTARY

They call me Crumpet Voluntary.
They say I am always willing.
The nickname isn't honorary,
an insult it's fulfilling.
I know I'm pretty easy,
I'm a lady in my heart.
I'm not dirty; I'm not sleazy.
I'm a friendly, happy tart.

A FRIENDLY, HAPPY TART.

I didn't choose to become a lady of the night. I had no choice. I was left by my husband with a small baby to support, when he ran off with a younger model of me. I say younger, but I mean much younger. I'm twenty-eight, and the replacement is only seventeen. She is attractive, I will grant her that, but she has cotton wool for brains, even if she has long, Bambi legs and wide open, blue eyes.

I don't hate her, but it beats me how Bill could be interested in a dumb blonde like that. I mean, I'm blonde, but I do have a string of A-levels, and I would have gone to university if I could. Sadly, my poor mum and dad had serious financial problems, at about the time I would have been doing research about what to read at Uni, and where to apply.

I decided to go out to work, in order to bring some extra cash into the Fleming household. It wasn't much, but my post as a junior clerk at the Acme Insurance Brokers office in Willingborough High Street did help a little.

My dad hadn't been able to work for years, due to his chronic respiratory problems. He was pretty much hooked up to a portable oxygen-cylinder, all the time. My mum did several part-time jobs, including working for that horrible snob, Digby Browne-Smythe. He had a posh house, in the Upper Hill area of Willingborough, and he needed a woman to clean his large, but tasteless, house, which had huge, stone lions on either side of the electric gates and a décor scheme that made your eyes hurt.

He thought that spots, stripes and faux animal skins went together well. The underlying premise of his interior design was that everything had to be expensive. He wouldn't pay Mum much, though. She earned a pittance for crawling round on her bony, red knees, washing and polishing huge expanses of parquet flooring, and she lugged around a massive vacuum cleaner to try to keep his fluffy carpets up to scratch.

One day she came home crying, well before I got back from the Acme office. When I eventually returned to our house, Mum was weeping, in the sitting room. She had a large pile of sodden tissues by her side.

"Wendy, I don't know what to do. I've lost my job. I was doing my usual chores, when Digby returned, blind drunk, from his club. He pulled me up off my knees, and he tried to undo my blouse. He was vile and stinking of whiskey. He crushed his fat, blubbery lips on mine, and he tried to put his tongue into my mouth."

All this happened when I was about sixteen, and mum was thirty-three. She had given birth to me when she was young, and she was still a very presentable woman, although she always looked drained and tired.

Mum continued, "He said, 'Come on Theresa, I know you're gagging for it,' I was gagging - that's right, but not for him. He was making me feel so sick. He tore my blouse – look; and he pushed me onto the sofa and tried to undo his flies.

"I picked up a large metal ornament and gave him a huge whack on the side of his head. I don't think he was hurt much, but it made him let me go. I grabbed my coat and ran to the front door. As I opened it, he shouted, 'You're fired. You never were a good cleaner, and you're a frigid lump of ice to boot. Get out!'

"I was relieved to be out, but I'm so worried about how we will manage. Your dad can't work; you try to help but can only give me a small amount from your salary, and I've tried to find other work, without much success."

"Mum, we'll manage. I'll get some evening work to help."

That's how I came to work in the Gladrags Club. I became a part-time barmaid, and I also helped them with their book-keeping, as their manager, Jake Weston, was useless. He was a lanky waste of space, but although he wasn't good at his job, he was a cheerful man with a good heart.

After he'd told me about the mess he was in with the club accounts, he gave me a great, big box of screwed up paperwork, going back at least six years, and he begged me to help him get things in order.

He wanted to get things sorted out, before Dave Solomon (the owner), found out about his terrible record keeping. Jake was grateful, but he couldn't pay me much extra money for helping with the accounts because the club was doing so badly. I did the two jobs at the club, as well as working for Acme, for a few years, but when I was twenty-two, after I got back from the office one Friday evening, my dad called me in to his bedroom, where he now spent his entire life.

His breathing was so bad that he struggled with every inhalation, and he was pallid and greasy looking. Even so, he was still my dear dad, but he was so frail. I loved him and was desperately sorry for him. It was painful to see him looking so wrecked.

"Wendy, I've got some very bad news. Your mum was out today, still looking for odd jobs to add to the other cleaning tasks she does, and she slipped on some wet leaves at the side of the pavement, and fell into the road. A bus was coming - Wendy, it was quick, and Mum was killed immediately."

Dad reached out for me, and we both sobbed and sobbed. I found out more details from my dad, and I started to do all those awful things that have to be done, when a loved one dies. Ringing round to people in the address book, talking to the doctor, making a list of all the red-tape jobs which have to be dealt with, and then endlessly following all those things up.

Dad was officially mum's executor, but I did all the donkey work. He was far too ill to be able to cope with the estate bureaucracy. We held the funeral quickly. It was a small affair, and the wake was just a few sandwiches and some wine at our house. The funeral was at the local crem.

Mum had insisted that she wanted *Fire* by Arthur Brown, as the coffin rolled away. She had scribbled her funeral wishes on the back of an old, shopping list, which we had found tucked in her favourite handbag. They were simple and modest, and the whole depressing affair was mercifully short.

Dad and I gradually got into a new routine. I made him sandwiches and a flask of soup, for his lunch, before I went to Acme, and when I got back, I prepared dinner for us both, after which I went to the club. Money was even tighter, but we just about managed for another two years or so, until Acme folded up. The business had been on the downturn for some time, and I wasn't that surprised when the boss, William Duncan, told me the bad news. Jake wanted to offer me more work, but Gladrags was still not doing well.

Dad and I soldiered on, and Dave Solomon called me into the office at Gladrags one day. He offered me a lot of money, for what he said would be an easy task. Dave was a handsome man, with a shrewish wife who never gave him a moment's peace. His offer was easily made, but it wasn't so easily accepted. He told me that a beautiful girl, like me, could always make money. He said I was sitting on my greatest asset.

"Wendy, I know you and your father have serious money problems. I could introduce you to clean, pleasant clients, who would pay good money to spend time with you. I could even be your first client. Do you know what I mean?"

I knew alright, but I wasn't having any of that, no thanks! I was a good girl, wasn't I?

"Dave, I should be insulted, but I know you're trying to help. I could never do that kind of thing for money, even with you!"

"O.K. Wendy, but if you ever need cash badly, that's how you could do very well."

Time went on, and I met Bill, my future husband, at the club, which by now was called the Zebra Bar. You've guessed it, everything was striped. Dave hadn't raised the subject of me earning a living on my back again, thank goodness. Bill was sweet, gentle and courteous. We hit it off immediately and were married quickly.

By then, Dad had also joined Mum in heaven (I hope!), and I had been forced to sell the house, as I just couldn't keep up the mortgage payments. There was hardly any equity, as Dad had been compelled to raise additional money on the house, and I'd moved into a squalid, one bed-roomed flat, in the seedier side of town. Bill swept me off my feet, and we ended up living in a respectable, three-bedroomed semi, in a good part of the town.

All went well, until I became pregnant, and when I found that I had completely gone off sex, Bill was furious. I tried to explain to him that later, when the baby was born, and once I had fully got back to normal, all would be well again. I began to suspect that Bill was seeking his comforts elsewhere. There were secret phone calls, hurried closure of computer screens, and other signs that I was no longer the centre of his universe.

I have to admit that he was kind to me, when I went to the hospital to have little Eric, and he promised that he would always love me, no matter what. He should have qualified that by saying, no matter what - except for a doe-eyed, blonde bitch, who was hardly out of nappies.

When I came home from the maternity unit, I was shattered. I'd been forced to give up my job at the Zebra Bar, a few months before Eric was born. I had been very tired, sick and unwell during my pregnancy. I was still not right, when I realised that Bill had found a new playmate. I found a letter, in his jacket pocket, which looked as if it had been written by a school kid.

Darling Bill
I reely love you Sweetikins, (Sweetikins?) *Once you leve yore wife we wil set upp home together and the world will be perfect...*

There was much more of this juvenile drivel, complete with spolling mastikes and terrible, grammatical howlers. I couldn't bear to read it all. I made a chicken pie and folded the letter into Bill's half. I set the table, put on my slinkiest dress, lit some candles and chilled a bottle of Pinot Grigio. When Bill came in I took his coat, and I kissed him before leading him to the table.

"This is lovely, darling!"

"Thanks, Sweetikins!"

He looked at me strangely but made no comment. I set his dinner down before him, including the letter-laden half of the pie. Bill cut into the pie, not even noticing that I hadn't started on my half, and he said, "Hey, there's a piece of paper in the pie."

"Oh dear, you'd better take it out and throw it away. I'm so sorry."

Bill had already pulled out the paper and unfolded it. He knew straightaway, that it was a letter from his new toy, Marybelle. (Even her juvenile name sets my teeth on edge.) He went deathly pale and had the good grace to apologise.

"I'm so, so sorry Wendy. It all happened because you never show my any affection anymore. I know you are a good wife, and I'm a shit."

I told him to pack and go immediately. I was surprised when he did so, but then I realised that he just wanted to be with his young, nubile bit of stuff. He tried to kiss me as he left, but I looked at him, as sternly as I could, and said, "I don't think that's a good idea - Sweetikins!"

He half-smiled and left the house. The next day I took stock of my situation. I was twenty-eight, with no job, a house to pay for, (assuming I could keep hold of it), a young baby and no job. Bill phoned later that day, and he told me that I could keep the house, but that he couldn't pay the mortgage. He also said that he could only pay me a tiny amount of maintenance, as his job as a self-employed, odd-job man was not bringing in much money.

I had a meeting with Mr. Thatcher, my dad's old solicitor, and he was blunt, but honest. According to Thatcher, any man who was self-employed could always show that his business was in dire straits. Thatcher told me to grab the house and then to see what benefits I could get. I made enquiries about nannies to look after young babies, but I was staggered by the potential cost.

I phoned Jake, who was still managing the Zeb, as it was often called by the customers. He said he would be happy to give me a few hours' work, in the evenings, provided I could get Eric looked after. The next week, young Charice (who lived next door), came round to babysit, and I started my job again, at the Zeb.

It wasn't too bad. The clientele was pretty much the same, and they made me feel welcome. I did this for a few weeks, but I began to realise that I could never make ends meet. I had found that the benefits I could obtain were quite limited. I was frantic with worry about how I would manage to stay in the black.

Dave came in one night and gave me a hug. I'm ashamed to say, that I burst into tears. He ushered me into the office and handed me his hankie. I calmed down and told him all my woes.

"Well Wendy, don't forget that you could earn good money as a.... sort of hostess."

Dave persuaded me to be introduced to a small number of respectable and friendly men. I was scared and nervous at first, but I always believe that you should do everything that you do, with a good heart. So here I am, with a dozen or so regulars, some of whom are skilled at lovemaking, but others who need a good deal of encouragement.

I make better money than I ever did before. Most of them are better at sex than Bill was, and all of them are good to me. I often get extra presents, and they frequently give me more money than I ask for. They are all clean and gentle.

As I said before, I didn't set out to be what I am now. I do my job well, and I like to think I am indeed - a tart with a heart.

Chapter 15

ONCE I WAS ELVIS

Once I was Elvis, in a rock and roll band.
I'd wiggle my pelvis, but it got out of hand.
I'd shout and holler, so my fans could dance,
Where I'd go, they'd foller, just to see me prance.
I live on Canvey, though the public think I'm dead.
I drink only cranberry, and I call myself - Big Jed.

I CALL MYSELF - BIG JED

When I was twelve I wanted to be Elvis Presley. I first heard him in 1956, and *Heartbreak Hotel* was the record which made me decide to be a singer. I practiced all that energetic, hip-swivelling stuff and tried to do the famous lip-curl. My singing was a tad squeaky. It wasn't at all like the moody and electrifying sound of Elvis' terrific voice.

I learned a few simple chords on a battered and aged acoustic guitar, which my dad had found in a dusty, junk shop, in a back-street in Bournemouth. Whenever a new, Elvis single came out, I bought it as soon as I had raised the cash (usually from car washing, which I did in the neighbourhood. I cycled round on my rusty bike, with a bucket and rags balanced precariously on the handlebars.)

If I didn't have the readies, my mum and dad often subbed me, until I could earn the money by doing small jobs round the house. Mum loved Elvis, but Dad preferred Mantovani. Can you believe it? If he had said he liked Jerry Lee Lewis better, I could have understood that, but those Mantovani records were so syrupy sweet - you could almost suffocate in their sugary mass of strings.

I formed a band called Alvis and The Bournmeouthaires. It wasn't quite as snappy a name as Elvis Presley and The Jordanaires, but we liked it. Our equipment was rudimentary and unreliable. This was towards the end of the fifties, and we couldn't buy good, cheap guitars, like the kids can nowadays.

We used Hofners mainly. They were German and were quite good if you couldn't afford Fenders, Gibsons or Gretsches. We had duff and underpowered combo amps, which rattled and distorted like mad.

We thought we could now, just about, make a half-decent sound. My voice was better than when I had started to sing, and we'd mastered easy harmonies, but our playing was still shaky. We started to get gigs at crumby dance halls. That was after we'd played in a few youth clubs - for nothing, or next to nothing. We added a few tunes by The Shadows.

Apache and F.B.I. were my favourites. My guitar had a tremolo arm, so I could try to play like Hank Marvin, but it kept going dreadfully out of tune. In spite of all this, we were building up quite a following in the area.

We couldn't afford the flashy, short-cut, Italian mohair suits which some of the other bands wore, in our area. My mum made us waistcoats in a shocking pink colour, and we wore them with white shirts, and those strange, upside-down bow-ties; or sometimes we had snaffle ties. Our drummer had started with just a snare drum and a cymbal, but he added other noisy bits and pieces. He soon had pretty good kit. We tried to do The Shadows' walk, but we couldn't manage to do that and play at the same time.

Elvis had been in the army and was back out of it, by that time. We were shocked when he recorded dreadful stuff like *Wooden Heart*. This was the man who did *That's Alright*, *Blue Moon of Kentucky* and *Mystery Train,* and now he was recording horrible things we had to pretend to like. His films didn't appeal to us either, except as an excuse to go to the pictures with girls.

There was a universal trick, which we all did. We sat in the back row, with our latest squeeze and yawned, raised our arm - and when we put it back, hey presto, it had slid round the girl's shoulders. Considering they were expecting this anyway, we wasted a lot of time just by being nervous, little tykes.

When The Beatles erupted onto the scene in 1962, we more or less stopped playing Elvis songs. We learned *Love Me Do*, and all the other Beatles singles. You know the ones I mean. The early ones were the best, before all that clever stuff, like the songs on the *Sergeant Pepper* album. We also sang a few Rolling Stones numbers, but, to be frank, I always thought that Jagger ruined a good band. He was a good showman, but what a whiney voice he had!

Like a lot of bands, we changed names frequently. We had become The Shadettes, Los Beetles, bypassed a Stones derivative, and then we discovered blues. Chess records was our favourite label at the time. Howling Wolf was The Man!

We changed our name to Whooping Walter and The Bluestones. What a daft bunch we were! We grew our hair long(ish) and tried to become grimy, but we were still at school and looked like what we were – well-washed, young boys who were still in education. Once we left school, we discovered soul music, and Stax became the label that we wanted to record for.

We shed our rhythm guitarist and recruited an organist. He had learned the organ at school, so he wasn't exactly Booker T., but he did change our sound dramatically. His organ was a Vox Continental. We yearned for a proper Hammond, coupled with that lovely, swirly sound created by those strange Lesley speakers.

We went to see the British blues and soul bands, whenever we could. There was a smelly, cellar-bar near the town centre, which hosted these acts regularly. The Stay-Rite Club was not the best place you'd ever be, but we loved it. We saw Zoot Money's Big Roll Band, Geno Washington and Herbie Goins and The Nightimers.

Screaming Jay Hawkins and John Lee Hooker also played there. We liked Zoot Money best. He was so funny. He was a proper comedian and had a Hammond too! We watched, astounded, when he stuck a knife in his organ to hold down a key, whilst he played fascinating lines round the sustained note.

Lots of bands of the time signed up to make records, and we were no exception. Plenty Records (a weak British imitation of Stax) got us to sign a three-record deal, where we paid for the recordings and then leased them to the record company. That was called tape lease. It was a good deal for the record companies.

Our first record (*Where Do the Heartaches Go?*) was released under the name Johnny B. Badde and The Heartaches. It was thin, out of tune and dreadful, but it became a Radio Caroline hit. The flip-side, *One, Two, Three, I'm Ready*, was written by the organist and me; Wallace/Smith was the credit on the B-side, and it was published by Radio Caroline's own sister company.

Our second single (another question), *Why Do I Do This?* was issued after we changed our name to The Wallace Smith Sound. It was a huge hit, as I expect you know. It sold an amazing three and a half million copies, and we toured all over the world. I hated touring. I didn't like the travelling, and the hotels were all boring.

We drank too much and used drugs too. I won't go into that in detail, as I'm not proud of what I became. Instead of being excited by the music, like we were in the beginning, we all used artificial stimulants to get us through all day, and all of the night. We wore ridiculous clothes, like most of the bands of the time. By this time, we were playing progressive music. Our first few singles had been pretty much like The Small Faces, but we submerged ourselves in prog. rock, and we allowed long, boring solos to be played, where the soloist tries to prove what a wonderful musician he is.

Our first album had featured the soul-flavoured songs we liked. They were, in effect, poppier versions of the much more authentic Stax stuff. By now we were just called Wallace, and it was under that name that we released a double album, with a ludicrous, gatefold sleeve picturing a young, fair-haired girl. In the photo, she was cuddling a sea lion, with a wolf's head. (The girl had the wolf's head - not the sea lion.)

The album bombed, and we tried to make some money by touring in Scandinavia, where The Wallace Smith Sound had previously been immensely popular. At first, we tried to play our newer, grown-up material, but all they wanted was our earlier, pop pap. One girl even asked me to autograph her breasts and a battered copy of *Where Do the Heartaches Go?* She was very persuasive if you know what I mean.

Tony Wallace and I had never been best buddies, and as we travelled through Norway and Denmark, he became even more arrogant. He said it was me – How ridiculous! In between shows he used to play jazz on his Hammond and said he wanted to play like Jimmy Smith. (The Hammond was miles better than the old Vox organ.) One day in 1973, he just walked out. There was no warning at all. He left me a rude note, telling me that he couldn't stand being in the same country as me, let alone in the same band.

I spoke to Oscar Jameson (our bass player), and he told me that he wasn't surprised. He took me aback a bit, by telling me that I was a prize big-head. I argued with Oscar, but I went and asked our drummer, Jerry Black, what he thought.

"Come on, man," he drawled, "Everybody knows what an arse you are. You're so fond of yourself nobody else can get a look-in. Jed Smith – Chief of the Jed Smith Fan Club."

I swept out of his hotel room and went back to mine. I don't know why (maybe it was all the drugs), but I sobbed hysterically for an hour. What a big softie! I was supposed to be "the lead vocalist with ultimate braggadocio," as the musical press had dubbed me. I thought I was a reasonable singer and a great guitarist, but it was the swaggering, posturing nonsense which had been mentioned the most, in the musical papers like Melody Maker and New Musical Express.

The next day I told the rest of the band that I would honour all of our commitments, until the end of 1974, but I said that after those bookings, I was out. Surprisingly, they tried to convince me otherwise. We agreed to add another guitarist, in place of Tony Wallace. We thought that if we went back to having two guitars it would give us a harder edge. Tony was a damned good organist, and we figured we couldn't replace him easily. We hoped that enlisting an additional guitarist might be easier.

The music scene was so different by then, and we thought we might join the pub-rock band wagon. We revamped our set lists and reintroduced some of our material from the first album. The next town we played, we did our revisited material, and it was a blast. The audience had expected interminable, twiddly solos for about five years, but we gave them snappy, rocky (almost punky), songs which lasted three minutes - tops.

The Scandinavian tour over, we returned to the U.K., only to find that we had been booked into cabaret venues and working men's clubs in the North of England. The audiences in these places were always difficult to please. They expected the acts to respond well to heckling, and we had to develop stock answers to abuse by rude and bluff men, who often shouted at us. Worse than that, our manager, Ricardo Belsize, encouraged us to learn some comedy songs and to tell jokes.

"You're on your last legs, guys. Make the most of it, and then you can go back to being office clerks, or whatever you want to be."

We hated him because he was telling us the truth. The tour of the North was awful. The clubs varied between being quite palatial, to depressing Bingo clubs, with us as unwelcome interruptions to the much more important task of playing Housey bloody Housey.

One club had unhealthy looking crocodiles, in small streams, round the dance floor. Luckily they were tiny, puny things, and they looked half asleep. We shared dressing rooms with comics, jugglers and strippers. The comedians expected us to play them on and off and to be ready to back them on a few songs, at the drop of a hat.

The only member of the band who could ever read music properly was Tony. He could sight-read well, but he was long gone. We did our best with chord charts, but we were useless, even when we tried to do that.

We also had to do two (or even three), gigs a night, and from sleeping in posh hotels, with large rooms for each of us, we had to share double beds, even sometimes with other acts. The last straw was me having to double up in a bed, at a tatty guest house, with a conjurer who kept fidgeting all night. At least I hope that's all he was doing.

One night we were watching the telly, in the lounge of a seedy place in Pudsey, when we saw a clip of us, when we were The Wallace Smith Sound, on one of those "Where are they now?" programmes. They asked the panel of vapid celebrities who we were, and none of them had even heard of us, let alone wanting to know where we were now. We sat there dumbfounded, and we decided that we would take no more gigs. We did the last few months with a cloud over our heads, and we breathed a sigh of relief when we did our last gig, in a cinema in Hendon. The next day, back in Bournemouth, I sold all my gear for a miniscule amount. The others did much the same.

I didn't touch a guitar again, until August 1977. The day Elvis died, I was so upset I drank a whole bottle of vodka, but I decided that I would like to play again. My wife Dot, was encouraging. Small and vivacious, she looked like Lulu, when I met her, only much better, and she wasn't quite as loud or raucous.

It was her idea that I should go back on the road, in an Elvis tribute show. I thought about it for some time, and finally took the plunge. I even managed to persuade some of the other guys from our old band to work with me again. I told them I now realised that I had become a monster, and I wanted to make amends. We found a new lead guitarist to play with us, as I wanted to be a proper front-man and to concentrate on the wiggle, and my showmanship.

I moved to Canvey because it was much cheaper than Bournemouth, and the other band members also relocated. They didn't move to Canvey, but they found houses nearby in Essex. We call ourselves The Big Jed - Elvis Show. I love it.

We do the early stuff in the first set, and I enjoy those rock and roll songs best. After the break, I don the Las Vegas jumpsuit, and we do all that nonsense. That really isn't my cup of tea, but our new guitarist has the James Burton sound (and his terrific licks), off to a tee. So, there you have it. Elvis Presley is really living in Canvey – where else?

Chapter 16

INN CONSEQUENTIAL

My favourite place is in the pub.
The real ones are going.
My local feels just like a club,
A social place, not foeing.
A pint, some nuts, a game of darts,
a sing along and some jokes.
The beer and snacks bring on the farts,
engender good high hopes.

A PINT, SOME NUTS, A GAME OF DARTS

Henry hated the new style gastro-pubs. What was wrong with pickled eggs and cheese sandwiches? The Sports Bars, with massive, widescreen Sky football screens, were even worse. Didn't they realise that not everybody like soccer? He yearned for the old-fashioned, proper pubs, with shove ha'penny, cribbage and a demented pianist, playing in the stride style.

Those were the days. A sweaty, sand and sawdust, public bar for all the oiks, and a decent smoke-filled, saloon bar for the others. Some of them also had snugs for the ladies. Henry and his pal Geoff were gradually working their way down a long list of pubs throughout the county, and they were crossing off the ones which had failed to meet their standards.

"What about this one, The Drunken Newt in Festerbridge, Henry?" asked Geoff.

"Oh no…far too modern for us. It's only got one huge bar. It's like drinking in an aircraft hangar, mate. Shall we try The Snail and Cabbage in Dreaconfield?"

"Pah, you wouldn't like that. They have blokes with backing tracks. They don't even have musicians with them. It's like listening to somebody singing with the wireless in the background."

Henry went to the bar of the pub in which they were currently sitting. He approached the barmaid and asked for two pints of real ale. He felt smart in his new, double-breasted blazer and his paisley cravat. The girl behind the bar looked him up and down, and she sniffed, which was not an attractive sound. She thought he looked like a charity shopper, with no realisation that his clothes were old hat.

"All our beer is - like, kind of real, I fink."

Henry asked for beer from a pump. The barmaid went to press a button.

"Stop! That will only deliver fizzy beer from top pressure."

"Is that a new brewery, Top Pressure? Ain't heard of that, mate."

Henry had now seen the only beer which the pub delivered from a genuine hand pump, and he asked for two pints of their Black Pearl beer. The young girl adjusted her nose ring, and she pulled two pints, reasonably expertly.

She passed them over to Henry and said, "There you go."

"I don't think so, young lady."

"Wot? Is sumfing wrong?"

"I'm not going anywhere. I want to drink my beer first, before I do so."

Henry's barely concealed irony was not detected by Marlene, even with the nose ring to guide her. She had taken his money and was trying to use a touch screen till to work out how much change to give from a ten-pound note, when each pint was £4.50. This inordinately complicated, mathematical sum was too much for the till. She offered Henry £2 change.

"My dear girl, that's too much change."

"I don't think so darlin', as that's what the till says, and so it must be right."

Henry took the coins and put one of them in the tin for a well-known and worthy charity (a point in favour of the pub, he reluctantly admitted to himself.)

"What took you so long, Henry?"

"A barmaid who doesn't know what real ale is, who thinks beer can be delivered reasonably by using gas, and who can't add up, even with electronic assistance."

Henry put the glass to his lips and took a long swig. The beer wasn't too bad, but it was far too cold. Didn't these people realise that proper beer should never be freezing cold?

"What was the name of this place, Geoff?"

"The Striped Hippo."

"That's another problem these days. Why do brewers call their pubs ridiculous names? What was wrong with The King's Arms and sensible names like that?"

Henry looked at the pub menu. Nothing surprising there, except for a twenty-ounce steak, he thought. Twenty ounces - wasn't that excessive? The two old men agreed that on their next weekly jaunt, they would try out "The Dingo and Shark" in a neighbouring village, Bodborough.

Henry had researched the pub, which described itself as "A fun, family experience with a soft-play area for children." Ignoring the obvious unsuitability of its name (and the unfortunate possibility of unwanted exposure to young progeny), they decided that it might be worth going to, as they had a micro-brewery. Henry was still searching for a good pub with real ale, within a few miles of home, and he liked the idea of beer made by tiny breweries.

"Hey Henry, that pub is what used to be called The Bricklayer's Arms."

"Really? That was a great place. They had a roaring fire, and on Saturday evenings they had a sing along, with that great, boogie-woogie pianist. He had one eye."

"One Eye Pete, wasn't he?

"Yes, but you'd probably be told off for calling him that, in this day and age."

Henry and Geoff finished their ice-cold beer, stood up and nodded to Marlene.

"Bye boys - be good."

They went out of the door, without bothering to point out that they were not boys and that at their age they had no option but to be good. Henry was driving that week, and he and Geoff took some time to get into his car, as they had some difficulty in entering a car which was too near the ground. Henry thought it was a bit like driving a car whilst lying down, and he hated the small, rear window.

Geoff was leaning over to look in the interior mirror, as he combed his few remaining hairs over his ever-increasing baldness.

"Come on, Geoff, you look exquisite!"

"More like extinct, my old chum."

They pulled out of the pub car park, without noticing a large, green lorry, which was coming towards them at an alarmingly high speed. The impact was inevitable and loud. The car was almost flattened, and the two pensioners (not Senior Citizens please!) were mashed into a bloody pulp, with no possibility at all of them still being alive.

Henry and Geoff looked down on the bent and wrecked car and the horrified lorry driver, who was unharmed except for some small bruises. He had leapt out of his cab, and he was trying to open Henry's car doors, but he knew that there was no possibility that there were any survivors. Marlene and Dean (the landlord of The Striped Hippo), had rushed outside when they heard the dreadful din of the collision, and they stood aghast.

A man in a smart uniform had taken charge of Henry and Geoff. He had a clipboard and checked their names on the list before him.

"Good day, gentlemen. We were expecting you today. My name is Richard Pankhurst, and I'm your Celestial Welcome Officer. I've been assigned, by St. Peter, to usher you into heaven and to give you meaningful tasks.

"We want you to be useful to us, doing something which will also be interesting for you."

"Are we really both dead, or is this a practical joke?" Geoff asked.

"I assure you that I'm not jesting. I've entered your details into my HeavenPad and it tells me that there are vacancies for men like you."

"Oh, and what would these be, sir?"

"We have many old fashioned pubs, with real ale, no sport on the T.V., and they have wonderful pianists. We need experts to visit them weekly, to ensure that they're not letting the side down by becoming too modern."

"That sounds like heaven to me," said Henry.

Chapter 17

MOUSTACHE

Some say I'm past my best, as I'm out of fashion,
but the mode is on or off; it's always changing.
I think I'm soft and warm, and I'm rather dashing.
My styles are up or down, and wide ranging.
I think I sometimes harbour, a little piece of food,
and the morsels are a useful extra stock.
The added storage means, I'm larder shrewd.
The curry sauce is pungent, nice and hot.
The crumbs and scrambled egg, they adorn my face.
My softly brushing hairs add to a kiss.
My owner thinks I really add, a touch of grace.
His wife says "Off - be gone! T'would be bliss."

A TOUCH OF GRACE

Roger regretted the fact that facial hair had gone out of fashion. He knew that some young chaps had esoterically shaped goatees, but he hadn't seen many full-face beards of late. He also liked moustaches. Ever since he was able to coax a little downy hair on his upper lip into a vague resemblance of a moustache, he had sported different variations on a moustachioed theme.

He'd had a pencil moustache like Clark Gable, a Zapata one (like most young men at that time), and he had experimented with a waxed model like Poirot's facial adornment. He had liked the Zapata one best - until he heard an ex-girlfriend say that he looked like a seventies, porn star. He did make that comparison an easy one, by favouring jackets with wide collars and nipped in waists. His favourite was a dark green, velvet one, which he wore with black, flared trousers.

His latest, brilliant idea was to join the Salisstown Moustache Club (S.M.C.) Each member had to have his (or her) moustache assessed by the club's experts to ensure that their facial hair met the strict club rules.

These rules were simple:

1. Moustaches must not be bleached or dyed.
2. Moustaches must be clean and free of dandruff.
3. Members found with food in their Moustaches will be fined £25, and will be reassessed every month, for the next three months, in order to ensure that they have seen the error of their ways.
4. Moustaches must not be treated with mascara, although wax will be allowed, as need be.

The S.M.C. had a formal constitution drawn up by Barrington Derwent, their President, who had been a solicitor before he retired. Mr. Derwent was as grandiose as you would rightly imagine, with a name like Barrington. The Committee (Officers and General Stewards), were elected by the members and could serve for periods of three years before seeking re-election.

The S.M.C. had arranged an outing to meet another moustache club in Somerset, The Hairy Mineheads. Barrington was vaguely dismissive of any club which could treat such an important matter as a moustache club in an offhand manner, with what probably purported to be a joke. Nonetheless, he was pleased that his club (note "his"), had been invited to dine with the young upstarts, whose club had only been formed six months prior to their contacting the S.M.C.

He telephoned his Vice-President, Alec Gormley. (Barrington would never do something as common as 'phoning; he always *telephoned* his friends, relatives and colleagues.)

"Good day to you, Alec."

"And to you, Barrington."

"Are we ready for our trip to Minehead to see that other club?" (Barrington grimaced dismissively, when he said the word, "other.")

"Oh rather, old boy. I'm looking forward to it immensely."

"The coach will be at the S.M.C. H.Q at seven a.m. sharp this Wednesday coming, so please make sure that all participating members are ready and waiting."

"S.M.C. H.Q. – Ha-Ha, you mean your house, don't you?"

"It is also my house yes, but it is the H.Q. of our illustrious and hirsute body of men. By the way, I know we changed the constitution to allow women to join, but I do hope we haven't had any female applicants for membership?"

"Not so far, Barrington. I've seen a couple of likely candidates in the High Street. Would you like me to sound them out?"

Barrington shuddered and almost told Alec off. Just in time, he realised that he was joking - again. He must put a stop to all this levity in the club. Surely their aim was to promote moustaches - with elegance, dignity and panache? After a few pleasantries, the two men concluded their telephone conversation, or rather Barrington did that very thing, whereas Alec just rang off.

The day for their trip dawned brightly, with a rosy tinge in the sky, which delivered a serious warning for shepherds. They had six members on the trip, as well as the President and Vice-President, both of whom are already on your radar.

The members were: Nicholas Sharpe, with his handsome, pencil moustache, Dennis Spring, with his Adolf Hitler monstrosity, Alistair Stannard, a man who elected to sport an upward-brushed, furry item, Roger Wetherby, reunited with his Zapata 'tache; Matthew Durnley, with a hairy ring around his lips - in a disgusting circle all round his mouth, and Ambrose Turner, who had an opposite moustache to Alistair, which he simply brushed downwards.

Nicholas was well-dressed and elegant, and his facial hair met with Barrington's approval. Dennis' Fuhrertache was disappointing and Roger's ornamental lip-hair only just scraped into the strict boundaries observed by the President.

Alistair and Ambrose were a jointly approved pair of candidates, and Barrington remembered seeing an interesting interview on the television (not the T.V. – please!) where Christopher Lee had explained to the interviewer that if he was a goodie, his moustache was always brushed upwards, whereas the reverse applied if he was a baddie. Barrington had always admired him, as he thought he was a charming gentleman, with a cultured voice and an excellent moustache, which he had grown after the Dracula films. He was also rumoured to be a real Count.

The worst moustache in the club was worn by that bounder Durnley, who had an awful ring of hair, which reminded Barrington of his wife, Ruby. (The other end - not the face. He was pleased that her demands on that score had ceased long since.)

Barrington greeted all of the members with the club signal:

"Moustaches Ahoy!"

The members all replied,

"We wear them."

Barrington examined all of the moustaches of the members and finally inspected Alec's handle-bar display. Barrington said that this was a proper representation of the club's aim. Alec returned the compliment, by tweaking Barrington's military style whiskers, and he patted his superior officer on the back. He clicked his heels and shouted, parade ground fashion, "All present and correct, sah!"

Barrington eyed him up and down and made a mental note to tell him off later. This unseemly jocular manner must be curtailed. Old Aloysius, the local garage owner had arrived with his mini-bus (his executive, luxury coach as it was described on his website.) Barrington lined up the S.M.C. officers and members, and they all entered the hallowed interior of the Mercedes coach.

Old Aloysius loaded their bags, including their packed lunches, as the trip from Essex to Minehead might take some six hours or so, barring any unforeseen eventualities. The Hairy Mineheads had arranged a dinner in honour of the S.M.C. at a small hotel, which they referred to in their emails as The Mariners Rest. Barrington remarked that there should almost certainly have been an apostrophe in Mariners. Old Aloysius asked him why.

"My dear fellow, The Mariner's Rest, or perhaps The Mariners' Rest, would signify that the Rest belonged to a Mariner or some Mariners. The Mariners Rest means that some Mariners are no longer active."

He then realised that this explanation only worked when written, and he was just about to elaborate on a piece of the S.M.C. paper, when he noticed that Old Aloysius wasn't listening anyway. The coach door was slammed shut. Old Aloysius revved up the engine, and they started their journey. After a short space of time, the only sounds within the coach came from eight sleeping, moustache experts.

Aside from a brief stop, at the services about halfway to their destination in Somerset, there was nothing to report - sah! They ate their sandwiches and drank their chosen beverages. Some had interesting things to eat. Barrington had granary bread with smoked salmon and horse-radish sauce, for example, and Alec had salt beef, with dill pickle, in a ciabatta roll - of which Barrington disapproved. What was wrong with ordinary bread, for goodness sake? The remainder had sandwiches which ranged from awful (Alistair had cheese and jam), to boring (Matthew had shrimp paste), with the occasional bit of wit and imagination, like the rocket and coriander in Ambrose's beef rolls.

They duly arrived in Minehead, and they drove down the pleasant street which runs at right angles to the esplanade, along which are ranged all sorts of restaurants. Old Aloysius managed to find The Mariner's Rest, and Barrington was pleased to see that the apostrophe had found itself a logical place in the name of the establishment, even though their website and their note-paper had divested themselves of this, apparently unwanted, punctuation mark.

The landlord was a jovial chap called Sean "But-I'm-Irish-Not-Scottish." Sean told them that all was ready for their special dinner, but The Hairy Mineheads, who had booked everything, would be slightly delayed, as they had been travelling together, and their vehicle had broken down.

"They've arranged a tab for you, and they say they want to pay for everything, in honour of an old-established moustache club deigning to visit, what they admit is a relative upstart," said Sean, consulting a piece of paper in his hand. "Furthermore, your rooms are ready upstairs, and there are several bottles of a special beer, brewed by one of their members, on each of your dressing tables."

Barrington was pleased by these gestures of civility, and he almost relaxed. The S.M.C. contingent went upstairs, and all of them were slightly the worse for wear, by the time they almost fell down the stairs.

The local ale, Sailors' Revenge, was potent, and it had an acceptable placement of the apostrophe. Barrington approved of the notion of several sailors exercising due vengeance.

They entered the low-beamed dining room, where a long table was set out for them and their hosts. Sean took Barrington to one side and said that the other club would be there as soon as possible, but they insisted that the S.M.C. should start their meal immediately. Barrington nodded and explained the situation to his fellow officer and the other men. They sat down happily, and Barrington asked Alec to say Grace. True to form, Alec said, "Grace."

Barrington elbowed him in his ribs, after which he did a proper job of thanking God, in advance, for the meal of which they were about to partake. There was a delicious, minestrone soup (which Barrington insisted was actually just vegetable soup.) This was accompanied by a deep and full-bodied red wine, of which there seemed to be plenty, as the dinner table was awash with empty bottles, before they had even finished their first course. The main course was Boeuf En Croute ("Steak pie," said Barrington.) More red wine followed the remains of the earlier red wine, which was a different sort of wine, but it was just as strong as the first sort.

Sean and his good lady wife, Dolly, worked like Trojans, and they kept the drink flowing. The S.M.C members had become rowdy, and they slumped in their seats like drunken, old men. This is, of course, exactly what they were. The dessert was Limoncello Pie (or Lemon Meringue Pie - according to Barrington, who was now finding it difficult to speak.) The pie was accompanied by a veritable ocean of a sickly, dessert wine called Apricot Sunset. Coffee and mints were washed down with several bottles of port, for most of the revellers, or cognac by the bucket load for the non-port lovers.

"Hey Barringt – hic-old boy wheresh the Herry Mernheads?" asked Alec.

"Dunno – shorry, don't know, behcurs I think I mebbe shlightly in – in – ineeb - drunk."

Alec noticed that he and Barrington were the only people in the room who were conscious. The others were fast asleep. Twenty minutes later, Sean looked into the dining area and was gratified to see that he had achieved his objective. He had been well paid by the young man who had arranged this deception. The person who had booked the whole charade was Alfie Timpson, who had been walking out with Barrington's young grand-daughter and ward, the alluring Sarah Derwent.

Sarah had been placed in Barrington's care formally, after his son and his wife had been killed, by a flash flood, in Asia. They had been holidaying, luckily without their young daughter, who was being looked after by Barrington and his spouse during the vacation.

Alfie had plucked up courage to ask for Sarah's hand, a few weeks before the S.M.C.'s visit to Minehead, and Barrington had grilled him about his job and his future prospects. Alfie had explained that he was a motor mechanic in a village garage. Barrington, being Barrington, had always imagined his grand-daughter becoming betrothed to a solicitor, a doctor, or maybe even a banker, in spite of their recent mass fall from grace.

He had curtly dismissed Alfie's request, and he had almost thrown him out, when he pleaded his case. Alfie had vowed to get his revenge. He had arranged this comeuppance with the aid of his friend Sean (and dear Dolly), who as well as being a land-lady had a part-time job as a dog groomer.

Dolly was, even now, setting out her clippers, scissors and other grooming accessories. She plucked hair, cut hair and shaved hair from all of the helpless victims, who had been drinking alcoholic beverages, which were dangerously laced with sleeping powders. At the end of her labours, she called in Sean and Alfie, who had been waiting for this moment, ever since he arrived earlier that day, well before the S.M.C.

All of the men were completely bald. They also had no eyebrows and no moustaches. Their hair was never likely to grow back, as it had also been treated with a special, laser device. Alfie settled up with Sean, and he unfurled a banner which would be the first thing that the victims saw, when they awoke. Its wording was simple. The message was:

To the President, Vice-President and members of the S.M.C.
Would you like the hair of the dog?
With love from the Hairy Mineheads.

Chapter 18

THE PRINCESS AND THE PEE

She slept quite well; she dozed 'til four.
On waking - she found that she was cold.
It crossed her mind; yes, she was sure.
The idea of a wee was gently sold.
She rang the bell; she quickly summoned aid,
The servant came. (If looks could kill!)
"Do a pee for me. You are my maid."
Her princess fell asleep, and all was still.

THE SERVANT CAME

Princess Agnes was beautiful, graceful and thoroughly spoilt. She thought that her lustrous, russet hair, her hazel eyes and her dimples made up for her conceit, and she believed that the world was at her feet, just waiting to do her bidding. Her maidservant, Bridget, was annoyed that she was summoned for tiny and useless tasks, such as blowing on her porridge to cool it, because Agnes didn't want to burn her tongue. When she was called to cut up Agnes' sausage, Bridget felt that she just had to object.

She waited until the princess was alone and knocked on the door of her boudoir.

"Enter!" The princess said, in her clear voice.

"Your Royal Highness, may I have a word with you please?"

"Certainly Bridget, what seems to be the trouble?"

"Madam, you frequently ring the bell, to call me to perform tasks which you could easily do yourself. Would it be possible to cut down on these duties?"

"Oh dear, give me an example."

"Last night, you asked me to have a wee for you. I told you that I would, but I found that I didn't need to go, and so I just went back to bed."

"My child, I thought that your kind intervention had alleviated my desire to urinate."

"No, Madam, it was just that you thought I had done your bidding. You relaxed and went back to sleep. That proves that you didn't need to call me."

"I fear that your concern is causing you to become impudent, Bridget."

"I'm fed up with running backwards and forwards, at your beck and call, only to find that you have a non-task for me to do. If you were a kind and considerate employer, you would understand that I work long hours in your service, and I need to relax once in a while."

The princess was red in the face by now, as she wasn't used to being spoken to like that, by a mere commoner.

"Get out, and pack your bags. You're sacked. Go home to your family, and see how they like housing an ungrateful wretch like you."

Bridget resisted the temptation to point out that if she was ungrateful, the princess was ungrateful - in spades. She stomped off, rather pointedly, but her stomping was wasted on the princess, who didn't care what Bridget thought of her.

As she was packing her battered leather bag, the head-chambermaid walked past the open door of her room. She could see that Bridget was red-eyed and had been crying. She also noted that she was trying to thrust all her worldly goods into the dusty bag, which had been on the top of her cupboard for five years. She didn't wish to intrude, so she carried on walking.

Bridget was a plain girl, with unremarkable features, until she smiled. It was then that her face lit up, and people noticed her sultry, grey eyes with long lashes. Just then though, she was feeling weary and unprepossessing. Sadly, she was right.

Bridget could feel a lump in the bag, and due to a typographical error, she found that it was really a lamp. It must have been put in my bag, mistakenly, by another servant, she thought. She looked at the lamp, blew some dust off it, and she rubbed it idly on her rough-textured dress. There was a blinding flash of light, and a gigantic genie stood before her. Bridget was astounded.

"Dear lady, I thank you for releasing me from my prison. I offended a fairy by trying to kiss her under the wings, and she cast a forbidden spell, which locked me in this lamp until a good, fair and honest virgin rubbed the lamp. Incidentally, are you really a virgin? If so, would you like me to help you to become something else?"

He twinkled at Bridget, and she almost forgave him for his cheeky joke, if indeed it was a joke.

"I am Alfredo, and I'm entirely at your service. Your intervention has earned you three wishes. Think carefully, and don't waste them. What are those wishes?"

Bridget said, without thinking, "I wish you would do something about my aching feet."

A cloud of smoke enveloped said extremities, and when it had disappeared, Bridget fell over before realising that her feet had gone, and they had been replaced by a fish tail, from the waist down. She felt herself carefully, and was staggered to find that she wouldn't have to worry about being a virgin (or not), because the velvet corridor, leading to the way of ensuring non-virginity, had also gone.

"Alfredo, that's not funny."

Alfredo was guffawing, at the top of his extreme volume capabilities.

"Oh, yes it is. That's one wish, now what are the other two."

"I wish you hadn't turned me into a mermaid."

A huge bolt of lightning flashed around the room, and, to her relief, Bridget found that she was a normal woman once again.

"That's two wishes. Think carefully about your last one."

"As you tricked me into the first one, I believe you should let me have an extra wish. After all, I did save you from the lamp."

"Very well. You now have two wishes."

"I wish I was the maidservant for the princess again."

There was no smoke, nor was there lightning. However, the princess' personal secretary soon knocked on the door and asked if he could speak to Bridget urgently. He didn't appear to notice that the room was full of enormous genie. Alfredo was easily seven feet tall, and his weight was in proportion, so there wasn't much space left for anything or anybody, except the genie and Bridget.

"Bridget, your princess has asked me to present you with this little note, written in her own fair hand."

Bridget took the rolled parchment from Daniel (the secretary), and read its contents with astonishment.

My dear Bridget,
I am so sorry we quarrelled. You are like a dear sister to me, and the unnecessary argument was entirely my fault. I would dearly like you to forgive me and to come back to work for me as a princess' companion.

Your salary would be doubled, and you would only need to spend three pleasant hours with me every afternoon, talking, painting and generally whiling away the hours, as equals.

Please give your answer to Daniel. A mere yes or no will suffice.
Yours ever, as a sister
Princess Agnes

"Please tell the princess that my answer is yes."

Daniel bowed and hurried out. He had no need to ask what the question was, as he had secretly unrolled the parchment and read its contents before knocking on Bridget's door. Alfredo loomed over Bridget and said, "You now have one more wish. Make it count."

Bridget thought hard, but she knew that she had no more requests.

"Can I save it for later, Alfredo?"

"No my dear, it must be used today, or its power is spent."

"I know! I wish that the princess didn't have to get up during the night to have a wee."

"Your wish is my command, Bridget."

Alfredo disappeared in another cloud of smoke. Bridget thought that the last wish hadn't worked. She heard the bell on her wall ring, summoning her to the princess. As she entered the princess' boudoir, she wondered what sort of reaction she would get from Agnes, now that she was officially a companion (and almost a sister.) She was surprised to see that the princess had a silk shawl over her lower body. The day was mild, but the princess had decided to cover her legs from the waist down.

"Oh Bridget, the most awful thing has happened. I was asleep, but when I awoke, I found that I had a golden catheter inserted inside me, and it was attached to a kid bag, with a waterproof inner. The catheter is beautiful, and the bag has a filigree, gold-mesh layer over the soft kid-skin, but try as I might I cannot remove this wretched thing."

Bridget thought she heard a booming and hearty chuckle, resounding throughout the boudoir.

"What was that noise, Madam?"

"I heard no noise, Bridget."

Bridget knew that Alfredo was having the last laugh.

Chapter 19

STINKER THE DRINKER

Whiskey, rum, lager, beer and gin,
Brandy, with schnapps and wine;
affect the crazy mood, that I'm in.
Drinking - leads to tipsy-fine.
This lasts a while, but not for very long.
I look at fancy good-time girls.
My balance then goes, awfully wrong.
All around, the whole room whirls.
And then I'm sick; I puke and I vomit.
My blood-shot eyes are blurred and dim.
This drink, it brings great trouble from it.
Now I've lost my daily vigour and vim.

THE WHOLE ROOM WHIRLS

Stinker the drinker had been called thus for many years. The smell referred to the alcoholic fumes, which he breathed all over any person who was unlucky enough to come too close. His name wasn't really Stinker of course; it was Marmaduke, and on balance he much preferred Stinker. However, balance was something he could only attempt physically, early in the morning, or before he had started one of his famous binges. Stinker repeatedly told people that he wasn't an alcoholic.

"I don't drink every day."

He said this often, and it was true. The problem was, that when he did drink, it could last as long as six or seven days, never mind his regular five day efforts. He had a devoted wife, called Gemma, who was indeed a jewel, and who did everything she could, to help him. When she had married him, she was a happy, well-rounded and attractive lady, with short, mid-brown hair, cut in an elfin style, and she had entrancing, expressive eyes.

As she struggled to cope with his addiction and its consequences, she lost weight, and her previously smart hair became lank and untidy. She looked ashen, and she wasn't coping very well with Marmaduke's problem. Nonetheless, she cleaned up the room if he disgraced himself, and she swept up any broken glass if he smashed anything. She had tried to persuade him to go to A.A. meetings and gave him examples of numerous well-known stars, who swore by their membership of A.A. Many of them said that the Twelve Step programme was the way that they had turned their lives around.

"Bunch of show offs, parading their problems in front of each other. What a load of rubbish. Anyway, I haven't got an alcohol problem."

"Marmaduke darling, you drink anything you can lay your hands on, for several days at a time. Every time you stop, you beg me to help you, until the next time."

"It's alright for you to drink! When you go out I bet you partake of the odd glass of wine."

"Yes I do, darling, but I stop after two, or maybe three glasses. You don't; you can't."

Marmaduke raised his glass to Gemma and slurred, "Sheersh."

Gemma picked up her bag and briefcase and said goodbye to her husband. Someone had to earn some money. They were heavily in debt, and she was worried that the building society might foreclose on their mortgage. She wasn't even sure that she could get back in. Marmaduke had taken to locking the doors, so she couldn't re-enter the house after work.

She left the right-hand patio door unlocked, just in case. She had tried to keep their problems a secret at work, but her colleagues were concerned for her, as she had lost so much weight. Her husband had so many accidents, and he was always in A & E. Many of these episodes were due to drunken pranks, like riding a bike into a lamp-post, or falling off a sea wall while walking along the top, when he was intoxicated.

Marmaduke had taken to threatening to do away with himself, and several times he had taken overdoses, or maybe pretended to do so. Gemma tried to smooth things over, but he was incredibly offensive in the hospital if she tried to be nice to him. On one occasion, the A. & E. Sister had threatened to section him if he didn't calm down.

"Bah, you wouldn't do that."

"Just try it, buster!"

Stinker had backed off.

Marmaduke could be so charming. He had used that charismatic quality to run up tabs at lots of off licences, until they realised that the bills were not going to be paid. His latest tactic was to go into pubs and to drink the dregs from half-empty glasses on the bar, where people had gone home and left a tiny amount in their used glasses, on the counter.

He also tried to pinch other men's drinks. One night, he came home with a black eye, and he told Gemma that he had fallen over. The landlord of the pub, Trevor, came round the next day, to see if Stinker was O.K. after being hit by another customer. The other man had taken exception to Stinker drinking his whiskey. Trevor knew that this was no mistake.

Poor Gemma was a shadow of her former self. When they were first married, she was a plump, healthy girl, with more than a dash of Dawn French about her. She was pretty, and she was popular. She had become so worried about Stinker's drinking that she was now gaunt. Her once chubby face was now angular and drawn. She wished that Stinker would try harder to overcome his addiction. One day, after a prolonged binge episode, Marmaduke asked her to help him – yet again.

"I know I've got a problem. How can I get back to normal?"

Gemma went with him to see their G.P. Marmaduke asked about "those tablets that make you sick if you drink."

Dr. Carver told them that although they did make people sick, when ingested with alcohol, the problem drinkers usually just stopped taking them, when they wanted to drink. Thus, they were not fool-proof. He proposed that he should send Marmaduke to a rehab. centre in Sussex, which had done wonders for footballers and pop singers.

"Mr. Stillgoe, I honestly believe the people there are top-notch and that they will be very helpful."

Two weeks later, Gemma drove Marmaduke to the *Halcyon Centre,* in Walborough, and after passing through the high gates, she parked the car in the turning circle, in front of the front door, before saying farewell to her husband. Stinker had insisted that she should go home, without coming into the rehab. centre. He wanted to be able to lie about his condition during the initial interview, without fear of her contradicting him.

He was there for several weeks, and a couple of times he and another patient absconded, and they tried to drink the nearest pub dry. The highly-qualified, resident psychiatrist, Dr. Bevan, was patient and understanding. He listened to Stinker telling him that his wife had caused his problem, because she was so possessive and controlling. Dr. Bevan sighed inwardly. Why didn't these drinkers accept that they had a problem and use the A.A. Twelve Steps, to help themselves?

After some weeks Stinker was ready to be released into normality. Gemma picked him up, and he asked if they could go somewhere to talk. She parked the car in a layby, near to the rehab. centre.

Marmaduke said, "Dr. Bevan says my problem has been caused entirely by you. He says you are a possessive control freak, and he wasn't surprised that I need a drink or two in order to live with you."

Gemma started the car, turned round and headed back to the *Halcyon Centre*. She told Marmaduke that she had left her handbag in the room where he had been staying.

"Stay there, darling. I'll be back soon."

Marmaduke started to read his daily paper. Gemma went straight to Dr. Bevan's office, and she entered without so much as a by your leave. She found that he was a forbidding character, with greying hair and aquiline features. His charcoal grey suit and crimson, silk tie reeked of money, and yet she could see a little humanity in his deep-set eyes. Dr. Bevan was surprised by the peremptory entrance, but he just raised his bushy eyebrows slightly, and asked her to take a seat.

"I'm sorry, but I've come to have something out with you. Marmaduke Stillgoe, my other half, said that you told him that his drink problem has been caused entirely by me. He also said you believe that I'm a possessive, control freak, and you weren't surprised that he needs a drink or two in order to live with me. I must protest most strongly. I've done everything in my power to help him."

"Mrs. Stillgoe - Let me stop you right there. I said no such things. Your husband told me that you had caused his problem, but that's ever so common. Alcoholics usually blame everybody, except themselves, for the dreadful state that they are in."

Gemma was embarrassed and ashamed. She muttered her heart-felt apologies and rushed out of the office. When she got to the car, Marmaduke was nowhere to be seen. She decided that she would have to make a tour of the town's drinking holes, to find him. This was something which she had to do frequently when he disappeared. At the fifth pub, she found Marmaduke with his arm round a brassy blonde, who reeked of foul smelling, cheap perfume.

"Hallo darling, I'm glad you found me. I was just telling Rita how wonderful you are. Have you got a tenner? I borrowed some cash from her, so we could have a drink, while we were waiting for you to come to pick me up."

Stoney faced, Gemma passed a ten-pound note to Rita and ushered Marmaduke out. He was soon fast asleep, and when she got back to their house she drove the car into the garage, and she left him, stinking of booze, in the car. She was sorely tempted to run a hose from the exhaust, to poke it through a half-open car window, and to leave the car engine running. She blinked, stood erect and walked out of the garage after taking the key out of the ignition – she was not a murderer!

The next morning, she woke up, showered and dressed, ready to go to work. She pushed her husband out of the car and left him lying on the garage floor, in a patch of oil. All morning long, at work, she worried about him. At lunchtime, she drove home, and he opened the door to her. He had cleaned himself up and shaved.

"Darling, I'm a new man. Tomorrow, I'll go to an A.A. meeting. Everything will work out fine."

Pigs might fly, thought Gemma.

Chapter 20

TOTAL ECLIPSE OF THE TUNE

Chanteuses of today, are scrumptious and are fair,
but they over-twiddle, with their needless notes.
They look quite good, but their screaming really scares.
And all the while - their family over-dotes.
The youngsters battle mockery, from smug and smirking judges,
As they sing a pointless, million, trillion quavers.
They joke and rile and scorn, the auditions are just fudges.
Their smarmy smugness never even wavers.

A MILLION, TRILLION QUAVERS

Damian Powell looked at himself in the mirror and was immensely pleased with his appearance. His dark hair was brushed back off his brow, and he had a manly, square jaw, which he thought gave him an air of a fifties film star. He was a good looking man. However, his smug and over-confident bearing rubbed people up the wrong way. He smirked at his reflection, and it smirked back. He raised one eyebrow, and then he practiced his, "My, how surprised I am! This person can actually sing," look.

The telephone rang, and Damian picked it up immediately.

"Good morning, Damian here, if you're looking for talent I can find it, and if you are talented, I can make the most of you!"

"Ah, finally run to ground, you jumped up lump of turd. My daughter was on your show last week, and you've ruined her life."

"How could that be? What's her name?"

"She's Phoebe Baby, and she will be the greatest singer since Aretha Franklin."

Powell remembered her well. She was a corpulent porpoise of a girl, aged fourteen, with delusions of adequacy. Her squeaky voice could never be compared to Aretha's, and he had only pushed her through the auditions because she looked fresh-faced, and had a sorry tale to tell. He often found that if a contestant had lost a mother, father or sibling, a bit of crying and trembling added to the show's pathos, and it attracted members of the public to that weeping wreck. He smiled, as he remembered the boy who said he was competing because his dog was ill.

"Oh yes, I remember her well. What's your name, please?"

"I'm Barnaby Davidson, Phoebe's father, and I want to know exactly why you turned my daughter down."

"Mr. Davidson, we can't have a show which only has winners. In life, there are winners and losers, and your daughter is definitely a loser.

It's my professional opinion that she can't sing and that she will never be a star. She's had her fifteen minutes of fame, and she should go and work in a pizza house."

"You're a no-nothing, pretentious idiot. My daughter is terrific."

"She certainly terrified me, especially when she tried to hold that long last note, on what she said was her best song."

"You'll be sorry! I know where you live."

The phone was slammed down by Mr. Davidson, and Damian sighed. This sort of thing was happening far too frequently nowadays. However, he wasn't worried. He had been warned before by over-zealous parents that they were going to make his life hell, that he would be beaten up, or his house would be set on fire.

He couldn't understand why these people wouldn't listen to him. He knew that he was the most influential person in the world of pop music. As he strode masterfully across the room, he brushed a hand over his mane of artfully darkened hair and licked a finger before smoothing it over his eyebrows.

The phone rang again, the ringtone being the theme tune from his well-known T.V. show, *Powell Presents!* He particularly liked the exclamation mark, which had been suggested by his then P.R. consultant, Amanda Hughes, who worked for Marketing Now! and was similarly over-fond of hyperbole. He had toyed with the idea of renaming Art King, one of his earlier protégés, as Exclamation! Art had dismissed the idea, and he had left Powell's management firm to form a band called The Periods.

"Good morning, Mr. Powell. I can see that your computer is running slow, and this is because you haven't claimed your P.P.I. refund. I also note that you had a car accident, which was not your fault, because the lorry in front lost some solar panels, you should have had installed, as the government is allowing a magnificent subsidy."

"What ho, Archie. You're an old villain."

He was quite fond of Archie, who was his fellow judge, and lesser personage, on *Powell Presents!* Although Archie knew next to nothing about music, the audience liked him. He was so nice, it almost made Damian want to throw up.

"Damian, earlier today I had a call from a man called Davidson who wanted me to give him your telephone number. He said he worked for Davidson and Davidson, a firm of solicitors, who are based in Islington.

"I looked them up on my mobile phone, while I was on the land line, and their website seemed pukka. I passed your number to this chap, who said he had details of a large legacy which was owed to you. I know you don't need the money, but every little bit helps."

"Archie, the man you spoke to is almost certainly nothing to do with that firm. He just rang me, and he's the father of that dumpy, little screecher we had on the show last week, Phoebe Baby. He was most unimpressed that I'd criticised his overweight brat."

"I'm so sorry old boy; I do hope that you weren't too upset."

"I just don't care what people say to me, I know I'm always right. He threatened me - but so what - I've had that kind of thing for years, while I've been laughing my way to the bank."

"O.K. matey, see you at the rehearsal on Wednesday."

"Ciao!"

Damien looked at the mirror again. It was always a pleasure. He smiled, but the reflection grimaced. He was puzzled. He tried again, but the reflection just pulled a face at him.

"What on earth is happening?" asked Powell.

"I am your good side, which has been hidden for too long."

"That's ridiculous; in a few moments I'll wake up and laugh at this silly dream."

"Oh no, you won't. If you don't mend your ways, I will make sure that Barnaby Davidson is made aware of all your movements. I will make sure that he is wound up so tight, that an unfortunate car collision will take place, thus removing you from the public's gaze once and for all."

Damian turned the mirror to the wall, firstly to see if there was any sign of wires leading to it, which might aid the projection of this other side of him - and secondly because he couldn't stand this sanctimonious clap-trap any longer. No wires. He turned the mirror back again, and the good side of Powell started lecturing him again.

"You can never be free of me. It's time you mended your ways"

Damian left the room and shrugged on his camel, cashmere overcoat, with a deep brown, velvet collar. He picked his keys up and went to his triple garage. Yes - the Bentley today, I think. The engine purred like a satisfied cat, when he started the car.

He pressed the button on the garage-door control, and he steered the luxury vehicle down the sloping drive to the road leading to the nearest town, Masseter, which is a beautiful place, and one of the most high-class towns in the Surrey stock-broker belt. The journey to his favourite wine bar would not take long.

As he came to an intersection, he saw a man driving a large van and waving a fist at him. He also realised that the other driver was swearing. Too late, he saw that the van driver had no intention of slowing down or stopping, and he was heading straight for a side-on collision with his maroon Bentley.

The crash was loud, and it jarred Powell, but he was only slightly injured. The Bentley had withstood the prang well, but the van was a complete wreck. The other driver was slumped over his steering wheel and looked in a bad way. Powell got out of his car and ran to the side-door of the van, which had Barnaby Davidson – Plumber Extraordinaire! written on the side.

The exclamation marks are proliferating, thought the pop mogul. Damian and another man, who had jumped out of a car behind the van, wrenched open the van door between them, but one look (or two looks if you counted both of them), told them that the victim inside was beyond saving.

An ambulance and a police car had arrived, and Damien was breathalysed. It was negative, and the policeman immediately became more friendly.

"Aren't you Damian Powell?"

"Yes, officer. I live in Highcrest Rise, just over there."

He waved vaguely, in the direction of his palatial home. The medics had left the scene of the accident, after putting Barnaby Davidson on a stretcher (in a black body-bag), and loading him into the ambulance. There had been much shaking of heads between the driver and his colleague. The Bentley was still driveable, and Damian did a cautious U-turn before returning to Powell Towers.

He unlocked the front door, threw his coat on the massive sofa in his study and poured himself a large drink. The brandy was gulped down in a flash, and several others followed. He went into his lounge, and looked at the mirror. He raised a glass to his good side, and the non-reflection said, "I tried to warn you."

The headlines in the papers the next day were awful.

Powell rammed by Phoebe Baby's father.
Phoebe Baby's father dies in accident with Damian Powell.
A million, trillion quavers couldn't save Phoebe's father.

Damian remembered how he had asked Phoebe if she thought a million, trillion quavers made for good singing. He tried to put this all out of his head. He was permanently drunk for six weeks, even though Archie tried to get him to snap out of it.

Amanda Hughes, with whom Damian had a brief dalliance a few years back, was much less forgiving. She had been ditched ignominiously, when Powell had found a larger breasted, blonder and more subservient mistress. She told Archie that Damian had been lucky the van driver hadn't hired a large lorry to do the job properly.

Damian spoke to the mirror every day, and his good side never varied the condemnation of all that Powell had built up. His detractor criticised Damian's record companies, the management company and the T.V. shows, including *Powell Presents!* All these counted for nothing

One day, Archie was unable to gain entrance to Damian's home, despite ringing the doorbell and knocking on the door for some time. He called the police, as he was worried. He hadn't seen Damian for several days but had spoken to him, on the phone that morning. His friend had seemed dazed and incoherent, but he had said to Archie, "It was all a waste of time, and I'm leaving you now. Goodbye."

Damian had hung up before Archie could say anything. When the police arrived at Powell Towers, Archie told them he was concerned about Damian. They rang the bell, but there was no answer. In the end, they used a large battering-ram, to break the door open. The police entered first, and Archie heard one of them say, "He's a goner."

He looked up and saw his friend hanging by the neck from an oaken rafter, which went over the top of the stairs. His face was suffused with blood, and his eyes were swollen. His tongue was lolling out of his mouth, and his head was at an awkward angle.

Archie sat down heavily on the chair by the door. He felt a lump under his posterior, and he found that there was a thick envelope beneath him, addressed to *Archie - My Friend!* Inside, there was a letter and a hastily scrawled document, which purported to be his last will and testament, replacing all others.

The letter was brief but to the point.

My friend Archie
I have written a new will. This leaves all of my estate to Phoebe Davidson. Her father is dead, indirectly because of me, and I think this is the least I can do to help Phoebe.
Damian (The good side.)

Archie was baffled by the reference to the good side. In time, Phoebe used part of her newfound fortune to set up a music foundation for disabled children who wanted to sing. She called it *A million, trillion quavers.*

Chapter 21

LEND ME A TENNER

My plea has been a failure; yes, it's been misunderstood.
Though I thought my requirement was, quite clear.
My order it has slipped, into faulty blunderhood.
The goods delivered, were all wrong; so I fear,
I'm returning the wrong item, to the sloppy sender.
Though he sent me a good singer of much note,
I asked him for a tenner, but he sent a regal tenor.
My instructions were exact; see what I wrote.

FAULTY BLUNDERHOOD

Cyril Fortescue was a serial, online shopper (as well as a Cyril, on-line shopper.) He had dozens of accounts with online retailers, and he looked forward to receiving goods delivered by the postman (or the courier), nearly every day. His home was gradually becoming swamped with unopened boxes and parcels, and there were many loose items from opened boxes and parcels.

He had even moved his dining table into the garage, so he had more space to store his merchandise. He tried eating in the garage, but the smell of damp, and the rusty, old tins of paint made him depressed. He sold his table on an auction site and spent the proceeds on a rare 1955 vinyl record by The Raving Rockabellos. The record arrived in fine condition, and Cyril had specially ordered a 78 r.p.m., wind up gramophone on which to play this scarce record, and other 78s which he had ordered in a nostalgic fit of retrospection.

He also ordered his meals online, and found that this gave him more time to browse the web for bargains. He bought records, books, old magazines and musical instruments, including a phono-fiddle which had captured his fancy, and he paid £250 for Daddy Lindberg's 1967 vinyl single, *Wade in the Shade.* His chum, Ian Buttershaw, pointed out that he could have bought it for $0.99 on iTunes, but Cyril was adamant that he needed to have the real record to hold and to put onto the spindle of his collectible, Dansette record player, the best medium (bar none), on which to play sixties records, (according to Cyril.)

His purchases were hit and miss, as he often bought them in the middle of the night when he had been drinking vino. This had also been ordered online, and he relied on Winetime for his supplies. Winetime loved people like Cyril, who asked for a crate of their specially recommended wines. They shipped a lot of wines that were not selling well, in these mystery crates.

Ian often came to Cyril's house, to ask him if he wanted to go to the bowls club or to a pub which used to be one of Cyril's favourites, The Halfway House. Cyril said, "I don't see the point of going out. I can stream films, or, better still, I can watch my Betamax cassettes of wonderful, old films. I managed to pick up some refurbished V.C.R.s which are compatible with Betamax. It was so much better than V.H.S., don't you know?"

"I'm sure you're right Cyril, but we now have H.D., Blu-Ray and 4K T.V.'s, and most of the new ones are Smart T.V.'s so you can stream films straight to your telly."

"I think I have a Smart T.V. somewhere, but it's under a lot of boxes and packages."

Cyril used to be a dapper man, but he had let himself go badly. At one time, he had been smart (not like the T.V. under the boxes and packages, but still presentable), and he had taken great care of his hair. He had grown it too long now, and it was tied back in a straggling, grey pony-tail. As Cyril never saw the light of day, his complexion was pale and wan. He had used insulation tape to mend his glasses, and he wore cheap clothes, which he had bought in online auctions. He didn't realise that these vestments were unwanted by any other customers. They were all baggy, but Cyril said he felt comfortable in these shapeless garments.

His long-time girlfriend, Beryl, usually went to see him thrice weekly, but she was becoming tired of his lack of interest in her, and in sex particularly. Cyril didn't appreciate that Beryl wanted some love and affection, and he spent many wasted nights, droning on about his model trains and the layouts which he planned, once he could find the box in which the tracks had been delivered.

Beryl tried to cook tasty dinners for him. However, upon finding that the saucepans were now all in the loft, and there was no dining table, she gave up in disgust. She finally left a note which said,

Dear Cyril
I'm leaving this note to you on the 18th August 2015. I hope you read it fairly soon. If I don't hear from you by 18th October, I intend to marry Bob Knowles. He's asked me many times if I would become his wife, but I had always been hoping that you would one day ask me, too.

If you do, I will accept. This is because I love you, even though you have some strange problems. However, I'm fond of Bob, and we will probably make a go of being happy together if you don't contact me.
With fondest love
Beryl
XXX

The note was left on the mantelpiece in Cyril's front room. The next morning, a large parcel arrived, containing a Norwegian Army Officer's Great Coat. Cyril couldn't find a space for it, and he rested it on the mantelpiece before taking it into the garage - which had more space in it, now that the intrusive dining table had been sold.

The parcel had some grease on the wrapping, and poor Beryl's note stuck to it, as Cyril lifted it through to the integral garage. In consequence, Cyril didn't see the note before the deadline, and in due time, Bob and Beryl were married. They weren't happy, and Bob left her after three years, but that is a different story.

When Ian told Cyril about the marriage, Cyril looked tearful for at least four or five seconds, and then said, "I want you to try some Orange Pekoe tea, which came this morning from Teatimeonline. It's a strange tasting brew, but I'd value your opinion."

Ian thought that the tea was probably long past its best-before date, but he told Cyril that it was refreshing. Ian had recently taken up with a striking widow, who had rather captured his fancy. She was sixty if she was a day, but she was still easy on the eyes, and she was chique and refined. She had a regal air, perhaps like a duchess, and resembled Audrey Hepburn (in her later years.)

Ian would have preferred her to look like Audrey in her earlier years, but he was still grateful to have her as a lady-friend. Ian had surprised himself in bed with Madeleine, and he had surprised her too, as she thought he would not be that energetic. What with all this romantic fervour and unaccustomed exercise, he died a happy man, after a particularly rigorous afternoon of passion. Cyril hadn't been told about Ian's death, and he wondered why his chum didn't come to see him any longer. However, he was resigned to the fact that Ian had obviously decided he had better things to do.

Cyril had been looking at women on the Brides2Buy.com website, and he had refined his search results carefully. His original search had yielded 46,765 hits for "pretty." After thinking about what he wanted, (what he really, really wanted), he searched for a potential bride who was pretty, brunette, slim, active, affectionate and who could cook. There were still 4,796 hits, so he added to his criteria: "likes music, cinema and model trains."

There were now no hits at all. After trying various different combinations of the filters, it became apparent that it was the reference to "likes model trains" which meant that there were no hits, and so he deleted that requirement. He carefully considered the 347 hits which he now had, and he made his own short list.

He had three potential brides to choose from. Birgitte came from Denmark (very much a plus), and she was the archetypical, Scandinavian beauty - slender, blonde and with limpid, pale blue eyes. Hilda was German, but she had a surprisingly friendly smile. Lottie, with the turned up nose, came from Southend-on-Sea. All of them offered to meet him, so that they could each see if they liked each other. Cyril took the unusual step of leaving his house, so he could do a recce, (or rather three recces.)

Birgitte had come to London for a nursing conference (another plus he thought, as he figured he might need a nurse, as he got older.) She looked more careworn than her profile picture, but she was sociable and knowledgeable. He decided he would see the other two, before making any rash decisions.

Hilda was brutally forceful, in spite of the misleading smile, and she was taken off the list mentally, immediately she met him in Munich airport. She set about organizing him, and she had a long checklist with her. She went through the list in the coffee lounge. After asking him questions about which side of the bed he slept on, what time he got up, and when he went to bed, she started to ask questions about sauerkraut and German music.

Cyril told her that they were unsuited, and that he had decided to book a flight home, that same evening. Hilda punched him on the nose. She made matters worse, by ignoring the bloody mess she had made of his face, and she stormed out of the airport. I need to see Lottie from Southend, thought Cyril. He went home and sent her an in-app message.

"Let's meet at the end of the pier in Southend, at noon on Wednesday next. I will be wearing a Norwegian Army Officer's Great Coat and will have a rolled up copy of The Times in my hand"

"O.K. – I'll be there at the time you suggested. I'll have a lime green mac on, and orange wellies."

Cyril was at the end of the pier at the prearranged time, but he couldn't see a garishly dressed lady. He was surprised when Lottie tapped him on the shoulder.

"Here I am, Cyril."

"But, where are your lime green mac and orange wellington boots?"

Lottie laughed.

"Come on Cyril, I was pulling your leg."

They spent a magical afternoon on The Golden Mile, and they watched youngsters enjoying themselves, in the amusement parks. They ate hamburgers, hot-dogs and candy floss, and they drank beer and gin in a side street pub, which had seen better days. As Lottie bade him farewell she said, "Will I do?"

Cyril nodded emphatically. He went home to Barnet and logged on to Brides2Buy.com. He added Lottie to his basket and pressed *Buy Now – See terms and conditions.* The payment terms were complicated. There was a one-off fee of £500, plus £100 per month after they married, for the first year, £50 per month during the second year and £20 per month during the third year. If they split up during this period, and Lottie said that it was his decision, the full amount would become payable immediately.

Cyril thought this over carefully. He was lonely and had really enjoyed Lottie's company. He pressed *Buy Now* again. The system said. *Are you sure? Review your purchase below!* Cyril obeyed orders and did so quickly, and then he pressed *Confirm your purchase.* The system responded, *Order confirmed. Your new wife to be will arrive tomorrow.* Cyril was so excited that he could hardly sleep that night.

At 10:30 the next morning a lady rang the bell. Cyril didn't recognise her, but she said, "I'm Lottie, your new bride."

Cyril was mightily disappointed. This was not the beautiful being, with whom he had flirted in Southend.

"Who are you? I've never seen you before. Come here and look at the profile picture of Lottie."

His deft fingers whizzed over the keys of his laptop, and a picture was displayed. It was undoubtedly the woman sitting opposite him. He sent her away and contacted Brides2Buy, via their complaints screen. Their response was rapid but worrying.

The lady whom you met in Southend was Lottie Fairbrother. The lady whom you ordered was Lottie Niblo. You confirmed your order twice, and you were also asked to check your purchase details carefully. You can either continue to buy Lottie Niblo, on an instalment basis, or you can pay the full amount and close your account.

Cyril transferred the full amount to Brides2Buy and closed his account. He was relieved that he had managed to get out of marrying the wrong Lottie. All he had to do, was to contact Lottie Fairbrother. He would explain what had happened, and marry the right Lottie. Bugger - he thought. I need to get back into Brides2Buy, so I can get in touch with my little friend.

He tried to access his account with his old log in details, but the system said that the profile did not exist. He also tried to set up another account in his name, but the system said:

In view of account difficulties in the past, we are unable to give you access to Brides2Buy.

Being a wily sort of fellow, he set up a brand new account in a different name. He searched for his Lottie again. After trawling through all of the Lottie hits, he was dumbfounded to find that the right Lottie was not available.

Cyril has spent every weekend in Southend, for the last fifteen years, trying to trace Lottie Fairbrother. There have been lots of Lotties, but never the right one. He is old and tired. The real Lottie moved to Canada to live with her aunt, shortly after Cyril failed to contact her, or to buy her from Brides2Buy. Cyril walks up and down the pier every weekend, muttering.

"What did you say?" asked one young man.

"Caveat Emptor!" replied poor Cyril.

Chapter 22

THE ANNALS OF CRIME

The annals of crime are dusty files,
or they were, before the web.
There were lots of drooping, cardboard piles
and folders, strewn and shed.
The search was long and painful.
Good results were few and far.
The eyes grew weak, and strainful.
Let's adjourn, to a club or bar.

THE SEARCH WAS LONG AND PAINFUL

Earle Spriggs had worked as an archivist for more years than he could remember. His whole working life had been spent at *The Museum for Clerical Perfection,* in the worst part of Dulwich. The museum was a dusty and dark place, a long way from the High Street, but his duties were not over onerous. He had perfected a fool-proof filing system, with colour coded ring-binders and alphabetical dividers, that would give the most nit-picking of filing clerks a rosy glow.

Ah, that was a name to conjure with! Rosy Glow was one of his first assistants at the museum. She was a slim, blonde girl, with a feline look and a wide mouth. She had the same exciting look as Carly Simon at her best, and she was rather naughty. (That's Rosy of course, although Carly Simon may well have been naughty too. Carly had been one of Earle Spriggs' favourites, back in the day, and he still remembered the pictures of her which he had taped to his bedroom wall, when he was growing up.)

He had been flirting with Rosy, one evening, after a long day's work in the basement, and he had been astounded when his timid chat up lines had resulted in an exciting skirmish, on the Director's sofa. (They had retrenched to Mr. Jackson's office, which housed his awards for services to filing and archiving personnel all over the U.K.) As Earle finished his important service to one of the most junior filing assistants in the U.K., the phone rang. Earle leapt up, almost tripping over his trousers, which were around his ankles. Rosy laughed at his predicament. He picked up the receiver and said, "The Museum for Clerical Perfection, Mr. Spriggs speaking, how may I help you?"

"Mr. Spriggs, I need to consult you about your wonderful filing system. My name is Tyrone Sutton, and I work in a more minor establishment than yours, in a small village in Norfolk. We're having great difficulty in deciding how best to upgrade our system. Your director met me, at The Filing Conference for Tomorrow in Brighton, last week. Oh my goodness, that sounds funny doesn't it?"

Earle thought that this fellow sounded like a bit of an ass, but he seemed quite harmless, even though he did waffle on a lot.

"Did Rolf Jackson suggest that you should contact me? I was on the point of leaving for the day, as I had just finished doing some important filing with my assistant."

"Yes, he said that he felt sure that you would be able to help me. I've taken the liberty of sending you a rail warrant, which can be used any time during the next two weeks. If you're able to come to Norwich, I'll pick you up at the station. I can then run you to our place, which is *The Spinning Jenny Museum* in Ragley."

"I don't have any leave due, and I'm not certain when I can come."

"Mr. Jackson said he was so pleased with your new system, that he wanted it to be adopted by other museums. He asked me to tell you that he will allow you three days off next week, during which you can show me how it's done. He said you could phone him at home to check."

"O.K. Mr. Sutton, I'll ring Mr. Jackson and will get back to you. What's your number?"

Earle wrote the number in his diary, in his beautiful, copper-plate handwriting. He then phoned Mr. Jackson. As Jackson answered, Earle could visualise his austere and vaguely frightening face. He confirmed, in his usual dour and unenthusiastic tone, that he had indeed said that he would be pleased to release Earle temporarily from his duties, for the purpose of showing Mr. Sutton what a really good filing system should look like.

"Take young Miss Glow with you. She knows the ropes. I know she'll probably bore the pants off you, with her silly chat and that terrible giggle, but it will be good experience for her."

Earle tried not to laugh. All this talk of pants being bored off, and good experience for Rosy, was making him feel a little flushed, especially as Rosy was doing something quite creative under cover of her dress, which was draped over her head.

"Very well sir, I'll go on Tuesday and will be back here in the office on Friday, so I can let you know how we got on."

They both rang off, and Earle allowed Rosy to finish her latest task, before gently pushing her away. He explained that they would be going to Norfolk and that she would be travelling with him to Ragley.

Rosy looked at him, wide-eyed.

"Golly gosh! Do you know what the sleeping arrangements will be?"

Earle said that under the museum's rules they would each be allowed to occupy a modest, single room, in an establishment with a shared bathroom.

"Oh, that would be terrific. We can squeeze into a single bed in one room and just mess up the covers a little in the other one, so it looks as if we did sleep in two rooms."

Earle allowed himself a small grin, even though he was worried about such an extended trip with his newly seduced lady-friend. Rosy was not worried at all. She was an experienced person who had already had five lovers, which was four more than Earle, who had only made love to one girl - Rosy.

Earle did have a girlfriend, when he was much younger. In those days, he was a handsome youth of twenty-one. He had been slim and dark, with the look of a Sun records era Elvis. Now, he was a prematurely aging fellow of forty-two. He recalled the night his girlfriend had given him his marching orders.

"I'm so sorry, Earle. You bore me. I was attracted to you because you're good-looking, but all you talk about is filing, and related dull topics. I'm sure you'll be able to find a steady, uninteresting girl with whom you can settle down, but it won't be me."

Earle had been relieved. Their attempts at making love had not gone much further than furtive fumbling in the back row of the flicks. He had been scared of taking things too far, too fast, as he was so inexperienced, and although he had read several smutty and inappropriate books about the subject, he would have run a mile had she stripped off and said, "Take me, take me!"

Earle instructed Rosy to make all the booking arrangements for their rooms and to look up the train times, so he could meet her at the station in Dulwich, in order that they could be in Norwich by two p.m., on the day of their outward trip.

After delegating the travel arrangements to Rosy, he phoned Tyrone Sutton and confirmed that they would meet him, as near to two p.m. as possible, on the Tuesday of the following week. All over the weekend, he kept remembering his exciting episode on Mr. Jackson's sofa with dear, little Rosy.

He thought she was a perfect angel. He realised that he was incredibly lucky to have snared such a poppet. Rosy thought about their lovemaking a few times, and she resolved to show him some tricks which would make him more proficient. She also hoped to show him how to slow things down somewhat.

Earle packed his clothes carefully, making sure that he had clean, white underwear and a smart, dark-grey suit with a faint, red stripe, which he had bought on a whim but never worn. He thought it was too racy, but then he remembered Rosy, and he decided racy was good. Rosy packed scarlet, satin underwear, which had cream, lace edging. She thought she would also take two flimsy blouses and a pencil skirt. Those clothes will make his eyes pop out, she thought.

Earle was not great in the looks department. He was bald and had entirely lost his youthful resemblance to Elvis. That didn't matter much, but he pasted his few remaining locks over his head with Brylcreem. That did matter, and it did nothing for him. She thought she might be able to persuade him to cut his hair shorter, and to buy some modern clothes.

They met on the station, and Rosy kissed him on the cheek. Earle was pleased, but surprised, at this outward display of devotion. On the train, they talked about filing, ring-binders and box files. After a while, Rosy said, "Can't we talk about something else?"

"How about politics or religion?"

"No, let's talk about loving!"

They chatted aimlessly for a while, and Earle fell asleep. As he was dozing, his mouth gaped open, and a little spit dribbled down his chin. Rosy watched as it reached the bottom of his chin, and she leant over and wiped it off with her hankie.

"What – what…are we there yet?"

"Two more stops."

When they stepped off the train, in Norwich, they looked round for Tyrone. A smiling man bore down on Rosy, and he kissed her hand, saying: "Tyrone Sutton at your service - Rosy I believe? And this must be Earle."

Tyrone shook Earle's hand, and he ushered them both through the doors of the station and towards a gleaming, silver Jaguar.

"This is my beast. I hope you like it."

"They must pay well at your museum, Mr. Sutton," ventured Earle.

"Tyrone, please! No they don't, but I'm a man of independent means. My father died a few years ago, and he left me two houses and a lot of money, plus some interesting investments."

Rosy could see that there was more to Tyrone than met the eye. That which met the eye was pleasing enough, but his houses, money, investments (and the Jaguar), were added attractions. He drove them to the Ivydene B. & B. establishment and promised to pick them up that evening, at six o'clock, for a spot of food and some bevvies.

He was as good as his word, and they had a convivial evening at a small Chinese restaurant, called The Choi Yin. Earle noticed that whenever he went to the toilet, Rosy and Tyrone seemed to be getting closer and closer to each other, on the red velvet, bench seat. They were talking gaily, each time he returned, but they quietened down whenever he spoke about filing systems.

Earle and Rosy worked together on the Wednesday and the Thursday, to implement Earle's system at the museum in Ragley. They didn't see much of Tyrone, who said he had some important correspondence to attend to. When Earle went to Tyrone's office, to tell him that all was ready for his inspection, he found him lying on a sofa - with a racing paper over his eyes and a half-empty bottle of whiskey, on the table next to him.

"Oh, I'm so sorry. I've been working hard, and I must have dropped off."

Tyrone looked at the system for just a few minutes, and he said he was pleased.

Earle had spent Tuesday night, with Rosy, in a tiny, single bed, but their attempts at renewing the physical side of the relationship were a disappointing fiasco. Rosy was not that interested, and she said it was because she was too tired. Earle was keen, but he needed some encouragement from Rosy, which was not forthcoming.

On the Wednesday night, Earle said he felt rather queasy and cried off the evening dinner, which Tyrone had said would be at a restaurant which served the largest steaks he had ever seen. Later that night, Earle waited, in vain, for Rose to come to his room. In the small hours, he went to hers, and it was empty.

In the morning, he asked Rose where she had been. She explained that she had just popped out for a breath of fresh air. Earle was not convinced, and he had been bad-tempered all day on the Thursday, their last day in Ragley. They had arranged to travel back on the six o'clock train from Norwich.

Tyrone had said he wanted to ask Rosy some questions about the filing system, and Earle reluctantly agreed to meet her at the station. Rosy was not there on time, and Earle decided to catch the train as planned. All the way back he seethed, and he cursed Tyrone. When he got home, he had a long, hot bath and went to bed.

At the museum in Dulwich the next day, he was called in by Rolf Jackson.

"That wretched girl, Rosy, has just telephoned. She's given in her notice and gone to work for Tyrone Sutton. Good riddance."

Earle was heartbroken. He put his heart and soul into his work but was staggered, when he received a phone call from Rosy, several days later.

"Earle, I owe you a huge apology. I was blinded by Tyrone, the man of so-called independent means. I found out too late, that he has no means, independent or otherwise. He's heavily in debt and has now been sacked by his boss, as there have been some financial irregularities. Please would you take me back?"

Earle was sure that he should say no. He wanted to say yes. He tossed a coin and thought, heads yes, tails no. The coin fell to the floor - tails up. Earle took a deep breath and said, "Yes, I will take you back."

Chapter 23

FLOYD, FLAWED AND FLOORED

Floyd was a useless, bareknuckle boxer,
a pugilist like a pugilisn't.
The crowd was one, which scorns and mocks a
man, both puny and wizened.
And Floyd was much more, on the boards
than an actor on the stage.
The watchers came in jeering hordes,
to watch Floyd falling, and aged.

A PUGILIST LIKE A PUGILISN'T

Floyd Charles was always a weedy and puny specimen. He weighed in at less than five pounds when he was born, six weeks prematurely. His mother, Irma, loved him, nonetheless. She telephoned his father with the good news.

He had been working up north, as a labourer on a large, building site, and had not expected that the baby would be born whilst he was away. He promised to rush back, even if only for a few days. His foreman was surprisingly sympathetic, and he told Cliff that he could take one week off - unpaid. He tempered his graciousness by saying that if he wasn't back by the eighth day, Cliff's place would be given to another man, who was on a waiting list for work. It was true that work was hard to come by, at that time, in 1909. Cliff was delighted that he had a new son, and he wanted to call him James, after James Figg, the first bare-knuckle champion of England.

The proud father caught a train back from his worksite, near Leeds. He hurried to the hospital when he arrived in Stepney, where the Charles family was renting a small flat, with one room to call their own. They shared a grimy bathroom and access to a tiny, back yard. The yard was always strewn with dog-ends and empty, beer bottles, quite a few of which emanated from Cliff himself. He peered round the curtains enclosing Irma's bed and saw that she was fast asleep. She looked drained, but she was still beautiful. Her curly, brown hair was wringing wet from sweat, and it was glued to her head with the dampness which had soaked into her normally springy ringlets.

Cliff walked over to the other side of the bed and looked down at the empty cot next to the bed. His heart took a leap, and he sprinted to the nurses' desk at the end of the maternity ward.

"Where's my son? What's happened to him?"

The nurse knew who he was, as he had spoken to her on the way in, and she said, "He's in a special ward. We're doing what we can for him. Come with me, and you can look at him through a glass screen."

He breathed a sigh of relief and followed her, trying not to look at her shapely legs. After all, he was a respectable father now.

"Look Mr. Charles, that's your boy on the end. Isn't he adorable?"

Cliff wasn't certain. The little scrap of humanity in the incubator didn't look like his idea of what a son should be. Mr. Charles was a big man with no fat on him, but with plenty of lean muscle. He worked as a mere dogsbody on the sites, but he earned money on the side, and a lot of respect, as a bare-knuckle fighter, each weekend. He called himself Cliff Hanger – The Human Mountain.

His other idea of fun was to leave Irma at home, to go to a dingy bar and spend every penny he had on booze, before staggering back into the flat and falling asleep, with all his clothes on. It was a wonder that the little boy had been conceived, as he rarely took much interest in "that sort of thing." He regarded himself as a man's man, with interests in the dogs, fighting, horse-racing and beer. He had no time for any cultural pursuits and had been hoping to have a big, strapping son, to carry on his boxing legacy. He swept past the nurse and muttered, "Got to see a man about a dog."

Cliff went straight to a rundown social club and sank four pints in quick succession. He was a hairy man, with a broken nose. (He had been set upon by two hefty debt-collectors, who wanted to teach him a lesson, as he was falling behind with the payments on a loan from a back-street villain.) His face was flushed, and his hair was red too. His doctor had warned him that high blood pressure could be the death of him, unless he cut down drastically on beer and whiskey.

He went out drinking all the time, even if Irma had earmarked the money for frivolous things - like food. She had taken to hiding any cash which she had saved from her pitifully small, housekeeping allowance, and he had found her tiny stash one day, when he had been in his cups. He had taken a hefty swipe at her head with his big, meaty fist, and she had sunk to the floor, half-stunned. The bruises were evident the next morning, and he had begged her to lie about their provenance, should she be questioned by any of her friends.

"I love you so much, little Irma, and I promise never to do that again."

Irma gave him the kind of look that a haughty cat gives to a dog, turned on her heel and walked out of the room. She wouldn't lie for anybody. She was a worker and a proud woman. She had been doing odd cleaning jobs and the occasional stint as a waitress in a local restaurant. She was an asset to The Bluebird, but the manager had tried it on with her, more than once. The last time he had pressed himself up against her, she had grabbed a large, kitchen knife and pointed it at his genitals.

"If you want to keep your crown jewels, stop touching me up," she said, in a cold, small voice which had frightened him, as he had no doubt that she meant exactly what she said. Since that day there had been an uneasy truce between Irma and Vincent, the manager.

When she had reported to The Bluebird, after having been punched by Cliff, he had offered to get some of the lads to pay him back. Irma told him that she could handle herself and that she was opposed to physical violence.

After sinking some Dutch Courage at that club near the hospital, Cliff went back to see Irma and his son. Irma was pleased to see him, as she still loved him, in spite of his callous indifference to her. He had never hit her again. In spite of his punch, there was a strangely warm relationship between them, fostered in the main by Irma's kindness and forgiveness.

"Hallo sweetie, what about this boy then? He's on the tiny side isn't he?"

"Cliff, give him a chance. He's here six weeks early and may not even make it. Let's pray that he survives and gets big and strong, like his dad."

"You can pray if you like. I don't believe in God."

"It's a good job he believes in you, Cliff."

As the weeks progressed, the baby became stronger but was still small. Cliff came less frequently to the hospital before Irma and the boy were discharged. Even after Irma and the baby went home, Cliff was often out drinking. Irma had asked Cliff what he wanted to call the boy. Cliff had forgotten about James Figg and told her that he didn't care. Irma took him at his word and registered him as Floyd Clifford Charles.

Floyd was a sickly child, and he was forever being teased and taunted at his school. However, by the time he was eight or nine, a change came over him. He learned that bullies were usually cowards, and after he had retaliated a few times, the tormenting stopped completely.

Cliff had been impressed by the change in his son, and he had started to give him boxing lessons. Floyd grew stronger, even though he was still skinny, and Cliff almost grew to love him. The boy was fiercely proud of his dad, and he admired the few boxing trophies of his, which his father had not sold or pawned. When he was fourteen, Cliff entered him in a fight, which took place in a disused warehouse, round the corner from the bedsit they now occupied. The rules were - that there were no rules. Cliff had hoped that Floyd would be a lithe and athletic fighter, who could be light on his feet.

Floyd was all of that, but his punches often went astray, and his opponent knocked him out with one casual blow, very early in the fight. Cliff picked Floyd up and took him home. He had come round by the time they were back in the bedsit. Irma had not known about the fight and was furious with Cliff. After a heated argument, Cliff left to go to the pub.

He poured out his woes to his pals, and his best chum, Dixie Driscoll, said, "Cliff, not everybody is a massive fellow like you. Floyd may turn out to be something else, rather than a fighter. Perhaps he will be an accountant or a shopkeeper."

Cliff harrumphed like a large Shire Horse and downed another pint. After too many drinks, he went home. He sang loudly as he walked up the stairs and slammed open the door to their humble quarters. Irma was lying on the bed. He pulled her up and tried to kiss her. She gave him a venomous look, and he ripped open her blouse. She screamed, and Floyd came into the room and said, "Leave her alone."

"And what will you do if I choose not to, you long streak of nag's piss?"

"I will only warn you this once. Please desist."

"Oh, do please desist," mocked Cliff, and he tried to pull Irma's skirt off her.

Floyd raised his fists into the classic boxing position, and he thrust a surprisingly fierce punch at Cliff's head. Cliff fell over and hit the other side of his head on the bed post, as he went down. Cliff didn't speak to Floyd or Irma until the morning, when he was truly repentant.

From that day on, Floyd and Cliff became firm good buddies, and Floyd gradually improved his boxing skills. He even won a few fights, here and there. Floyd never put on any spare flesh, and as he grew older he became wizened and haggard. He was knocked out more times than I care to recount. Irma had long gone, after being mown down by a badly driven dustcart. Cliff was in a home; the punches he had sustained to his head, over the years, had left him dazed and confused.

Floyd saw sense when he retired from boxing, at the ripe old age of thirty-one. He worked hard at a shop, in which he was employed to sell groceries, and he finally settled down with Eliza, a flaxen haired treasure of twenty-six. She fell for a child quickly and produced a huge baby, who obviously took after his grandfather. Eliza asked Floyd what he wanted to call the child. Without hesitation, he said, "Clifford Elmer Charles."

Chapter 24

THE GIDDY GOAT

I am a fine young ram, with much to recommend.
My horns are sharp and twirling, and imposing.
My problem it appears, when I turn a dog-leg bend,
and I do the skilful move, you are proposing.
I've always been this way; on the mountains I have trod.
I trip, I slip and fall, and I am dizzy.
I'm in a spinning tizzy; I fear it's all slip-shod,
because I am a silly, wayward Billy.

I AM A SILLY, WAYWARD BILLY

My mother always told me that I was very handsome, and after a while I began to believe that I was. I know now, that mums always think their sons are special, and they reinforce the bond between them and their infants, by selling them the blatant nonsense that they are the best looking young rams in the world.

I think I'm quite dashing, with my sharp and twisted horns, but I was disappointed when mum told me that we goats are related to sheep. I ask you! They are bleating little nobodies, aren't they? They are so meek and mild; it makes me want to poke one of my horns up their bum, every time I see one. That would make them baa and scrape.

Although I look pretty good, I suffer from dizzy spells, and that's a bit of a problem for a mountain goat. My brothers and sisters (all of whom are scraggy and not strong like me) are sure-footed and clear-headed specimens, but if I turn quickly or get up from a snooze too soon, I feel my head spinning, and it makes me want to be sick.

We tried to find out why I was feeling this way, my mum and I, and we even asked my mother's mum, whom we call Nanny Goat Nanny. She didn't seem all that interested in helping her grand-buck, but I wasn't worried. Mum said I would probably grow out of my giddiness. I wondered if it was too much testosterone. I am a whole ram, in a search of a ram hole.

There must be over a billion goats in the world, and as I am the best looking one (just ask my mum!), it should be easy to find a partner. In the meantime, I try to eat well. I have a four-chambered stomach, so my digestion is a breeze. I love eating tips of bushy shrubs and - well, anything really.

My mum, siblings and I are all owned by Tanya Maynard, who is quite tiny by human standards. She is a strange girl with arched eye-brows and masses of dyed green hair, but she's kind to me. She strokes my beard and fiddles with my horns, but I don't mind as she gives me tasty titbits.

Mum says that I should be looking for my ideal nanny goat, as I am at that stage, and that if I eat well, I should be good for breeding. I am interested in this idea, and I've asked my sisters if they would let me experiment with them. They ran away, when I approached them. They said it would be incest. Mum told me that they were too small, and that anyway I should seek a non-family member for this experience.

So, there I was - suffering badly from being a sort of romantic outcast. I was pleased when Tanya's father, Lance, opened the gate to our field and led in four beautiful, young does. At first, they tried to avoid me, but within a few days I noticed a marked change in the behaviour of one of the new inhabitants of our field.

Diana, a black and white beauty, started to wag her tail furiously - like a flag, every time she saw me, and there was a wonderful smell coming from her. She told me, that I too had a lovely aroma coming from near the base of my horns. I won't go into the gory details. (I didn't gore her, honest), but suffice it to say, we had a truly scentsational frisk, in the meadow. A little while later, she became fat, and Mum told me to be ready to be a daddy goat in about 150 periods between sunrise and dawn.

I actually saw my son and daughter born. Twins are quite common in goats, but mine were the best looking offspring ever. They were a doe and a buck, and Tanya called them Spick and Speck. I was such a proud billy goat. As they grew they became intelligent and curious. I tried to get them to stop eating cardboard and empty crisp packets, and Lance was very helpful. He laid down the law to Tanya and her brother Dominic about litter.

Spick (the doe) is beginning to be an interesting specimen to other bucks in our field, but I hope she finds a thoughtful and respectful partner. Oh and by the way - I am no longer a giddy goat. My dizziness has gone completely. I stopped feeling sick, and I got better after I impregnated Diana.

Isn't it wonderful, what love can do?

Chapter 25

DIAL EMMA

I was an agony aunt, for a local weekly paper.
I'd offer help and tips for star-crossed lovers.
I wish that I had been, a tailor or a draper,
but I read about their antics and their covers.
I also ran a service, for the ones who liked to phone.
Dial Emma helped them make the right decisions.
They liked to tell me all, and to share their griefs and moans,
and I'd answer them so neatly - sweet precision.

THE RIGHT DECISIONS

I'm Emma Cartwright, and I'm twenty-eight, and at the time this story begins, I was unmarried. I'd had various boyfriends, and most of the relationships I had with casual admirers were fairly light-hearted.

It was more serious, and so different, with Jonah. When we first met, we were both journalists for one of those free papers which are mainly filled with boring adverts. Our local paper, The Sunbury Advertiser, had several features in each edition, and Jonah was their resident I.T. expert. You know the kind of thing - Let's look at the latest operating system, its features and glitches, and how you can learn to love the new release.

I suppose you could say that I was smitten with Jonah, right from the start. I soon found out, that he looks much better than he is, just like a luxury box of chocolates, which has some wonderful selections, but also has the usual orange and lime crème filled dross, that nobody really likes. He spoke well, dressed well, and he looked wonderful. He had a floppy quiff and was slim and muscular. The trouble was that he was as vain as he was good-looking, with his long, fair hair and indigo eyes.

I was taken on originally as an advertising Sales Executive. That's a laugh. It meant I had a poor basic salary and high commission, a deal guaranteed to make the sales people chase all opportunities. Jonah was doing quite well already with his own one-man I.T. consultancy on the side, so his low pay at the paper didn't really worry him.

The editor, Aaron Wednesday (which I strongly suspect is a fictitious name), called me into his office early one morning, and he asked if I would be willing to grasp a new opportunity. I nearly laughed as Aaron always tended to speak in clichés, and this conversation was no exception. He also dressed in clichés – that day he wore a blue shirt with a sparkling, white collar, flashy cufflinks and a shiny, mohair suit (yuk!)

"We're really pleased with the way that you have buckled down and made the stage your own, Emma. Some of our Sales Executives don't realise that the world is their oyster. I mean, we have to admit that there is always an elephant in the room, and so we have to push the boundaries, by thinking out of the box."

"Oh yes, Aaron. I always think that the elephant is a hard tusk master."

Aaron blinked his eyes like a baffled Husky, but he had the good grace to laugh.

"I have a new nettle for you to grasp. Our Agony Aunt, Delilah Dandridge, is leaving. Her marriage is in absolute tatters, and she's been drinking like a fish.

"She is going into rehab. next week, and although I am sympathetic to her troubles, she's no longer a shining recommendation as an adviser, dealing with other people's personal problems.

"That's where you come in. We can double your basic salary, and all you have to do is to provide calm and collected solutions to problems raised via letters or emails."

I demurred. (If you agree, do you mur I wonder?)

"I'm glad we had this little chattette, and I can think of no better person than you, to turn this challenge into an opportunity. Pick up the details from my P.A., Kitty, and off you go. You will still be Delilah Dandridge, as that's not a real name. I pulled the first name (and the surname), out a virtual hat."

"I'm staggered, Aaron. I always thought that was her real name and that she just called herself Esther Bloggs in the office, as a joke."

Aaron didn't even know that I was being whimsical.

"Oh yes, I'm a mine of information and a creative light in a desert."

On that note, I left him. I wasn't sure that there were any lights at all in deserts, let alone creative lights. Kitty handed me a thick, bulging folder and rolled her heavily mascaraed eyes at me. Well, the lashes were mascaraed, not the eyes – Oh, you know what I mean. She knew that talking to Aaron was like wading through a treacle sea of sticky clichés. Oops, I think it must be catching.

I took the folder back to my desk. Inside there were a few snail-mail letters, and a whole lot of emails, which had been printed. Esther wasn't a great fan of emails. These three communications tickled my fancy.

Dear Delilah
I am a bachelor and find that I am attracted to you immensely. Your compassion and the way that you evaluate potential solutions for readers' problems speak volumes. As I write these words I feel a burning sensation which I attribute to my longing for you. How can I deal with this desire, other than the obvious way?

Please would you meet me in The Sunbury Arms at seven p.m. next Wednesday, so we can discuss this delicate matter? I will be wearing a black, polo-necked sweater and a dark grey suit.
Yours, in anticipation
Louis Letherbridge

Esther had clipped this letter together, with a few other papers, with a sticky note on the top of the pile, on which was written one word: Perverts.

The next letter I looked at was comical, or it would have been, had it not been so sad.

Dear Delilah
I love wearing Boy Scout uniforms. I have been doing this now for over sixty years. At first, this was not a problem, as I was actually a Boy Scout. When I left the scouts, because of an argument with another scout, who was picking on me, it was no longer possible to

wear the uniform in public. I continued to wear it every evening after school, and later on, after work.

I am none too young, and I have been lucky enough to meet a wonderful lady, whom I am hoping will do me the honour of becoming Mrs. Anon. Should I tell her about my harmless longing to wear Boy Scout apparel?
Yours Sincerely
Mr. Anon

The last of the three examples was an email print out and read as follows:

Dear Delilah
I know who you are. I follow you each evening and need to talk with you about inappropriate advice which you gave my wife, resulting in her leaving me after thirty years of marriage.

I am inconsolable, and I want to understand why you felt it necessary to ruin my relationship with an ideal partner.
Yours Sincerely
Wesley Branson.

Aaron walked past my desk and said, "Glad to see you are getting stuck in to that project. I knew I could count on you. Let me have your suggested answers to a few requests for advice, and if they are the icing on the cake, the cherry on the top will be that they are published next week."

I drafted my answers, and these were the replies I showed to Aaron, for him to decide if they should go into our next edition.

Dear Louis
Bachelors are often looking for that someone special. You may think that you are attracted to me. That is only because you are searching for your own perfect lady.

I am pleased that you value compassion and have an analytical mind, which should help you to decide your own future path in life.

The burning sensation will vanish in time, when you meet, woo and marry, your wonderful bride. Rather than just hoping to meet ladies in public houses, why not join a social club run by a church, or possibly a cycling and walking club? This latter idea would enable you to meet new people and to be in the fresh air.

I note that you take an interest in your appearance and suggest that you continue to dress well.

Yours Sincerely
Delilah Dandridge

I was pleased with that reply. However, the reply to letter number two was more difficult.

Dear Mr. Anon
Boy Scout uniforms are smart, but they are not the right wardrobe for a gentleman of your age. If you have been doing this now for such a long time, it will be a wrench for you to stop doing so, but stop you must.

I would caution you against telling your intended about this habit. She may well misunderstand the reasons for your problem. I use the word problem because you should endeavour to find another elegant form of clothing, which will help you to wean yourself off the Boy Scout garments.

Have you considered becoming a Lollipop Man? They look dashing, in their caps and high visibility coats.

Yours Sincerely
Delilah Dandridge.

The third reply was very tricky. I therefore wrote the following stern missive.

> *Dear Mr. Branson*
> *I think it is possible that you do know who I am, as you have contacted me by a private email address. If you really follow me each evening, please stop doing so. Perhaps I gave advice to your wife, which resulted in her leaving you, but it was her decision and not mine.*
>
> *I am sad to hear that you are inconsolable. I cannot advise you any further until you tell me your real name, as we have no record of advice given to a Mrs. Branson.*
>
> *If you wish to meet me face to face, that can certainly be arranged. The meeting would have to be in the offices of The Sunbury Advertiser, and there would be two security guards present.*
> *Yours Sincerely*
> *Delilah Dandridge*

Aaron thought the letters which I wrote were brilliant. They appeared in the next edition of the paper, and I worked as Delilah Dandridge for several years. Wesley Branson never made an appearance in our offices, and although I looked behind me when I left work, every evening for several weeks, there was no inconsolable wretch following me.

Jonah suggested that I should set up my own telephone advice service and even came up with a great name, Dial Emma. The Agony Aunt telephone service was a great success, and in the end I had a thirty-strong team of "Emmas" working for me.

In the meantime, Jonah had asked me out, and we quickly became an item. I found out that his vanity was a façade for a loveable man, who wasn't nearly as confident as he appeared to be. We married after two years and lived in a modest townhouse, on the outskirts of Sunbury.

Jonah was attentive at first, but I noticed that he had started to come home later and later. He sometimes smelt of booze, and he carried the scent of a particularly cloying perfume, like the one Kitty used, usually too liberally. I thought Kitty was his sort of girl. Everything about her was obvious, especially her pushed out, and thrustingly ridiculous, conical breasts.

One day, I was in my Dial Emma office, at about eight o'clock in the evening, in an industrial site out of town, when my phone rang.

"Hallo, is that Emma?" said an obviously disguised female voice, "I mean the real Emma, not one of the team."

"It is. All of my professional advisers left ages ago. I was just packing up myself."

"I work for a local newspaper, and I'm friendly with one of the journalists. If he was interested in me, I'd be happy, but he loves his wife and is worried that their marriage is crumbling."

"Why does he think that?"

"She never talks about anything else but your Dial Emma outfit, which is where she works. She does long hours. They haven't had a holiday for several years. Sometimes he takes me to a pub and weeps. I have to put my arms round him to comfort him, but he only wants to be with his wife."

"This is a difficult situation. Why not suggest to him that he should broach the subject of a holiday in the sun, to his wife? When they are away from his work and her own job, things may seem easier to patch up. I suppose she must be one of my ladies. I do expect them to work long hours."

The voice on the other end sounded non-committal.

"Thanks. I'm not convinced, but I'll try that suggestion."

A few nights later, I managed to get home at a fairly reasonable hour for a change. Jonah greeted me at the door with a huge smile and a glass of wine. He took my coat and showed me the delicious lasagne that he had made. As we sat down he said, "You've been working so hard. Why don't we have a week in the sun. How about a little place in Montepego, near Denia?"

"That would be fantastic, Jonah. Oh, and by the way, how is Kitty?"

Chapter 26

GNAT KING COLE

The king of the mosquitoes sings, a bit.
He chants, serenades and warbles.
And on his nightly jaunts and flits,
his song shines bright; it baubles.
Its refrain is full of heart and soul,
the emotions, they are stirring.
He knows he has a major role.
His music leaves us purring.

NIGHTLY JAUNTS AND FLITS

Leon loved walking at night. His best times were in foreign climes, very late, or perhaps in the twilight period just before dusk, when the warmth of the sun had not yet dissipated, and it was still hot enough to stroll along the prom in shirtsleeves.

His wife, Jeannette, was not a fan of these nightly jaunts because of the hordes of hungry mosquitoes, who aimed themselves at her delicate skin, with the sole aim of having a bloody feast.

"Come on Jeanie. It's such a beautiful evening. We can wander down to the other end of the town and sit in the taverna, with a table overlooking the bay. You'll love it."

"Do I have to come Leon? I've nearly finished my book. I might read the last few pages and then have a long bath and an early night."

"Please darling, I want you with me, and you can read that book on the beach, tomorrow."

Jeanette hoisted herself up, as gracefully as she could. Moving from a prone position on the bed, to sitting upright, was not nearly as easy as it used to be. She had made her mind up to go on a serious diet, when they returned to Hastings, where they lived in a pleasant cul-de-sac, not far from the sea front.

"O.K., but I must warn you that before I go, I'm going to spray that new anti-gnat aerosol all over me. I'll be stinking like a chemical factory."

Leon laughed and asked her to meet him in the bar downstairs, once she had protected herself from her arch-enemies. He picked up a light bomber jacket, in case it was chilly on the way back to their accommodation, and he whistled softly to himself as he left their room, reminding her to bring the room key.

Ten minutes later, Jeanette appeared in the bar, tucking the key into her handbag. The bag was a massive one, which seemed to have everything a lady might need, and then lots more, stuffed into its spacious interior.

"Do you want a drink here, before we go out?"

"No, let's have a stroll now, Leon. It's a lovely night after all; we might as well take a walk to the last taverna in the bay, and we can have some Ouzo."

They left the Hotel Anastasia and wandered over the road, to the paved promenade. Leon felt his wife slip her arm through his, and he smiled to himself. All was well with the world. They sauntered along, at a slow pace, and he thanked his lucky stars for his good-natured, and still pretty, wife.

He was not over bothered that she had put on such a lot of weight, but her doctor had insisted that twenty-one stones of woman was about eleven stones too much. Leon had told her that whenever he heard *A Whole Lotta Woman,* by Marvin Rainwater, he always thought of his delicious wife. Jeannette loved the compliment but knew that she had to slim down.

When they had first met, although she was still technically a whole lotta woman, the lotta was much lessa. Nonetheless, he loved his wife with a passion, even if real passion was not that easy, now that she was so huge. He made his mind up to persuade her to cut down on the carbs, after their holiday. He was lucky in that he could eat and eat, and he never put on weight. He was a short man and only weighed around nine stones.

Jeanette was swinging a parasol around, which she had extracted from her huge bag, in true Mary Poppins fashion. She seemed not to be aiming at anything in particular but just gently stirring the night air, which admittedly had more than its full complement of midges. Gnats never bothered Leon. Perhaps he had a natural anti-gnat force-field? He liked hearing their gentle buzzing and also wanted to stop to listen to cicadas, whenever they passed one of their hiding places.

"I wonder if gnats are singing when they buzz?"

"Don't be daft Leon, they just do that automatically. They aren't trained opera singers, dear. Unless you have heard of Gnatarotti?"

Jeannette gave a throaty chuckle. Her husband had always had a touch of whimsy about him. That was what had first attracted her to him, she supposed. He found it difficult to be serious about anything and always looked on the bright side of life. His whole aim in life appeared to be to make the most of whatever he was doing, right that minute.

He had retired early, after selling his three shops, which specialised in rare and hard to find vinyl records. Leon was glad he had done this at the right time, before streaming and downloading of music had made that much impact. The man who had taken over the shops had struggled for a while, but he said that some customers would still pay good money for a sought after record.

Jeannette was puffed out by now, and they sat on an iron bench overlooking the sea. The waves were gentle. The air was balmy, and if he didn't sit too near Jeannette, he could smell Jasmine.

"Do you think gnats have kings and queens, Jeanie?"

"I don't think they could understand the concept of royalty, Leon. You do talk rot sometimes."

"O.K., but do they have an alpha male, like wolves?"

Jeannette had to laugh.

"Look it up on Gnatipaedia when you get back to the hotel. Maybe the wi-fi will be working."

They stood up. Leon did so gracefully, but Jeanette uprighted herself more slowly, and she arose in an ungainly way. They continued their walk and spent a couple of happy hours, sipping much too much Ouzo, at their favourite taverna, which had small tables, covered with blue and white chequered cloths, facing the sparkling sea.

"Come on darling, we should be making a move, before it gets much later. We have that boat trip planned tomorrow, and they told us to meet at the front door of the hotel, at seven thirty in the morning."

Leon smiled. They had really asked the people going on the trip to be there by eight a.m., but Jeannette was always late for everything, so he added half an hour's leeway into any appointment times. Jeannette grinned. "That means eight o'clock doesn't it? I'm not as stupid as I look."

They resumed their walk, this time in the direction of the hotel, after Jeannette had managed to get her breath back. Halfway back to the hotel there was a man lying on the ground, with just his upper torso protruding from a small alleyway, which led off towards the back of the town. Leon hurried over to help the man, and to see if he was injured. The man jumped up and grabbed Leon by the throat.

"Don't be a fool. I'm twice your size. Just hand over your phone, wallet and your wife's jewellery."

Leon just managed to say, "Never. I worked for anything I have in life, and you should do the same."

The ruffian took a cosh out of his inside jacket pocket and gave Leon a sharp tap on the head. He went down like a sack of bricks. Jeanette had also been grabbed by another man.

The two men had only reached the small Greek island a few days ago, after being rescued from a tiny boat which had been sinking, although it was only a few hundred yards from the shore. They had expected things to be much better in Greece and were hoping to head for England eventually. They had left their families in their home country, and they intended to send for them, when they had made their fortunes.

They had both been drinking from various bottles of drink, which they had pinched from taverna tables or dust bins. They had not eaten for two days and were more drunk than they would have been, had they been fully fed. The two men pulled Jeanette into the alley and took her roughly, one after the other. They left her in a crumpled heap, crying and worrying about Leon, as she thought he was still out cold. A passing couple who had also been to the taverna, happened upon Leon's body, and at first they thought he was dead. He groaned and said, "Where is my Jeanie? Is she still in the alley?"

Mr. and Mrs. Haverstock had recognised Leon as one of their fellow hotel guests, and they looked around, only to see his wife prone and crying, with her clothes all torn. To their dismay, they noticed that there were a pair of panties and shoes lying at the entrance to the alley.

Mr. Haverstock phoned the police, and they came promptly. He was going to explain to the two officers what he thought had happened, but there was no need. It was so obvious. The policemen called an ambulance, and Leon and Jeanette were taken to the local hospital. It was surprisingly modern and well equipped, and the medical staff assessed the condition of both of the patients immediately.

Leon had come round by now, and he was taken to a separate cubicle. Jeannette was led, still weeping, to a small room where she was questioned about her attackers, and only then was she allowed to be treated. The nurse also took D.N.A. samples. She spoke to the waiting police officers.

"There has been sexual activity, and I can tell from her injuries that this lady was forced to have intercourse. There's also the presence of semen, which I've sampled for D.N.A. analysis."

Jeannette had been sedated. Leon had also been calmed down, with the help of an injection. There was a sudden and almighty commotion in the reception area of the hospital. A man was half leading and half carrying another fellow, and he was shouting, "Help, help! My brother is suffocating. His face has gone all blue, and he seems to be having difficulty breathing."

The policemen ran to see what was happening. One of them bent down and noticed something strange about the man who had been brought in. He could smell the same acidic aroma on this man, which was present on the woman who had been raped. He was just about to charge him and to arrest him, when the man grabbed at his throat and screamed that he could not breathe. He yelled that his throat was closing.

In only a few minutes, even with the intervention of a nurse and a doctor, he had died. The doctor said he thought it was due to anaphylaxis, and he asked his brother if he had been eating anything unusual, perhaps peanuts? His brother shook his head woefully.

"We haven't eaten for two days."

"It can be caused by medication. Is he taking anything?"

"No sir. He has no medicines."

The police took the dead man's brother away. The deceased was put onto a trolley, and just as it was being wheeled out, Leon and Jeannette came through to the reception area.

"Look Leon, that's one of the men who raped me."

Leon was absolutely shattered. He was still hurting from his physical injuries, even though they were only bruises and minor cuts. However, he was much more worried about what had happened to Jeannette. She looked at the body again and told Leon that this was definitely one of the men, who had taken her by force. Leon leant over the corpse and recognised the stink of Jeannette's anti-mosquito spray.

"It served him right. He had it coming."

He took Jeannette's hand, and they were escorted to a police car, as the officers wanted to make sure that they were back in the hotel safely, before talking in more depth with the doctor. Leon leaned back on the seat of the car. He suddenly felt hungry. He and Jeannette had only eaten some peanuts in the taverna.

Chapter 27

AL MOST-HUMAN

I am a large and virile lad.
I'm tattooed, dyed and pierced.
I hope I'm not so very bad,
although I look quite fierce.
The lager and the laddery helps
to make my life so special.
I like my studded leather belts.
My face is full of metal.
I shout and bellow, every night.
I frighten my pub's clients.
I yearn to argue and to fight.
I run from great big giants.

I'M TATTOOED, DYED AND PIERCED

My name is Alan Ferguson. That name sounds a bit girlie to me, so I encourage everybody that knows me, to call me Al. I have some wonderful body-piercing in all sorts of intriguing places, but the best one is a skull that hangs from a sort of metal rod, that's jammed through my septum. I always thought my nose looked too refined and delicate, so this has achieved the brutal look which I wanted.

I've also had my hair shaved off, and the result is brilliant. That is, brilliant because I like it, and also brilliant because the lights shine on my polished cranium. In addition to my tattoos, I have some splendid body art. I like the eagle on my forehead and the vulture on my left shoulder best of all, but I have thirty tattoos altogether.

I had to toughen up. I was always bullied mercilessly, at school, because I spoke too nicely and didn't really like rough sports, like football and rugby. My dad was a Don at one of the Oxbridge universities, and I learned a lot from him as I was growing up. He was a placid man and always seemed to persuade others to do what he wanted, by explaining the potential outcomes and encouraging them to adopt the one that would achieve the desired result.

I inherited a love of books from him. I read voraciously, when I was in my early teens, and my love of the literary classics was also a trigger to spur on the bullies at Metherwick Grammar School for Boys. They called me Fergie the Turd. They said it was because there were two other boys who were called Ferguson in our year. A sledge hammer type of wit, I think.

They started pushing me down the stairs. I could usually hang on to the bannisters, and I avoided any serious injuries on most occasions. One time though, the biggest of those toe-rags took me by surprise, and I tumbled down a flight of thirty steps. Luckily, I managed to roll most of the way, but I broke my arm and had to have it in a plaster cast for several weeks. I liked the ugliness of the rough cast and wrote all over its surface. I drew some fake tattoos on it, but they weren't convincing.

When the cast came off, I did my first real tatt. myself. I bet most thirteen year olds haven't got any tattoos. I used a pencil, a sewing needle and blue-black ink. It looked terrific at first, but it became badly infected. My dad had to take me to the doctor, and he managed to sort out the infection, but I was stuck with the tattoo, which was a hawk, with Al Most-Human written underneath.

Dad drove me home. He hadn't said a lot since I had shown him my tattoo and the infected area all round it. As we got out of the car, he asked me to put the kettle on, and he said, "We need to talk about this, Alan. I will talk first. You must listen, and only then are you allowed to ask questions. Understood?"

"Yes, Dad."

I owed him that. Most fathers would have hit the roof. He was his usual cool, measured self and had simply taken the right steps to sort out the poisoned mess on my right arm, before starting to give me what I thought would be a good telling off. I made the tea. He had his favourite, Earl Grey, and mine was ordinary, breakfast tea.

I took the two cups and saucers (never mugs), into his office, with a plate of Garibaldi biscuits. He picked up his tea, stirred it thoughtfully after adding half a teaspoonful of sugar, and he said, "I think tea experts would be horrified to see me drinking Earl Grey tea with milk and sugar. That is the beginning of my lesson for you today."

I started to speak, but he told me to hush.

"Alan, the deal was that I speak first. People are all different. Those tea experts would think that I am a sad little man, with no taste, for despoiling their delicately-flavoured tea. The point is that I do not agree with them, but I respect their right to their own opinion.

"When your dear mother and I married we had our first argument over a trifling matter. She said that she liked Craig Douglas, but

I pointed out that his cover versions of great songs (first recorded by people like The Drifters), were infinitely inferior to the originals. We batted our views back and forth for a while.

"Arguments between man and wife often start about a particular point, but they usually degenerate into a slanging match where one says, 'You always do this, et cetera.' and the other one retaliates by saying that it's because of some terrible fault of their spouse.

"I would wager that if you taped arguments between husbands and their wives for a given period, all over the U.K., that at least eighty per cent of the rows would feature lists of what was wrong with the husband or wife, according to their spouse.

"Anyway, back to this debut argument with your mum, I listened to the litany about my shortcomings, during this row, for some time, and then I said, 'Dorinda, I respect your right to have an opinion which differs from mine. You can't help being wrong.'"

I couldn't resist interjecting, "I bet that annoyed her."

"On the contrary, old lad, it stopped her in her tracks. She looked at me in a bewildered fashion and then laughed like a drain. Don't you see, my boy, these bullies are not so different from anyone else."

"They are vicious, nasty thugs."

"But you have to ask, why? I bet they are threatened by your obvious intelligence, the fact that you love Charles Dickens and that you can string a sentence together with eloquence."

"They call me Symphony Cissy, because I foolishly admitted that I like Beethoven. I've listened to your classical music L.P.s many times, and I can't see why that's a crime in their eyes."

"That's because you're different to them. They are entitled to be wrong. You have to stand up for yourself, but it can be done in two ways. There is a difference between assertion and aggression. The former is the best attitude to adopt. The other thing you can do, is to act like a cat."

"What on earth do you mean, Dad?"

"If a cat's frightened, it puffs itself up, and its fur makes it look like a much larger animal. Just that small thing, can often save them from whatever they are scared of."

"I haven't got fur, so that won't work."

"Of course not, but you can walk tall, keep yourself erect, wear bulkier clothes, and you can meet them face to face rather than scurrying off if you are challenged."

I had to admit that if I saw them coming, I usually tried to get away from them.

"The other thing to do, is to identify any unusual likes they might have. Then you should talk to them about those things. I guarantee that they will share their oddities with you."

He cleared up the tea things and cooked us a simple but tasty repast. Since Mum had left him, when I was eight, he had prepared all of our meals. She had run off, with a used car salesman from Bradford. He had sold her the idea that life with him would be absolutely blissful. Dad had told me later, that he had given her two choices. One was to stay with him, ditch the lover and to start all over again. The other was to go immediately, but she would have to agree never to contact him again, once the divorce proceedings were over. She chose the latter. She never saw me again either, so I was raised from that age by Dad.

The next day (after the talk about the difference between assertion and aggression), I was walking down the corridor at school and saw Mortimer Morris, the sort of second-in-command of the bullyboys, looking at a book which he was holding in his hand. I saw that it was about spiders. I took the bull by the horns.

"Morris, what a coincidence. I love spiders. I know that some people tread on them, but I'd never do that."

He looked all round, as he wasn't sure whether to speak to me or not. None of his cronies were present.

"They are fascinating creatures…," he started.

He then told me all sorts of things about spiders, most of which were revelations to me.

I also bought myself some big boots, a thick jumper and a bulky, donkey jacket. I walked tall and spread my shoulders. The bullying didn't stop instantly, but the next time one of the other thugs tried to push me around, Morris called him off, and as they walked away I heard him say,

"Did you know that Fergie likes spiders? It just goes to show you that nobody's all bad."

One by one, I found out their likes, dislikes and foibles. For example, Ike Dansie hated his surname. He had been teased about it sounding like a weedy, ballet dancer. He was the ringleader of the bullies and had lost his mother when he was seven. That was so nearly my age, when my Mum ran off. I actually felt sorry for him. Ike's Mum had been thrown from a horse, broken her neck and been in a coma for weeks before slipping away.

I saw him looking at a faded photo of a smiling lady, which he had been carrying in his wallet.

"She was so pretty, Ike. Was that your mum?"

Without thinking he replied, "Yes, you're right. She was perfect."

We talked for some time, and I told him about my Mum, who had never tried to contact me. He took me by surprise by crying. He brushed away his tears and said, "If you ever let on that I'm a cry baby, I'll throttle you."

"You're not a softie, Ike. You just loved your dear mum, and sympathised with me."

After that episode, either Ike Dansie or Mortimer Morris intervened when the others tried to rag me. As I grew up, some of them even became my close friends. I always remembered the lesson my dad had taught me, and I continued to be like a cat.

I also started having some professionally designed and executed tattoos done, when I left school, and although Dad hated them, he respected my right to be wrong. Some body piercings followed. These were in places covered by clothes, but I finally had my skull-shaped, nose ring inserted. All Dad said was, "That looks totally ridiculous, and it's probably unhygienic."

I'm a loud person now. I drink a lot. The lads at the pub sometimes have contests to see who can drink the most lager, or eat the hottest curries, but I always win. I wear a lot of leather, usually with masses of studs. When I go into my local, and there are newcomers at the bar, they finish their drinks and rush out. They don't know that inside I am a frightened Symphony Cissy.

Chapter 28

A GOOD EGG, NO YOLK

Albumen, is my real name.
I'm part of staple diets.
The white stuff isn't quite the same,
although they like to try it.
The sunshine stuff is what they need.
I think they must be yolking.
The egg-white is a jolly feed.
I'm sure that I'm not joking.

THE WHITE STUFF ISN'T QUITE THE SAME

I have a singular aversion to the white of an egg. This is not just an affectation, and I seriously wonder if I am allergic to albumen. On the other hand, I love the yolk of eggs, and if I could buy white-less eggs I would definitely do so.

Anita, who is my lovely better half, and a sort of latter-day Francoise Hardy lookalike, thinks I exaggerate the effect that the whites of eggs have on me. She's wrong. I always find that if I eat any of that horrid stuff, my eyes stream, and my throat closes up, so I can hardly swallow the slimy, snotty mess. I can eat eggs at home, as I don't have to worry about the whites. Anita uses them for meringues. However, even if I eat a pre-prepared meal which has the dreaded albumen as a constituent, I still get that awful, instantaneous reaction.

I can't eat at restaurants, unless I have something really simple - like a grilled steak or a pan-fried chicken breast, perhaps with a few chips. This has been going on ever since I ate an egg which was well past its best before date, and I found that the soft-boiled egg, to which I was looking forward, was absolutely repellent, and it made me sick. Anita says I should remember that I ate eggs (including the whites), for more than sixty years with no problems.

She persuaded me to consult my doctor. Dr. Hemmings was his typical blunt self.

"Mr. Rayner, this over-the-top reaction has only been caused by one episode of food poisoning, due to a rotten egg. You must put this behind you, as it's just in your mind. The thought that the albumen of the egg might have the same deleterious effect again is illusory."

"Doctor, I can assure you that the way I sweat, the streaming of my eyes, and the immediate restriction of my throat cause me real problems."

"I'm not disputing that, but the very fact that the problem manifests itself so rapidly, leads me to suppose that it's caused by your own dread of egg-whites.

"I'm going to prescribe some mild sedatives which will soothe you, and I'll make an appointment for you to see Mr. Hyde-Mayhew in Harley Street. He's a renowned expert on aversion therapies and combatting phobias, and I'm sure he will be able to help."

I left his surgery feeling unconvinced. However, as I had told poor Anita that I would do anything to try to tackle this problem, I was resigned to an expensive (and probably useless), visit to see the consultant. My son, Jason, who is au fait with the wretched Internet thing, looked him up, and Mr. Hyde-Mathew does seem to have a whole string of letters after his name (and many plaudits on his website.) Jason says he's written heaps of books about phobias.

Anita said she would come with me, from Crawley where we live, to see Mr. Hyde-Mayhew, when we got the appointment. She wants to buy some more shoes. She's only got about sixty pairs of shoes, poor thing. I wonder if H-M can cure her Imelda Marcos style addiction to footwear?

The letter confirming the appointment came fairly soon, on fancy, headed paper, which felt more like vellum than writing paper. There was also a long questionnaire to complete. It had strange questions, such as:

Do you have this reaction if you eat albumen on its own, or just when it is mixed with other foodstuffs?
Do you find that the aversion is present when you eat egg-white with the following foods?
Tomatoes
Kale
Meat
Other: (please specify.)

Anita asked me if I had finished completing the questionnaire. I said I hadn't, but she raised the subject again, after our morning coffee.

"Joel, let me look at your answers to those questions."

I huffed theatrically, and I chucked the papers at her. She spent some time tut-tutting at my sparse responses. She offered to fill the replies in herself and started to ask me additional questions. After a while we had answered all of the queries, and she said it would have to do.

It has now been two weeks since we finished the form for H-M and three days since I saw him. Anita had a successful day and bought five pairs of new shoes. My day was strange. I went into the reception area, in a posh surgery which was about halfway down Harley Street. The room was pretty much what I had expected. There were several dark brown, leather couches in the waiting area, lots of nicely bound books and framed certificates on the walls, all proving that Hyde-Mayhew was a recognised expert in just about everything to do with phobias. Strangely enough, there were no photos of the great man on the wall.

A cold, but spectacularly beautiful, blonde took my details, and she asked me to wait, in a plummy voice. She looked as if she would discipline me harshly if I talked out of turn. As I crossed the room to my seat, I idly turned over in my mind the thought of being disciplined by Ms. Iceberg. After a long wait, the chilly blonde had a call on her intercom, and she said, "Mr. Hyde-Mayhew will see you now. Would you like to come with me?"

(Fancy that, just exactly what I had been thinking of, as I sneaked a peek at Ms. Zero Minus Ten, every now and then. Unfortunately, she was just asking her to follow her.) We went through a frosted-glass door and down a passageway, which had a carpet about six inches thick. This is where the money goes, thought I. She stopped at a maple door, on which there was a brass plate. Mr. J. W. T. Hyde-Mayhew was engraved on the plate, and there were lots of initials thereafter, as referred to earlier in my tale.

My chilled-date fancy, rapped on the door loudly, and the summons: "Enter!" came from the room where H-M was sitting. When I opened the door, he was sitting behind a massive desk, with green leather on its top and gold tooling round the edge.

I was taken aback, as Mr. Hyde-Mayhew was the spitting image of Tommy Cooper. I don't mean he was just a bit like him. If Tommy had not died I would have thought that he had merely changed his job from being a comedian, to conducting sessions for people with phobias, in flashy and expensive accommodation in Harley Street.

He motioned for me to sit in a chair opposite him, and he started to question me about the answers in the form which I had posted to him. As Anita had done most of the work, I wasn't really sure what she had written, and I hadn't even checked it. I think I have made it clear that my feelings about this meeting were ambivalent, to say the least.

"So, why do you think that mangoes exacerbate the physical reaction to albumen?"

I knew I had to bluff.

"I wonder if the sweetness of the mangoes, gives me an expectation of fruity pleasantness, which is immediately offset by the slimy albumen?"

He muttered something and jotted some notes. This charade went on for an hour. He asked many questions, and I answered all of them with ridiculous, made up replies. At the end of this hour, he sat up straight and said, "I believe that you have a mother fixation and that albumen reminds you of suckling at your mother's breast.

"The conflict of longing for the milk (represented by the albumen, particularly if it is not well cooked), and the revulsion that you feel for this close contact with your mum's mammary glands, heighten the reaction to the milk/egg-white and causes you to stiffen up your muscles which control the swallowing reflex.

"You perspire because you desire the intimate, physical contact with your maternal relative - and yet you wish to stop swallowing the dreaded, white fluid. This can be cured but not just like that."

I tried hard not to roar with laughter. Tommy Cooper was spouting a lot of stuff and nonsense, and then saying, "just like that."

"Are there any techniques which I can adopt, to make me think of something else, and which might help to relax me while I am eating egg-whites, Mr. Hyde-Mayhew?"

"Oh yes, you could think of something ridiculous initially, to make you laugh. Once you have done that, you could start to eat the albumen, whilst imagining something you really want to do. Perhaps this might be an activity like walking on a sandy beach, with a well-loved dog, in the sun and with plenty of fresh air."

"I'd really like to try these suggested steps, to see what happens and to report back to you, after whatever you think is the best period of time."

"Excellent, my friend. You will recover."

On the way out, I stole a surreptitious look at the receptionist. Oh yes, she was a sight for sore eyes.

Anita had promised to meet me at a small bistro, in Soho, and when I arrived, I found she had taken a corner table, for an early dinner. She looked at the menu and tried to select something for me with no trace of egg. I jumped in and said, "I think I'll have a prawn cocktail, followed by rump steak in a hollandaise sauce."

"Joel, is that wise? Both those dishes use egg-white."

"I think I know what to do."

We ordered our meals. (She wanted smoked salmon followed by a chicken dish.) We sipped a pleasant, white wine, whilst we waited. My prawn cocktail was placed before me. I closed my eyes and imagined Tommy Cooper diagnosing a mother fixation, just like that. I imagined a baby's bottle and a breast, and Tommy saying bottle - breast,

breast - bottle (almost like the bottle - glass sketch.) I couldn't help it - I roared with laughter.

"Are you O.K., dear?"

"I'm fine. Watch this."

For my next trick, I imagined Ms. Iceberg on a bed, with no clothes on at all, but with just a light coating of egg-white. I started salivating and ate the prawns, which were drowned in marie rose sauce (including the dreaded egg-white.) I had no problems at all.

The main course, a medium-rare steak, with hollandaise sauce, was similarly treated to a preparatory, Tommy Cooper sketch and then more mental images of the delectable, even if Arctic, blonde. I've never had any aversion to egg-white since that day. I wish I could see my unofficial muse, Ms. Iceberg, but that might break the spell. I reckon the yolk is on Mr. Hyde-Mayhew, as I only needed to pay for one expensive consultation.

Chapter 29

OLD WIVES' TAILS

It is a well-known fact,
that as our neck skin sags
at the bottom of the back,
comes a tail that wiggly-wags.
It is always there for women,
though the men have none, oh brother.
It helps when girls go swimming
It's a very useful rudder.

OUR NECK SKIN SAGS

My name is Danny Vertigo. You must have heard of me. I've been making films since the seventies. The best known one is *The Secret Mysteries of the Terrestrial Minds.* I played a hypnotherapist, who also doubled as a Secret Agent for the powers that be, in the U.K. I was very dashing, though I say it myself.

When I look at the stills from that epic, I can truthfully say that if I had been a young girl, I would have fallen for me. I have nicely shaped eyebrows, and before I was contracted to do the secret agent film, I had jet-black hair. O.K. - to be honest it was jet-black after a treatment of Grey Be Gone, every few weeks. I was slim and rangy, but I had the rippling muscles of a big cat.

Moonbeam, my leading lady, was a stunning girl with luxuriant, blonde hair, in that big-hair style, which a lot of ladies favoured, in them thar days. When we went to town and partied, the gossip columnists had a field day. She also got me the part - all will become clear. On more than one occasion, the press announced our wedding date, or reported that we had been secretly married in a far off location, like Bali. They were wrong of course, although we did get married later.

We fancied each other and had a few great nights together, but Moonbeam lived secretly, with a special girl friend called Sassy, and Moonbeam and Sassy truly loved each other, with a force that almost terrified me. For two young girls (Moonbeam, who was a major star, and an aspiring starlet - Sassy), it was important to keep their relationship under wraps, so that menfolk could worship from afar, as excited fans, without knowing that Moonbeam's lover was little Sassy. She was pretty enough, but she wasn't in Moonbeam's class, by any means.

I made many films. Some of them were huge money earners. Initially, I was taken aback, but I became even more fond of myself, when my very first film became a ginormous success for Tarantula Films. I was cast as a teenaged singer who worked his way up to become a worldwide star, selling millions of L.P.s. They called me Danny Vertigo in that film. They thought my real name, Jack Nicholson, was unimpressive - little did they know!

The press announcement said, *Watch the way that Danny Vertigo makes the girls' heads spin.* That was the appalling standard of the P.R. for the beach films of the day. I was a muscular lifeguard in the film, with a hankering to be the next Tab Hunter. The film was called *Beach Ahoy!* Don't blame me for the daft title. It was a smash here, and in the U.S.A.

I was an awful singer, but that didn't hamper me. My records were produced by an independent guy, who worked in a studio, on his small estate, in Berkshire. He used a lot of echo and reverb on my voice, which was just as well, as I was terrible. Where the vocals were rough, he dubbed on strident, backing singers, who could do it properly, and then he mixed my voice judiciously, so you couldn't hear it properly. If that didn't work, he substituted a great vocalist, whose name escapes me. He sang the notes which also escaped me.

The film was released at about the time that my first L.P., *Spin with Danny Vertigo,* and a track from the album, called *You Saved My Life,* went straight to the top of the hit parade in thirty-four countries. There were three more beach films, *Beached Again*, *The Boy and The Buoy* and, wait for it, *Sand and Sunshine.* I suppose that must have been before the famous three S wish - for Sun, Sand and Sex, was expressed in exactly that way. The subsequent films did reasonably well. The second film was a hit (but not a huge one), the third earned them enough money to balance the books, and the fourth film only lost a little money.

Walton Hamilton the Third (no, I haven't heard of the other two either), was the head honcho of Tarantula Films. He was fat all over. By that, I mean his corpulent body, his neck, his limbs and his jowly face. He made a clumsy pass at me, when we first met, and I explained to him that I was secretly married to a lady from Doncaster.

He shrugged it off with ease, and he said that he supposed he was being given the Doncaster Bypass. After that we got on well, especially when the first two films were bringing in the loot. Later on in my acting career, he called me into his opulent office, and he poured me some red wine, which he said was the bees' knees. I really preferred brown ale, but the wine was O.K.

"Danny boy, we are going to let you go. We had an agreement to do four films with you and an option to do four more, but I think the time has come for you to spread your wings, and you should work elsewhere."

He had left the protection of his huge desk, and he was shaking me by the hand, as he led me out of his office. He started talking to his secretary, who had a desk in the room just outside his, much more palatial, working area.

"Linda, Danny has decided to leave us. Please take care of the paperwork. Oh, Danny please don't forget to surrender your parking badge and your ID card to get into the film lot. Goodbye old sport, it's been great knowing you."

My singing career was also more or less washed up, as the singer who had performed the notes I couldn't reach had sold his story to a gossip rag, and the songs which I had recorded of late had been tame and boring. I was happy though, as I had met a dazzling actress, called Sophie Morgan, a ravishing English Rose.

We'd been sort of dating, on and off, and she was already well-known. She rang me one day, to tell me that she had landed a part in a film with that dreadful title, *The Secret Mysteries of the Terrestrial Minds.* She was known as Moonbeam, and had been cast as the love interest for Adrian Adair, who was a fading heart-throb.

His best work was well behind him, and he had taken to drink. The film company, Spire Inc., had given him a last chance and cast him as a secret agent, who uncovers a plot by aliens to take over the world. The aliens would do this by guiding the thoughts of key terrestrial leaders.

Adrian couldn't remember his lines, and he was often in a bad state on set. A few days previously, he had been asked to kiss Sophie (sorry - Moonbeam), and had been sick all over her. He was sacked on the spot. Spire had been desperate to rescue their investment in the film. They tried several other reasonably well-known names, but they were all working already. It was then that Moonbeam had suggested me.

I was called by Dexter Phillips, the head of Spire, and after a short conversation I agreed to replace Adrian. The deal was that I would be paid no money down, but I would earn a small percentage of the receipts for the film. I suppose that Dexter thought he had achieved a good deal for Spire, but in the end I earned a lot, and I mean a substantial amount of money, from that terrible film. They told me that I had to stop using that horrible, black dye on my hair. After it was washed out, and it was revealed that my hair was silver all over, the make-up girl told me that I looked much better without the black gunk.

Dexter was taken aback to see my grey hair. He asked Moonbeam what she thought, and she said I looked super sexy. Moonbeam assured him that the ladies would go wild when they saw me. Dexter asked us to do the rounds at the parties and receptions, and it was proved that Moonbeam was right. What a lucky break.

The film was shot on a tight budget, and it was wrapped up in a short time span. Spire used some sets from another film, and most of the cast, except for Moonbeam and me, were on small basic wages to appear in all Spire's movies. The story was laughable; the script was appalling, and Moonbeam and I took to playing for laughs. Dexter was furious, but the director, Grainger Storm (who sounded like a pop singer, but wasn't), told him that we had the film crew in stitches every day.

Dexter asked for some rushes to be played in his film room, with a small, selected audience of critics invited. They loved every minute of the showing. The next day their columns sang the praises of Spire, the talented writer and "the funniest pair of actors since Laurel and Hardy," yes – Moonbeam and me.

The rest is history. The film was a huge box office smash, and Spire made a great deal of money. Dexter had tried to worm his way out of my percentage deal, but the agreement was water-tight. My bank account was full to the brim, and I was investing wads of loot in all sorts of ventures, many of which also came good.

I made twenty other films in all. There was a follow up called *Even More Secret Mysteries of the Terrestrial Minds, The Cat with Five Feet, Twisted and Snarled* and other films which gradually earned less and less money. I never managed to get another percentage deal, except for *Even More...*

My relationship with Moonbeam had taken an immense turn for the better. By this time, Moonbeam had split up with Sassy, who went to Los Angeles to be with her new girl-friend, Tandy Curtis, who was a successful country singer. Moonbeam had been distraught, and I had consoled her when she was sobbing copiously.

We'd been drinking red wine heavily, and we'd also been partaking of the weed. I kissed her pretty eyelids, her neck, her lips and various much more private parts of her, and we ended up in bed for thirty-six hours, in a posh hotel. We only got up to go to the loo, and we ordered all our food from room service. I don't know if she was really a half-hearted lesbian before, or if she was really a converted hetero-sexual after that mammoth session, but she and I became a closely linked item.

Moonbeam also worked with me on the sequel, but after a few months she caught me misbehaving with the pretty make-up girl. You know who I mean - the one who had been the first to admire my silver hair. We were doing something energetic in the bedroom of my house in Hampstead (which Moonbeam and I had bought just before we got married.) My darling Moonbeam, the love of my life, walked out, and we never spoke for years.

Monica, the make-up girl, moved in, and we did fairly well, I guess, but she lost interest in our relationship, and she left me quickly. When she walked out she gave me a hard time, saying, "Unless you cut down on the booze and drugs, you'll soon lose all your work. You've already lost your pretty boy looks. Look at that thinning hair and the flabby cheeks. And that turkey neck is gross!"

I laughed, but when she'd gone, I took a good hard look at myself in the mirror. Sadly, she was right. I had plenty of money, so I had a face-lift. That tautened me up a bit. I carried on working for years, in films with ever more awful names, and matching dire scripts.

I had a few more injections of this and that, and I also had facial operations; it seemed to help. One day however, I heard Darren Thimp, the boss of the budget film company for whom I was working at the time, say to his aide, "If Danny Vertigo has any more face-lifts we could cast his as the monster in our next film - without even paying for make up."

I swallowed my pride and rang Moonbeam. At first she wanted to hang-up, but I begged her to see me. She agreed to come to my house, (the one we used to own together), and when I opened the door I saw that she was still a very attractive woman, albeit with greying hair and tiny wrinkles at the corners of her eyes.

She saw an ageing tortoise with no hair. She must also have noticed that I had a face so tight, I could hardly speak. Moonbeam surprised me by kissing me gently, on my tightly pursed lips. I could hardly move them. She touched my shiny, smooth neck, and she sighed. She came in for coffee, and I told her that I had kicked the booze and the drugs. I also admitted that I had been with many women, but there had never - ever, been one in my life like her.

"I know that this is too little, too late, but I still love you, Sophie."

She replied, "I've always loved you. To prove it, I will move in again. I don't know how things will pan out, but you need me."

If my face had been more flexible, I would have smiled the widest smile, just for my Moonbeam.

Chapter 30

MOANING ACID

As I grow old and placid,
I'm serene and quiet and more.
I dispense no moaning acid.
Yes, of that I am quite sure.
I was worried and would falter,
when the going, it got tough.
With my troubles on the altar,
if the path was steep and rough.
The solution that I sought
was to be so much more smiley.
The answer can't be bought,
but I'm getting far less riley.

I'M SERENE AND QUIET AND MORE

I'm a seventy-three and I'm a recycled teenager. Or that's how I think of myself at least. My lovely wife, Violet, says I am just a big kid, but wives don't understand men do they? She says they understand them too well. I know better than to argue with her. She's always right, in her opinion. She is wrong about her always being right, so she may well be wrong about lots of things. Only this morning, she said to me, "Amos, I found the bathroom towel on the floor – again. I wonder who left a sopping wet towel by the side of the bath?"

That's a good example of a useless question. It was I, and she knows it. I know it too. Therefore, there is no need to argue about it at all. That's my usual philosophy. If there is no need to argue – don't. Conversely, if there is a need to argue - do. However, at my advanced age it's taxing, and I never win. I don't think a husband should automatically just say, "Yes dear, no dear, three bags full dear," as we used to be encouraged to do - by the distaff side of a relationship.

Some people choose between these options:

1. Do exactly what your wife asks you to do, at all times.
2. Do exactly what you want to do, at all times.

I discarded another option:

3. Sometimes do what your wife wants, and sometimes do what you want.

That's far too difficult. I've now adopted a sort of fourth option. I just agree with Violet, but I do whatever I had already made my mind up to do anyway. It was working fine until she said, "I think we should move to a smaller house. Lots of people downsize when they get older and let's face it, we are older."

In all honesty, I have no desire to move, and I will not do so unless they drag me kicking and screaming to another house, or they put me in a ridiculously expensive care home. I gave her a non-committal "Hmm," and I went on reading my book all about rare, vintage guitars.

I have forty-six guitars. I have Fenders, Gibsons, Gretsches (is that the plural of Gretsch?), Martins, Macaferris plus many other lesser instruments, including twelve old Hofners, which I picked up for tuppence ha'penny each, in the early seventies, when their asking price was low.

Violet has about four million pairs of shoes, and yet she seems to think my guitar collecting days should be over. I've been doing some sneaky buying. I get them online, have them delivered to a mate's house, and I spread them round our large house, as evenly as possible, so they are hardly noticeable to the naked eye.

To keep the peace, I have even taken an interest in the food shopping. However, I try to avoid supermarkets when Violet's with me. I offer to do the shopping, take a list and whizz round the aisles p.d.q. If she still wants to come with me, I invent an important meeting that I have to attend, immediately after the shopping, maybe like visiting the accountant.

I usually top up my beer levels at The Sinking Sun, in Meldersham, where it is unlikely for Violet to run into her errant husband. The other day, I was just downing my second pint, when I saw her out of the corner of my eye, through the pub window. She was about to walk along the pavement, towards the door of the saloon bar. I slumped down as far as I could.

She walked past my little cubicle, and she sat behind me, in another high-sided nook. Luckily, the sides were six feet or so from the floor to the polished, brass railings on the top, and she couldn't spot me from where she was sitting. I was just about to creep out, when I heard my friend, Julius (the one who takes delivery of my illicit guitars), say, "Hallo Violet, my goodness, you're looking prettier than ever!"

"Get away with you, and fetch me my gin and tonic."

I heard Julius stand up, and he made his way to the far side of the bar, where neither of us could see each other. After a while, he returned, presumably bearing the G. & T. and another pint for himself.

"Violet, I can't wait to rub my hands over that beautiful body. Those lovely curves and rounded parts are just what I need."

Violet giggled and said, "Sssh, that's supposed to be a deadly secret, Julius. Supposing any of Amos' other friends heard you talking like that. They might give the game away."

"My wife will be out next Thursday, and I'll be waiting for you at eleven a.m. Can you make it? I think I'll be able to surprise you, when you see what I've got to offer."

My first inclination was to dash round the partitions, and to punch Julius on the nose. All of my usual leisurely and relaxed leanings seemed to disappear. My second inclination was to bide my time, to go round to Julius' place a few minutes after eleven on Thursday, and to see if I could then catch them in the act.

I had a copy of his front door key, which he had given me a long time ago, and I reckoned I could open the door quietly and get proof positive of their adultery. I could then make plans for a divorce. It would be a bit of a shame, as I had always thought that Violet probably loved me. You can never really tell, can you? I loved her, but if she had been up to no good with my best pal, I thought I could unlove her pretty quickly.

I returned home, after taking a walk through King Cedric's park. I had managed to extricate myself from my cubicle and the pub, without being discovered. I got home before Violet, and when I heard her key in the door, I decided to see if she would own up to seeing my erstwhile chum.

"Hallo dear, where have you been?"

"I went to see Naomi Sinclair."

"Did she say where her husband was?"

"No, Julius was out somewhere. I think he was bowling."

"You were quite a while. Where else did you go?"

"I just had a coffee and a Danish at Naomi's place, and then I came home. Oh, by the way, I've got to see the dentist on Thursday at eleven a.m., so would you mind doing the weekly shop for me? I'll give you a list."

"That's fine, darling."

Inside I was fuming, but I decided to say nothing, until I could catch them in flagrante delecto.

On Thursday, we both left at about the same time, but my journey was supposedly in the opposite direction, so it was easy for me to encourage Violet to take her car, whilst I took my lovely old Rover. I went to Julius' house by an indirect route, and I parked the car round the block.

I got there at about five past eleven, and I sat for a while, trying to calm down. I had Julius' spare key with me, and I'd coated it in WD40, so it would slide into the lock noiselessly. The door opened soundlessly, and I waited a few moments until I heard them talking, upstairs. I mounted the stairs as softly as possible. "Violet, I've never seen such a beautiful body."

"I've been waiting for this for such a long time, Julius."

"Oh Violet, what a fantastic action. I can't help rubbing my hands all over those curves, and I love the delicate places at the top of this wonderful neck."

I pushed open the door and saw Julius holding a fantastic 1959 Fender Stratocaster, with a rose-wood neck and a maple fretboard. The three-colour sunburst finish on the beautiful body was amazing, and it had one of the original, single-ply scratch plates, with ten screws, rather than the later, three-ply one with eleven screws. The rounded curves, and the delicate parts at the top of the neck, did indeed make it a special guitar to hanker after. I closed my mouth, before I could say anything that would make me look a perfect fool.

"Oh darling, what a shame. I bought this guitar for you with Julius' advice, and this is your birthday present for next week. I know that you haven't bought any guitars for years, and I wanted to show you how much I love you."

"Er..., I thought I might have left my pipe here the other day. I took the liberty of using your spare key, Julius."

"I don't think it's here, but it was a good idea to check. Just try this!"

He offered the precious and very expensive guitar to me. I played a few simple runs, on the perfectly aligned and intonated neck. As Julius had said, the instrument had a fantastic action. I decided that Violet did love me after all.

Chapter 31

BONKETTE

Ernest made a visit, to a squalid place of pleasure.
He was hoping that the treat would help him relax.
The skills the girls all had, were entirely his to treasure.
They were helpful, when it came to bare, brass tacks.
He heard about a service, a special thing on offer,
and they asked him to recline, on a banquette.
He was sure they were mocking, what he wanted to proffer,
when they told him, he could have a small bonkette.

A SQUALID PLACE OF PLEASURE

Ernest was a sad, unattractive and heavy man, with no friends or relatives. His mother and father had been killed in a terrible, boating accident, when their holiday pedalo was washed out to sea by strong waves, off the coast of Guernsey. There had been freak, current conditions, which would unfortunately see young Ernest orphaned, at the tender age of nine.

He had been at home in Manchester, being cared for whilst his parents had what they termed a second honeymoon. The baby-sitters were the Meads - Edith and Bryn, and whilst they had not relished the idea of looking after a morose and taciturn child, they had been persuaded to do so by the payment of a modest, but welcome, fee. Bryn worked in the Post Office sorting department with Ernest's father, Gabriel. They were more like colleagues than friends, but they spent much time together working at their various tasks, and neither of them enjoyed their work.

They had fallen into the habit of having lunch together in the canteen, where Bryn would talk to Gabriel, and he would nod and grunt. He was a poor conversational partner. That suited Bryn, as he could give long, boring dissertations about his pet hates, without being interrupted, like he always was by Edith. (That was definitely one of his pet hates.)

When the subject of nannying Ernest for a fortnight had been raised by Gabriel, Bryn had been surprised that his workmate had actually started a new subject, all by himself. Bryn made a request for money in respect of the Ernest minding service, and Gabriel agreed.

The holiday had been booked, and Ernest's grateful parents had travelled by car to Portsmouth, breaking their journey halfway to the port, so they could drive straight onto the ferry, when they arrived at the dock (subject to the queues, of course.) They planned to use their own car from St. Peter Port to their chosen destination, St. Martin. The guest house was clean and comfortable, and the sun was shining, as they drove to Fermain beach.

They found a little shack, which rented beach essentials and water sports equipment. It was Edith's idea to rent a pedalo. At the time, it seemed a good notion, but once they were out on the ocean wave, the wind picked up, and the undertow was very strong. They were carried out to sea, at an alarming rate of knots. Just exactly how many knots, I'm afraid I can't tell you, but the resultant collision with another ferry, this time bound for Portsmouth, put paid to the only living relatives of little Ernest.

Ernest was notified, by Bryn Mead, that his mum and dad had been killed, and he did it as gently as possible. Ernest was generally a glum child, and his normally sullen expression became sullen to the nth degree. He didn't speak for three weeks, and although both of the Meads tried to comfort him, his natural tendency towards solitude increased, and soon he hardly ever left his room, save for bathing and the natural, bodily functions which made journeys to the lavatory mandatory.

Edith, a youngish, fifty-year old, had sparse but flowing hair of a strange, pale, ginger colour, which she called strawberry blonde. She also had a lovely face and warm, brown eyes, which sparkled. Sparkling those eyes at Ernest became more and more of a laborious task, and even when she pulled him into her impressive mammaria, he was unresponsive, or so she thought. Little did she know, that she was the first subject of Ernest's secret, fantasy love-life. Forever after, the smell of Chanel No. 5 had an unfortunate effect on him.

The Social Services people intervened, like they always do, and the lad was eventually whisked away to a children's home, called St. Martin's Refuge for Boys. The irony of its name was totally lost on Ernest. He waved goodbye to the cuddly Edith and her slimmer husband, with his hooded eyes and distinguished features, his round specs and his faint smells of tobacco and mints.

Ernest was fostered several times, and some potential adoption candidates were interviewed. Everything usually went well, until they met him. He was coming up to eleven, and he had grown into a fattish globule of a boy, who was exceptionally plain. However, the photos shown to couples who might be interested in adopting him were flattering, and they made him look trimmer than he really was.

Some of the candidates persevered, and they tried to talk to him. Well, that's not quite right. They did talk to him, but he didn't answer. It may have been a special sullen gene passed down from his father. One by one, the offers of possible homes for Ernest all but vanished.

On a fine, spring day in March, he was summoned by the matron, Daphne Gaffney, whose mother and father must have had a poor sense of humour, or just thought it was a wheeze to land her with a rhyming name. She was still a spinster at fifty-eight, and she was doomed to be an unmarried, walking couplet for the rest of her life.

"Ernest, we've seen a lovely couple, and they'd like to talk to you. They are the Williamsons, and their names are Joseph and Nicola."

Ernest grunted, and he resisted the temptation to ask how he would be able to tell which one was which. In the day lounge, he was introduced to Nicola first, and he caught the unmistakeable scent of Chanel No. 5, as she wiped her brow with a clean, white hankie.

She took him by his shoulders, and he soon found his nose buried in her soft, warm breasts. He again had the strange, stirring sensation which was alluded to earlier in this story. The man with her, presumably Joseph, held his hand out and, extricating the boy from his wife's appendages, he shook him by the hand in a matey, man to man way. Ernest actually smiled and said. "Good day sir, I'm so pleased to meet you and your lovely wife."

After all the tedious form-filling had been complied with, the boy went to live with his new mum and dad, as they had asked him to call them thus. Everything went well, even though Ernest was still a quiet person, until he was sixteen.

One fateful day, he was found in a disgracefully intertwined position with his step-mother, who should never have encouraged him to do what he did. It turned out that the pair of them had been involved in a sort of step-incestuous relationship for several months, before Joseph caught them in bed together, when he had popped back from work one day, to pick up something he had forgotten.

Joseph parked Ernest with a friend and his wife, for a few days, whilst he talked to Nicola about their future.

"Nicola, until now you've been a loyal, loving and good wife. I'm prepared to forgive you, provided Ernest leaves this house and you never see him again. I will pay rent for a small flat for him, until he is eighteen, and then he's on his own. I've asked a client of mine, to take the boy on as a junior clerk. My solicitor has instructions to forward a small monthly allowance to him. He will advise Ernest that if he ever tries to contact you or me, he will be evicted from the flat, and the allowance will cease immediately.

"Furthermore, if he does try to contact us a sealed envelope, addressed to Social Services, explaining your disgusting and inappropriate relationship, will be forwarded by Mr. Murgatroyd (or his successor at the solicitor's office.) Those are my only and final terms."

Nicola had thought that she would be thrown out of their elegant mews house. She nodded and cried, and she said, "I agree. You've been merciful, and I'll make it up to you, I swear."

Ernest was soon ensconced in the studio-flat which his step-father had supplied. Murgatroyd had explained the strict terms of the arrangement to the boy and supplied a final, terse (but abundantly clear), letter from Joseph Williamson.

Dear Ernest

I am not a vengeful man, but your conduct is such that you cannot live in our house any longer. Provided that you never attempt to contact my wife or myself, I will pay the rent for a small flat for you, until you reach the age of eighteen.

You will be taken on next month, as a trainee with a firm whose details will be given to you by Mr. Murgatroyd. He will also forward a small, monthly allowance to you.

If you try to contact either of us, you will be evicted from the flat, and the allowance will cease immediately. I will also tell Social Services about your disgusting and inappropriate relationship with your step-mother. This has been detailed in a letter lodged with Mr. Murgatroyd, and he has instructions to release it on my say so.

I need hardly add, that I could also ask the firm who will be taking you on, to sack you if you break these terms.

Goodbye

Joseph Williamson

Ernest thought he had got off quite lightly. He became used to his tiny flat, and he almost enjoyed the mundane job with a small shipping company, where he had been taken on as an office dogsbody. He was pleasantly surprised to find that he could save a modest amount each month, after paying out his living expenses from the allowance, which was paid into a bank account, on the first of each month.

He took to having a couple of pints every now and then, in The Flying Donkey, a normal pub with a stupid name. This fairly peaceful existence went on for a year or so, until he was approached by a friendly and good looking girl, who had been eyeing him up for some time.

"Aren't you ever going to buy me a drink, darling?"

He looked at her in surprise. She was small and pretty, with masses of dark hair and a delicious, dainty nose.

"O.K. What's your poison?"

Ernest and Candice (with the nose), chatted for a long time, and then she dropped an unexpected bombshell.

"I work at a brothel near here, and I was hoping you would come with me, to try out my services."

Until then, Ernest had been becoming more and more ready to avail himself of the girl's temptations. However, talk of payment made his desire wither immediately. Nonetheless, he finally agreed to go with her.

They walked half a mile or so, to a small house called Wanderlust. The owner must have a funny sense of humour, thought Ernest. Candice took him into the front parlour of what looked like a normal family home. He took his duffel coat off, as he was far too hot, and she poured him a large measure of Scotch.

"Are you ready to come to bed with me now?"

She also told him what the rates were for some sample services.

"Candice, I don't want to be rude, but is there anybody a little more, motherly and rounded? That's the kind of woman which I am used to."

Candice laughed.

"Don't worry. I think I know just the lady for you."

She ushered in Emily, a youngish, fifty-year old, with sparse but flowing hair of a strange, pale, ginger colour. She had a lovely face and warm, brown eyes which sparkled. Ernest had the strangest sensation of déjà vu. As she sat next to him, he could smell Chanel No. 5. He breathed a sigh of relief. Everything would be fine.

"Emily, I love strawberry blonde hair. Do you mind if I call you Mummy?"

Chapter 32

REIGNING CATS AND DOGS

Cats are feline fine, but dogs are more canine.
Their owners have their fads and proclivities.
They snuggle on our laps, and in our open hearts.
Are these pets, real family members? (Possibility!)
Cats are purring tigers, in their dreams and aims,
but dogs are faithful servants of the world.
The animals all kid us that they really have been tamed,
when all cosy they are lying round, all curled.

DOGS ARE FAITHFUL SERVANTS

Rover was always a troublemaker. When his brothers and sisters did all they could to please humans, he told them off.

"They are not so special. Their sense of smell is poor and as for their hearing – they can't even hear very high frequencies. What good are they? They feed us and stroke us, but they only do it to make themselves feel good."

Topsy, his favourite sister, looked at him askance.

"This is heresy, Rover; it goes against all that our mother taught us. I bet if we knew who our father was, he'd say the same."

Rover wasn't convinced. He was fed up with being called Rover, too. His real name was Bark, and his sister's dog-name was Lick. As for the rest of the litter, they also had proper dog-names, like Growl, Rumble-in-the-Throat and Grrr.

One day their human (and surrogate alpha male), Glenn Travis, gathered up their sisters, Growl, Rumble-in-the-Throat, and their brother Grrr, and he took them away in one of those metal carts, with no horse in front. Bark and Lick were devastated. (They'd already lost their mother who had died shortly after they were born.) It was right after this human treachery, that Bark formed the Dog Not Human Party.

The D.N.H.P. started to have meetings every few days. At first, only Bark and Lick came to the meetings. Lick admired her brother. She thought he was compelling, when he spoke at length. He managed to convince her that they should throw off the yoke of human oppression, and she started to fully support his protest movement.

Whenever they could get out of the garden, with its faulty latch on the back gate, they toured the neighbourhood, and Bark lectured to all the dogs that would listen, about the way that humans treated dogs like babies, "when we are really fierce hunters." Bit by bit, he managed to persuade many other dogs that humans were taking away their very dogness, by putting on collars, inserting micro-chips and making them wear ridiculous coats.

Bark knew that marking the carpets in the Travis household was forbidden, but he could never understand why this was so. He sprayed all of the carpets and rugs and encouraged Lick to do the same. Bark advised other members of the D.N.H.P. to wee all over the houses in which they were imprisoned, to chew slippers and skirting boards and to eat slips of paper that looked important to humans, such as bills and cheques. Hattie Travis was dismayed to find urine stains and to be assailed by nasty smells, all over the house.

"Glenn, I think Rover or Topsy must have a problem with their waterworks. Look at the state of these carpets. They smell of dog pee. They've also started to chew everything, and one of them has even nibbled my spectacles."

Glenn sighed, lowered his paper and took a begrudging look at the protest pees, which had been performed with great exactitude by Bark and Lick. He sniffed, but could smell nothing. That wasn't unusual, as he had lost his sense of smell when he was fourteen, following a severe head-cold. No matter what the doctors tried, they could not resurrect his olfactory sensation.

"The carpets do look a bit grubby, but I can't smell a thing, Hattie."

Hattie wrinkled her nose. At any other time, Glenn might have appreciated the beauty of her pretty schnozzle, and he knew that the rest of her was equally perfect. However, right now he was trying to do the crossword, and he was stuck on 2 down.

Rover and Topsy entered the lounge, and the male part of the crime team lifted his leg and peed copiously on the T.V. His female cohort squatted, and a pool of hot, steaming liquid was dispersed on the rug in front of the fireplace. Hattie was dumbfounded. Glenn threw his paper on the floor, and he grabbed the collars of these ungrateful mutts, before dragging them into the back garden.

Bark howled, and Lick followed suit. The gate to the garden was not securely fixed, and other dogs poured in. They lined up in front of Bark and Lick.

"On my command, howl continuously - until I ask you to stop. After three: one, two, three."

An awful din drew The Travises to the back door. They were astounded to find twenty-seven dogs, of all shapes and sizes, howling for all they were worth. After about half a minute, Rover barked imperiously, and they all stopped.

"Let's do that again, fellow members of the D.N.H.P. Here we go: one, two, three."

Once again, there was a loud chorus of canine ululation. Glenn ran into the garden and shooed off the invaders. Bark thought about getting them to bite him, but he decided that, although this would demonstrate the power of the D.N.H.P., he didn't really want Glenn to be hurt.

Hattie suggested that it was time to take the ungrateful pets to the vet, to see what might be causing the problem. She backed the car out of the garage, and she opened the cage in the back. She was pleased to see Rover and Topsy acting normally and running up the path to jump into their cage, with eager expressions on their faces.

She sat in the driving seat and waited for Glenn to come out, after doing his usual, laborious checks. Lock the back door, spectacles, wallet, keys - and finally set the burglar alarm. He came out of the front door, pulled it shut, and he double locked it. Hattie was used to his annoying plodicity. She had invented the word herself, but she thought that it summed him up beautifully.

"Let's go, Hat!"

At the vets, they announced their arrival to the receptionist, explained the problem, and the girl behind the desk, known always as "Sandra from the next road," told them that quite a few other dog owners had brought in their cherished pals, with exactly the same problem. She said, so far, they had not been able to find any reason for the sudden difficulties which the local pooches had been having, like drastic incontinence and unusual chewing practices.

They waited a while, and then Mr. Patel asked them to bring Rover and Topsy into his consulting room. He examined them thoroughly, but he could find nothing wrong with either of them. Bark and Lick couldn't resist making a fuss of him, as they knew they normally had some treats at the end of these visits.

"Well, Mr. and Mrs. Travis, I've now seen about thirty of these local dogs, all with exactly the same problem. If they were humans, I would have assumed that this was an orchestrated protest, over some imagined or real wrong.

"However, they are not, and I firmly believe that a chemical in the air has been released from an industrial process in the vicinity, and it's causing this involuntary loosening of the necks of the dogs' bladders. Take them home, and bring them back in a week. If the situation is no better, we may have to euthanise them. We can't allow this to continue."

Hattie started crying, and Glenn gulped. His eyes looked red, and he screwed them up, to stop tears appearing. Hattie said, "Do you really think that we will have to put these lovely dogs to sleep? I'd hate to be without them. They are our babies. We've never had children, and they made our life whole."

Bark looked at Lick.

"Did you hear what he said? I didn't know what that word meant, but Hattie has spilled the beans. I don't want to die, Lick. What shall we do?"

"We'll have to disband the D.N.H.P., and go back to being lap dogs. I know you said we shouldn't sit on their laps anymore, but I really liked being cuddled and stroked."

When they returned home, Bark and Lick went into the garden and Bark summoned the D.N.H.P. members with his usual howling. Once they were assembled he said, "My dear D.N.H.P. members, we've had a great victory over the human race. They've learned that we can use special methods, by which we can show our dissatisfaction, so we can now relax and go back to normal. You've all done well."

The dogs acquiesced with low, murmuring growls. As they went out of the open gate, Lick heard one of them say, "Thank goodness for that. He's off his head, that Bark."

Chapter 33

MY TRUE LOVE

True love is always better,
than a million loves before.
A scent, a touch, a letter
makes me happier, yes more.
I made mistakes, I didn't learn.
I think that's pretty usual.
For goodness sake, that's my concern
although, it's very crucial.

A SCENT, A TOUCH, A LETTER

My first love was a girl called Bonnie Carr. I always thought she sounded like a posh automobile. She was blonde, curly and twelve years old, the same age as I was at the time. I thought the world of her, and we took walks in the local park, had some milkshakes in the Eldorado Coffee Bar in Wetherton High Street, and we shared our first kiss (for both of us), in the back row of the local fleapit, The Rialto Picture House.

The cinema was dusty and always smelt damp, and the atmosphere was smoky, as was the case in all cinemas in the early sixties. She leaned her darling head against my shoulder, and I caught a greasy whiff of fish and chip fat. Her dad owned Dermot's Plaice, the best chippy in town, by far, and in consequence Bonnie somehow always had a slight aroma of cod about her. That didn't put me off at all. I looked down at her face, and raised my hand to her chin. She did her part and looked up at me, and then, somehow, we were kissing. It was an exciting evening, and we repeated the osculation procedure many times that night, and then on other dates, sometimes at the flicks and sometimes in the back room of her parents' house.

They had an enormous radiogram, on which you could stack records, on a sort of metal spindle, and they would play automatically, one after the other. Our choice of music was a trifle limited. I only remember *Go Away Little Girl* by Mark Wynter, *Til I Kissed Her* by The Everly Brothers, *Lipstick on Your Collar* by Connie Francis and *When My Little Girl Is Smiling* by The Drifters. I don't think we really cared about the music. We had to listen out for interruptions from Dermot Carr and Evelyn (his wife), who popped in to see if we were alright, as they did it a lot more times than was strictly necessary.

We went to parties together and to a youth club, and we even discussed getting married, when we were older. We had in mind a cottage in the country, with roses round the door. After two months or so,

Bonnie made it clear that she thought we were seeing too much of each other. I wished we really were, but it turned out she meant we were seeing each other too frequently. (I was a pedant, even then. I always liked everything to be expressed clearly.)

The final straw was when we were at a party, playing a ridiculous game which involved kissing the next person you saw, when you were found after hiding. The next person always seemed to be a dreadful creep called Carl something or other, who appeared mysteriously, each time Bonnie was found. Bonnie came to my home one day and delivered the coup de grâce. She said we were much too young to be talking of marriage and that silly cottage. She then finished me off with this final, extra blow. "I want to have some fun, Hugh. I'm afraid you are far too serious, and you're not much fun at all."

I was shattered, but not for long. A few days later, I was helping to stick some egg boxes to the walls, in the basement of a local coffee house. This was a primitive method of sound-proofing a place in the early sixties, so that beat groups (as they were called in those days), could thrash away at songs which were in the hit parade, or in some cases play a little rock and roll and rhythm and blues. I took a well-earned rest. I sat in an alcove, under the stairs leading down to the basement, and as I did so I noticed a young beauty I had seen before, but to whom I had never spoken.

"Hi, I'm Hugh."

"I know, and I'm Laura Ryan."

I don't know what came over me. I suddenly became brave and put my arm round her and kissed her several times. This bravado must have been acceptable because we started to go out together, and I tried hard to pretend not to be serious. This must have worked, because we were together for nearly a year, before I realised that I would rather be with another girl, who was called Maria Webster.

I'd like to be able to report that this was a good move. The differences between Laura and Maria were many and marked. The main one was that Laura was a lovely, friendly girl, but Maria was a total bitch. Maria drove me crazy with jealousy, and she delighted in twisting the knife, by making vague references to old boyfriends and to other men she knew, and whom she admired. Jealousy over old boyfriends, and other male friends of my girls, was one of my most ridiculous habits.

My best pal, Patrick Hat, said, "You shouldn't be worried about things that happened in the past, when you were snogging the face off several other girls. And all girls know other men, but it doesn't mean that they are shagging them behind your back."

I realise now, that this was fair comment, but it was hard to take from a boy called Pat Hat. What were his parents thinking of?

Maria dumped me, just before I did the same to her, citing my jealousy and over-protective nature as the reasons for our break up. My usual method of becoming involved with a new girlfriend was to slough off the old one like a discarded snake-skin, and I moved on quickly, to what I thought was a better prospect. I was fourteen and desperate to get laid. Name me one single fourteen-year-old lad who isn't?

I was desolate for at least four or five days, until I saw a cute, little brunette working behind the counter in Woolworth's. Pat dared me to ask her out. I told him that this would be easy, but I almost bottled out. In the end it was as simple as I'd boastfully predicted, and she agreed to meet me in The Eldorado, on her day off.

Tess was a laugh. She was friendly, and she allowed me to take some interesting liberties with her (heavy petting no less!) She was good company. We courted for three years, and a little while before we parted, I was awarded the golden prize by my Tess. I could hardly believe that I was no longer a virgin.

I went to work in a book shop in the High Street, and now that I had a little spare cash, I sometimes treated us to burgers and chips in the Wimpy Bar. Tess took me to one side after one of our burger fiestas, and told me that she was pregnant. I was gob-smacked. We had only been together "like that" once.

I offered to marry her, and she just laughed. She reassured me that the father was a squaddie, who was stationed locally. She had been seeing him for some time, although she had more or less dropped him just before I asked her out in Woolworth's.

She'd seen the doctor on the same day she dropped the bombshell to her ex-boyfriend. With simple calendar calculation, she was certain that the soldier was the dad. She therefore told me that she had seen him and given him the bad news. The good news for me, was that he had agreed to marry her.

That was a close shave. Talking about shaves, I used to have my hair cut by a local barber, and he always asked if I wanted "something for the weekend" or some "night flyers." Pat told me that these were nicknames for Durex condoms, and I bought some, when I next had a trim. They weren't to see any action for a few months, but by golly did I make up for it with Yvette, my next conquest, whom I met at a club.

She and I were at it like rampant rabbits, and we stayed together for four years before getting married. I was twenty-two, and she was eighteen. I was naïve and foolish, like most boys of that age, but she was a little more street savvy, like most girls of eighteen. She tried to change everything about me. She didn't like my hairstyle, my job, my shoes and my clothes. She didn't laugh at my jokes and hated my friends.

I bet you can see what's coming. I met a girl in the park, by the stagnant pond (of all places), when I was sitting on a bench looking at the ducks, and wondering how I could be free of Yvette.

"Penny for them."

I looked up to see the most gorgeous, and I really mean stupendously, terrifically, gorgeous girl I had ever seen in all of my twenty-seven years. She was sophisticated, cool and calm, and she exuded almost tangible waves of femininity. She even had a classy name – Imogen. We chatted for some time and had watery coffee, with a couple of Wagon Wheels, in the small café on the other side of the smelly pond. I asked her if we could meet again. She looked at me carefully, and she asked, "Is there anybody else in your life?"

I decided, luckily as it happens, to tell the truth. I told her all about Yvette, and she told me about her rough husband, Martin. She said he was a big and brutal man, who beat her up frequently. I almost gave up when I heard that. I've always been tall, but I was thin and gangly, and Pat said he was surprised I didn't blow away with the slightest breeze.

"He's already chucked me out. The place where we lived was a small, rented flat. I've got no savings, no kids and no future. I've just taken a room in town. Would you like to come and have another coffee? I promise it will be a bit stronger than the dishwater we just drank here!"

We went to her place, had much better coffee, and we went straight to bed. She was tender and affectionate, laughed at all my jokes and was appreciative when I stroked her - and so on. We've been together now for thirty-six years. I won't say we have never had a cross word, but she is my perfect partner.

When we got married (after the divorces of each of us from our previous partners), we entered into a state of marital bliss that was truly wonderful, but it even changed (for the better), as we grew older, wiser and closer. We take an interest in each other's hobbies. We talk about important and trivial things with ease, and she's my one true love. The others were a part of a tricky, learning process.

By the way, did I tell you that it was some time before I discovered that she was Bonnie Carr's little sister? The last time I had seen Imogen, she was only five, and what with me being a mature twelve-year-old, I don't think I had even noticed her, as a snot-nosed youngster. How was I to know that she would be so knock 'em dead gorgeous when she grew up?

Chapter 34

THE MEMORY STILL LINGERS

I left it while I went inside, to warm my frozen fingers.
It was very cold and dismal and the wind was wet, so bleak.
I came back to find it gorn, although the memory still lingers.
I searched for it for several days, or maybe for a week.
It seems while I was gone, a sunny spell was started,
and my poor snowman, he was called to paradise.
I hope he didn't feel too bad, or chilly and down-hearted.
He left me, just his hat, his coal black pair of eyes.

HIS COAL BLACK PAIR OF EYES

I've enjoyed all my reincarnations as a snowman. The good thing about water, ice and snow is that every part of those substances mixes easily, and each part remembers any water molecules, with which there has been previous contact. I've been involved in rivers, streams, muddy ditches and rain-water, but I like being a snowman best of all. I suppose that the air must be similar, with mix and match, interchangeable molecules, but I'm not an expert.

Allow me to introduce myself. My name is Wet Face. I was, until only recently, known as Cold Wet Face, but as the sun has started shining today, I think I will soon be Slush Man and then Puddles.

The main thing is, I really enjoy being built into a snow, humanoid figure, and each time, I am surprised to be comprised of at least some new water molecules, but I'm even more astonished when some of my old molecule pals turn up, as a part of the new, snow me.

I always know how I was built, and I'm instinctively aware of how many times parts of me have been included in previous snowmen. This time I am 98.98% new, but the 0.02% which is returning, is comprised of water that has previously been part of my contribution to the snowman universal consciousness, on other occasions.

The children who made me are the Miller twins, Bridey and Claude. They are only six, but they are expert builders of snowmen. I always try to talk to the kids, and sometimes they seem to hear my voice. It's not loud, and it does sound a little like car tyres going through the snow. If I say something simple like, "Woosh, wooshey, swooshey, whoosh," they look up and peer in my direction, but they always come to the conclusion that a car just went past which they heard, but didn't see.

I wanted to ask them to build me a snow-wife. I've never had a female companion, and I was eager to have one, before I melted. I was therefore surprised and joyfully expectant when Claude suddenly said,

"Have you ever seen a snowwoman, Bridey? Let's build one quick, before this snowman melts."

Claude is my favourite of the Miller twins. He has a smiley face, even though his teeth are goofy. His hair resists any attempts he makes to control it, or to part it, and it stands up in unruly and spikey tufts. The rest of him is similarly ungainly, but even though he usually has muddy trousers and scuffed shoes, he's a sunny chap.

Bridey is like a little old lady. She's immaculately turned out, and is always pristine. The only time I saw her looking less than perfect was when Claude deliberately tripped her up, and he rubbed her face in the muddy flower-bed alongside the Miller lawn. She is a tad too wonderful for me. All that politesse would be a strain to cope with all day, I'd think. Give me a nice, carrot nose and coal eyes, and I'm happy.

I was beginning to slide towards the ground slightly just then, and I tried to stand up straight, but part of my left arm slipped off. Claude rolled up some more snow and repaired my arm. They'd found an old hat belonging to their dad, at least I hoped it was an old hat, and they set this at a jaunty angle on my head.

They rolled a large ball of snow, and when it was about two feet in diameter, they rolled another one, and set it on top of the first ball. They'd positioned the first giant ball about eighteen inches away from me, and I could have reached the ball if my snow arm was more flexible. I would have liked to put my arm round my headless companion, but it was joined to my body.

They quickly rectified the no head situation, when another smaller ball was placed on top of the torso ball. Claude went to fetch some small lumps of coal for her eyes, and although he couldn't find another carrot for the nose, he came back from his mum's kitchen with a small banana. Once the banana was pushed into her face, it made a grinning, yellow mouth.

"Hallo sexy," said the snow temptress, "How 'bout some fun before we melt? I think I have some molecules which you've used before, so we should really connect."

If I could have done so, I would have blushed. I thought she was too forward.

"My name is S.N.O. Queen. What's your name, hunky?"

"I'm Wet Face. What's with this posy S.N.O. business?"

"Just a passing fashion, I think. As we're also passing snow creatures, I thought I'd have a modern name. These kids just called me Donna. Sounds like a kebab to me."

Part of her slipped off, and her left arm ended up on the floor, next to where my right foot would have been (if I had any separate feet that is.) Bridey quickly repaired my new girl-friend's arm. "Look at those two. Why don't we have a wedding for them, Claude?"

Claude looked round cautiously. He had to see if any of his friends were within earshot. Although he thought it was a good idea, he couldn't admit as much if his pals were around. They would have thought he was wet. Claude could see that the twins were the only children in the street, and he nodded vigorously. Bridey allowed her brother some temporary seniority, "You can be the vicar. I'll be the witness; I think that's all we need."

Claude started off, "Dearly beloved, we are now going to marry these two snow people."

He carried on with some meaningless words, and extemporised about water, snow and sky. He thought he was being clever, but Bridey was getting impatient.

"If you don't hurry up, they'll both be gone before you reach the bit about, what the Snow God has joined, let no man put asunder."

I knew that she was right, but I was enjoying this romantic interlude before being swept away, when I would become a pile of grey and uninteresting slush. My bride had collapsed somewhat, and she was leaning on my shoulder.

"I do feel weird, with your head on my shoulder. What will happen now?"

She ignored me, but Claude said, "Bridey, why don't we roll them both into one giant ball. That will be like - they are really joined, at least until they melt completely."

They worked hard, and soon S.N.O. Queen and Wet Face were indeed one. We felt a strange sense of union, and the world was a better place, now we'd been rolled up together.

"Woosh, wooshey, swooshey whoosh," I said as I wanted to thank the infants for their good deed. The sun was shining and I was enjoying the warmth, until I saw part of us dripping down into the gutter.

"S.N.O. Queen – Thanks for being a part of my life - and now a part of me."

We were a pile of slush by now, and I never heard her speak to me again. I wanted to cry, but I was afraid the children would make fun of a sentimental, snow heap. I admit though, I did weep in the end, but my tears just looked like drops of water glistening on the lawn of the twins' front garden.

Chapter 35

FLIM FLAM

Humbug is a boon, given to the true pragmatic,
a loosening of the pressure to be sensible.
This nonsense of the mind, with nowt in the attic
and an urge to be quite reprehensible.
The current vogue for sense and style
makes it hard, to be ridiculous.
I'd rather walk a thousand miles,
than be forced to be, meticulous.

NOWT IN THE ATTIC

Clint Burton relished his ridiculous name, that is the introductory Clint part, not the Burton afterthought. It seemed to him that being named after the man with no name (in those spaghetti westerns), was a wonderful oxymoron. He had made the mistake of telling his pals at school that he thought like this, and they had nicknamed him, Poxy Moron.

Clint didn't even mind that much. They still treated him well, even if he didn't seem to be as bright as his peers. He didn't look like a moron at all. If anything, in his Clark Kent glasses and his smart cardigans, he looked more like a male model in a sixties knitting pattern.

After he left school, he looked for a job which was undemanding, having failed all his exams, mainly due to a lack of concentration. He was also afflicted by a severe tendency towards persistent boredom. Every time he had to read or write anything, even if the task was relatively easy (and well within his capabilities), he felt like dozing off.

He was a little smarter than he pretended to be, and that suited him because his new employers only gave him easy tasks. He could daydream at will. Daydreaming was a favourite occupation of his, and he built elaborate pipe-dreams mentally, such as becoming a world famous pop star, an Oscar winning actor or Prime Minister of England, after having been elected to lead The Daydream party.

He remembered Screaming Lord Sutch and his Monster Raving Loony Party, and he thought that this had been a much more interesting outfit than any of the current serious, confrontational and narrow-minded factions in England. They spent so much time blaming the previous incumbents in office, and none of them ever did what they had promised to do. They were therefore all labelled as no-hopers by Clint.

He had a lowly and menial job in the packing department of a small factory. The company manufactured cheap umbrellas, and Clint's tasks were easy. He was friendly with the other two people in the department, Tara Goodman and Una Malloy. They flirted with him outrageously, thinking that they were safe in the knowledge that Clint was so dozy, he probably wouldn't even know one end of a woman from the other.

Tara and Una were physical opposites. Tara was blonde, tall and lissom, whilst Una was brunette, short and pleasantly rounded. Clint was not so unaware of their charms as they thought. He daydreamed about Tara and Una separately, and Tara and Una together (his favourite thought.) He also daydreamed about Tara with him, Una with him, or even better - Tara *and* Una with him.

Clint had been told the facts of life by his shy father, a little while before his dad had died. The circumstances of his death were strange. He had simply decided not to eat or drink, and nothing could persuade him to stop this fast. He had never been all that healthy and had been a frail specimen all his life. He loved his wife Melanie, but she had become indifferent to him, even though he had tried hard to get their marriage back on to a stronger footing. She was cold and unfriendly to Sid, and he had gradually stopped going to work.

He was signed off sick, due to depression. At first, he had sat in an armchair in his sitting room, all day. After several months, he decided that he would spend most of his time in bed. He never had a big appetite and gradually ate less and less. His final decision, not to eat or drink anything, was discussed with a succession of doctors and nurses. Eventually he was persuaded to go to hospital, but Melanie was warned that the end was near.

Sid had asked to see his wife Melanie and young Clint, who at that time was only twelve. Sid wanted to see Melanie first, and then Clint. When Melanie entered the Intensive Care ward, she saw her poor spouse, encumbered with various tubes and other medical trappings, and she was alarmed to observe that he was little more than skin and bones.

The doctor had warned Melanie that Sid was unlikely to last more than a day or two. She tried to keep from crying. Sid had been a good husband, who had always worked hard and never strayed from the dutiful marital path.

"Melanie, my love. I'm on the way out."

"Hush Sid, that's not true, they can do wonderful things nowadays."

Melanie raised her exquisite face towards Sid and kissed his damp brow. He looked into her purple eyes (like Liz Taylor's but even better, he had always said.)

"I want to say two things to you, and then I must see Clint. I love you and have provided as well for you as I can. Talk to Edgar. My brother will help you with all the boring bureaucracy. He is my executor, as you know, so he's the right person to help you do whatever is needed, when I die.

"The second thing I wanted to say is about Clint. He is a decent, truthful and loving boy, but he's not been blessed in the groves of academe. He needs strong guidance and parental care. A replacement, father figure will be essential. I've always been faithful to you, but I know that you and Edgar have been having a relationship for some time."

Melanie went deathly pale. She was so ashamed, as she had thought that the awful secret was just that. How did Sid know? He seemed to anticipate her enquiry.

"I came home early one day and saw all the evidence. Edgar's car was outside. Two glasses, an empty wine bottle and his fags and lighter were on the coffee table. I saw male and female clothing strewn all over the room, and up the stairs. I made a point of checking the house several other times, and I spotted the same sort of things on other days. I can be very quiet, when I want to be. It was then that I resolved to give up on life."

Melanie gulped and started to say something, but Sid stopped her again.

"I haven't got time for your apologies, and I haven't finished what I wanted to say. I think you should allow a decent interval, and you should marry Edgar, so that Clint will still have a father in his life, albeit a step-father. Edgar's been a bachelor all of his life, and I'm sure he will jump at the chance. Will you do that?"

Melanie knew when she was beaten. She and Edgar had been trying to envisage a future together anyway, and although neither of them would have wanted Sid to die, his suggestion made sense.

"Go now. You have my reluctant blessing. Send in Clint."

Clint went in to see his dad, a few minutes later. He mumbled something, but although Clint leaned over to try to hear what he was saying, he couldn't make sense of his last words.

"Oh Dad, I'm sure you'll soon be back home."

Clint's optimism was wasted, as Sid simply nodded, drew a deep breath, and he expired.

In due course, Melanie married Edgar, and they made a good job of looking after Clint. His job at the umbrella factory was more or less unchanged, except the company now imported even cheaper brollies from China, so the packing department took goods in, unpacked them, and then repacked them in the firm's own boxes.

Clint's days were humdrum, but for his thoughts of the two ladies who were his constant companions at work. They sent him on fool's errands, like the usual ones of buying striped paint and of fetching a long weight. He pretended he didn't understand the jokes until they explained them to him. Clint took their joshing in good part, and they found that they both became fond of him.

He was a serious, abstemiously clean, twenty-six-year-old, and he had never kissed a girl, let alone experienced anything more ambitious. Edgar had made a strict, sensible step-father. As Clint was unaware of them betraying his dad, he had a happy upbringing, once he had got used to the absence of his father.

Tara and Una used to go to The Green Dragon, in the Walcott Centre, two or three times a week after work, to drown their sorrows. After a particularly heavy drinking session, Una came up with a plan to give Clint a special treat. She told Tara that it was obvious that Clint had never had a woman, and she said, "Let's give him a night he'll remember forever. We ought to draw straws, and one of us will let him have his evil way. He's spotlessly clean, not too bad looking, and he's a gentleman. He'll need a bit of coaching, but it will be a laugh, and it'll make a man of him."

"Wow – that's one out of the blue, Una! I think it's a fab idea. Let's draw straws right now."

Tara went to the bar and asked for two drinking straws. When she got back to the round, copper-topped table at which her chum was sitting, she cut the end from one the straws, with a pair of nail clippers. They asked a neighbouring drinker, on a similar table, to hold the straws. They told him that they were deciding where to go later that evening. He laughed and helped them as requested. It was decided, by this means, that Una would be the scarlet woman. They talked about how best to encourage to Clint, and they decided that a sudden drunken approach by Una would be best.

The next day, she asked Clint if he would go with her to The Green Dragon, as she had a problem and wanted his advice. When they got there, she said she needed a drink, before she could reveal the nature of her problem. Clint was happy to buy some drinks, and Una reciprocated. This alternate procedure was repeated many times.

Before too long, Una was slightly merry, but Clint was definitely one over the eight. Una snuggled up to Clint and "accidentally" put his hand on her breast, whilst she was looking at his watch to see what the time was. She smiled at him, and told him he was a naughty boy. More of this and that (but not yet the other), occurred in the pub, and at the end of the evening, Una asked Clint to escort her home.

"I'm a little tipsy, and I need a strong man to get me home safely."

Although Clint was not the quickest thinker in the world, even he had realised that this might be his golden opportunity to let slip the tiresome shackles of purity and inexperience. They went back to Una's flat, and she said she wanted to go to the bathroom to freshen up. When she emerged she was very fresh. She was also naked, and she led the delighted, but nervous, Clint into her bedroom.

They had an amazingly successful time, and Una was pleased that her mission had been so well-received. With some helpful coaxing and expert tuition from Una, Clint had proved to be a good lover, especially for a first timer.

A little while after his premiere, Clint could feel some encouraging signs. He stiffened his resolve too, and soon they were at it again. Clint suddenly sat up and said he had a pain in his chest.

"It's probably just indigestion."

"It's quite a sharp pain, and my arm feels funny. The left arm it is, and it's a sort of dull ache, which has more or less joined up with a pain in my chest. I'm a bit dizzy, and I feel sick. I'm so sorry to interrupt this wonderful evening, but I may need to just lie down."

Clint lay back on the bed, but he sat up almost immediately, made a chilling noise because of the pain, and he shuddered before taking a few deep, difficult breaths. He then slipped away. Una was thunderstruck. She couldn't think what to do. She had the presence of mind to dress Clint, before rigor mortis set in.

She phoned Tara and gave her the dreadful news. Tara told her to ring an ambulance, which she did, and it came quickly. The paramedics confirmed that Clint was dead, and explained to Una that a doctor would have to come, to certify death. They also said that as it seemed likely that a heart attack was the cause, there shouldn't be any further difficulty for her, at this troubling time.

"We are so sorry about your boyfriend."

With that, they left, and Una waited for the doctor to arrive. (He had been called by the paramedics.) He came an hour and a quarter later and certified death by heart attack, almost absent-mindedly. He had been given access to Clint's medical records and had noted that he had been suffering from an irregular heartbeat for some years.

"I expect you know all about that, love. He probably told you."

"No, he kept that to himself."

"I have to ask you this. Were you doing anything energetic, before he died? You must tell me if you were, so I can make a note on the file."

"We'd been making love. He was such a kind man."

"I'm so sorry for you. But he would have died happy."

Chapter 36

MR. ALUCARD

He retired as a vampire, after many years of duty
to the wicked, evil and the downright scarey.
He hoped his undead memory would evade the posh and snooty
men, who thought his eyes were red and very starey.
He was once a role model, for those wanting to suck blood,
but he found that he'd developed a red allergy.
As the touch of any scarlet turned his meal to tasteless mud,
it sapped his strength and drained his frame of energy.

A RED ALLERGY

Hubert, Ezekiel and Gideon took great pride in having unusual names. All of the other boys at St. Andrew's Academy for Boys had common, run of the mill names, like Tom, Dick and Harry. The three boys in The Gangsters had posh names, and they liked to sign them in full and to be known by their grand, real names, rather than by common monikers. After all - who could call them Hub, Ezy and Giddy? Their classmates tried to do so, but the lads just ignored them until they reverted to their proper, but snooty, handles.

The Gangsters loved horror films, and as they were all tall for their age, they managed to get in to see X-rated films without any difficulty. The Rio cinema was their favourite. It was a rundown place, which smelt mouldy, but it was cheap, and they smoked their illicit fags whilst watching their all-time hero, Christopher Lee, in films like *Dracula - Prince of Darkness*. They enjoyed many other films of that ilk, with actors such as Peter Cushing, Boris Karloff and Vincent Price being their joint second favourites.

It was definitely Christopher Lee who stole the show for them, and they all read the original *Dracula* book by Bram Stoker, many times. The tall and distinguished, gravitas of their preferred Count Dracula (who was much better than Bela Lugosi in that role, in their opinion), encouraged them to stand up straight and to wear black at all times.

One evening, after they left The Rio, they were strolling down a side street when they saw a cadaverous gentleman, in a dark cape, walking towards them. He walked straight at them, with no obvious intention of moving to one side of the pavement, to allow them to pass him. He carried a cane and swished it at them, in mock menace.

"What have we here? Three young tearaways up to no good, I think."

He spoke with a foreign accent and a slight lisp, but he had a deep, dark brown voice, reminiscent of their hero's timbre. He pulled his cape tighter around his shoulders and thundered, "Will you allow me to proceed, or do I have to unleash the forces of darkness to make you move?"

Hubert was the first to stand up to the stranger.

"Who are you, and why do you attempt to frighten small boys?"

"I, sir, am Mr. Alucard, and if you are not terrified of me by now, then you soon will be."

Alucard pushed Hubert aside and walked off without looking back. Ezekiel was trying to pretend to laugh but was actually worried. He had immediately realised that Alucard was Dracula backwards, and he started to make foolish jokes about reverse vampires or seripmav, which he found difficult to say. Gideon took the bull by the horns (or the bat by the wings), and made this grim pronouncement.

"Gentlemen of The Gangsters, I fear that we haven't seen the last of Mr. Alucard. We come to The Rio frequently and have often walked down this road. I'll bet he's only moved here recently. Perhaps he is a retired vampire, and he's lying low, waiting for some red-blooded young teenagers, on whom he will pounce for his gory meal."

"What a load of tosh Gideon, he's just an old man with a funny accent and a daft cloak. Did you take a look at his teeth? They were slightly pointed, but they weren't like real fangs," Hubert pointed out.

The boys pretended that they were not fazed by this meeting. They hadn't expected to come up against a potential vampire pensioner in a dark side street, on a cold and wet evening, and they carried on walking to their homes, laughing unconvincingly, to keep up their spirits.

The following week, The Rio was showing the original Bela Lugosi, *Dracula* film, from 1931. The Gangsters decided that they would give old Bela a second chance, to see if he could compete with Christopher Lee. After seeing the film, they walked along the side road, mimicking Bela Lugosi.

"Listen to them - Children of the Night."

"That's not right, Ezekiel. Bela definitely says, 'Children off the Night.'"

They all chanted, "Children off the Night, Children off the Night, Children off the Night."

That doesn't sound like much fun to me, but to fourteen-year-old boys with Dracula complexes, it was surprisingly entertaining. That is, until old Mr. Alucard put in another appearance. He seemed to emerge from thin air, and he whispered, "Listen to them - Children off the Night. What music they make!"

The lads were mightily impressed with this cross between Christopher and Bela. Hubert took the lead and asked Mr. Alucard if he liked vampire films.

"I am a renowned expert on vampires and the undead. I could show you my collection of books and pamphlets relating to demons and spirits. They were in existence for thousands of years, before it was realised that they were indeed, Children off the Night."

The Gangsters were desperate to prove how unscared they were, in the face of the undead.

"I'm Hubert. I'm the leader of this rabble, and we're called The Gangsters. I think we should change our name to The Children off the Night. We'd definitely like to see your collection. When would that be possible?"

"Very well, come to the small house at the end of Rushmore Street on Wednesday. Knock three times and wait for ten seconds before knocking again - this time twice.

"I will know who you are by that sign, and I will admit you. You must come after nightfall, as I will be elsewhere before then. I bid you good night"

With a swirl of his cape, Alucard strode off.

"Look, look, there's no shadow."

"Don't be silly Gideon. There's no sun, how could there be a shadow?"

Hubert snorted at Ezekiel.

"I bet there would be no shadow, even if there was a lamp-post behind him, although he couldn't come out when the sun was shining. I bet that before he comes out, he really is - elsewhere, in a coffin full of earth from his homeland."

Wednesday dawned, and it was bright and clear, with the sun shining all day. Hubert thought that Mr. Alucard was right to steer clear of the sun, and he hoped his coffin was padded and comfortable. The boys had agreed to meet at the front of The Rio at 11:30 p.m., and they noted with glee that *Nosferatu*, a film from 1922 (with Max Shreck as Count Orlock), was showing that weekend.

"I know where I'm going to be, on Saturday evening," said Hubert. The others grunted their agreement.

They went down the same side street that Alucard seemed to frequent, and they turned into Rushmore Street, after a few hundred yards. The allegedly small house was in fact a lumbering, faux-gothic mansion, with creaking gates, and there were stone griffins on the tops of the side pillars.

The house itself was in sore need of repair, and the boys were worried that the gargoyles, atop the roof, might come toppling down as they walked past them. Hubert gathered The Gangsters (sorry The Children off the Night), at the door and handed them each a clove of garlic, which he had stolen from his mother's pantry, and he also showed them a tiny jar of water.

"This is Holy Water. If we have any trouble with old Alucard, I'll sprinkle it on him. I also have more protection in here."

He had carried a battered portmanteau from his house to their meeting place. He opened it and showed them a sharpened stake, courtesy of his father's gardening shed, and a heavy mallet. This latter was borrowed from his dad's tool cupboard, in his garage. As he closed the portmanteau, a chill wind blew up the drive of the mansion, and they shivered. Gideon knocked three times and waited for ten seconds, before rapping on the door twice.

"Who is it?"

The voice was shrill and piercing.

"We've come to see Mr. Alucard."

"Who?"

"The tall, distinguished looking gent who lives here. He wears a cape."

They heard shuffling and moaning, and the sound of heavy bolts being drawn back. Gideon thought he would tremble to death, as he shook with fright. The door opened and a stocky, but otherwise unremarkable, middle-aged woman, in a nurse's uniform, stood in the hallway.

"I'm the matron here, Mona Fielding. Who might you be?"

Ezekiel stepped up to the front door and said, "I'm Ezekiel, this is Hubert, and the other one of my friends is Gideon. Mr. Alucard invited us to see his collection of items relating to vampires."

Mona looked at Ezekiel to see if he was jesting, but she realised that he was deadly serious.

"You'd better come in. You'll catch your death of cold out there. The gentleman to whom you refer was really called Montague Lawson. I'm sad to tell you that he passed away last night. He was once an actor and wrote a play about vampires, called *Alucard and His Children of the Night*. The play toured to half-empty houses, but forever after, he used to take people back to his house to talk about his play, and his collection of memorabilia.

"When he moved in here, he continued to take people to his room, to show them his souvenirs. His stuff wasn't just about vampires. It was mainly posters and mementos from the places in which he played as an actor. He was here for ten years, and lately Alucard was gradually taking over from old Mr. Lawson. He passed away peacefully."

No need for the stake and the mallet then, thought Hubert. They thanked her for her time and walked back to the large wrought iron gates. As they left, Ezekiel saw a huge board, which was propped up against one of the pillars. He turned it round, and he realised that it had probably fallen down and been left there leaning on the pillar, awaiting being re-affixed to the stone wall. It read: *Homeview Care Home – For Elderly Vampires.*

Chapter 37

IS IT A POEM?

Does metre matter, does it scan,
Is it written well, or terribly?
Should this little rhyme be banned?
I'll continue on, so merrily.
Is this an ode with poor intent?
Is it ripe with intonation?
The timing may have strange accent.
Pentameters live in Spain.
They resemble woolly mammoths, not a horse.
The terror dactyl bird, flies o'er the plain.
Trochees come from Italy, but of course.

THEY RESEMBLE WOOLLY MAMMOTHS

Gervaise Hoffman fancied himself as an all-round, artistic intellectual. He could play the virginal, lute, ukulele, double bass and violin (but not all at the same time, as he wittily replied to his admirers when they showed appreciation for his amazing and diverse musical talent.) He was amazing alright – yes, he was amazingly bad at all of these instruments, although he was quite good on the kazoo.

His talent was limited, but his ambition was unbounded. He could also paint, again not well. He had now decided to become a poet, in addition to his other skills. He affected a vapid air, and he allowed himself to be photographed, draped over Art Deco furniture, with long, flowing curls. I should clarify that it was Gervaise who had the curls, not the furniture. He fancied himself as the new Lord Byron.

Gervaise couldn't write poetry, and he definitely wasn't as handsome as Byron. He knew as much about poetry as John Bobin (and his other friend Warren Cohen), the difference being that John and Warren admitted that they knew nothing, but Gervaise pretended to understand iambic pentameters, and the like. He had a few poems accepted by dedicated magazines, with limited circulation, but lost interest when the submissions he made began to come back with rejection slips.

You may be wondering about his flouncy name. Gervaise was really called Toby. He had never liked the name, as he thought it was too perfectly matched to his actual surname, which was Shaw. Yes - Toby Shaw of one thing, his new name, Gervaise Hoffman, was not much better. Nonetheless, he liked it. It was different, and he thought it lent class to his identity.

He had previously had very little success in the musical ventures which he mounted. His band - consisting of lute, accordion and banjo plus a washboard player, had not been rebooked anywhere. (They should have been called The One Night Stands.) They called themselves The Hoffman Ensemble, but ensembling was not something they did well.

His art installations had been more well received. He thought that if Tracey Emin could get away with her mad, bad efforts, he could do much better. His first project was *Men Sitting*. He hired a church hall, and he persuaded thirty-six gullible men to sit cross-legged on the floor. One art critic said, in the Elderbrough Gazette, "Hoffman's *Men Sitting*, is a master work, reminiscent of Guido Milano's *Men Standing*, although the standing men installation had twenty-five men, and they were not sitting down. The freshness of his work is remarkable, and his inventive streak has prompted me to make a note in my diary to visit his next installation, due to takc place in March."

That project was to be called *See Gulls*. The beach at Tyminster on Sea was roped off, and Gervaise had spent the time between his last installation and the opening date of 14th March, collecting three hundred dead sea gulls from all over the South Coast, which were in various states of decomposition.

The gulls were mounted on tall poles driven into the sandy beach, and twenty-three, high-powered, blue floodlights were trained on the eerie installation, which was only officially open between sunset and dawn each night, for three weeks from the opening date. The audiences were encouraged to take their own photos and to post them on various social media sites.

The resultant pictures were of poor quality, but the number of Gervaise Hoffman followers for his Facebook page shot up to 305,876 in the first week of the installation. Gervaise was immensely pleased to note that other social media sites all had large numbers of hits, likes, reactions, comments and retweets.

The stench of the decaying sea gulls in the *See Gulls* project grew worse and worse, as the days went by. Gervaise said that the decomposing seabirds, and their accompanying, putrid aroma, added to his vision of the breakdown of society, and portrayed the festering dishonesty of politicians and bankers. On the final night of the installation, he performed sea shanties with The Hoffman Ensemble, and one person even "liked" their rendition of *What Shall We Do with the Drunken Seagull?*

The reporter who had reviewed his *Men Sitting* work, asked him if he would do an in-depth interview for the magazine, *Paint, Music and Rhyme.* He edited the mag. from his tumble-down, converted barn, which was on the outskirts of a dairy farm, a few miles outside Elderbrough.

Gervaise decided that now he was an expert musician and artist, it was time he delivered more poetry. He had concluded that attempting to be Byron was much too difficult. He now fancied himself as a cross between Laurie Lee, John Lennon and Spike Milligan. The obvious difference was that each of those renowned gentlemen had talent, but poor Gervaise did not.

His first new poem was called, *The Dawning of Peace.* It was a piece alright, a piece of merde. The poem was written in many styles; some of the lines rhymed, and others did not. The lines were of ragged and uneven lengths, and the imagery was naïve and unappealing.

The poem started just as a bloody battle had ended, and it was written from the viewpoint of a badly injured soldier, who was lying, (and rhymingly dying), in a muddy field, watching the sun rise, as his lifeblood ebbed away. Most astonishingly, it won the Golden Pentameter award for "its ambitious and deliberate flouting of all the known rules about poetry and its bold and contentious setting of death as a new beginning."

The critics spouted drivel like this, in many newspapers and on the television. Gervaise himself was surprised. Privately, he had thought this poem was lacklustre and laboured. Once the other critics came on board, the Hoffman effect began to be felt in other spheres, like arty farty radio programmes and open mic. nights.

He was commissioned by Sprecher and Tinsley, the leading art world publisher, to produce a volume of poems for the masses. Gervaise took a few months to finish his book, which he entitled, *Germaine Vaise to Make You Talk.* His publishers asked him to change the title, but he refused.

The poems in his anthology had various subjects. One was about a dead duck viewing his earthly remains, which had been rolled into a pancake. If you think that sounds bad, the other one which comes to mind is about a rip in the fabric of the universe. The laughable title of that poem was *The Teary of Everything.*

When the book was published, there were protests about its offensive title from various well-meaning organisations, and the German Embassy sent a formal complaint to the publishers. Sadly, this only added fire to the publicity blaze. Every day, the papers carried headlines about Gervaise.

He installed a new art wonder in a huge gallery in Zurich, which was a converted warehouse. He had the gall to call it, *Headlines and Cant.* For this venture, he bought five hundred sheep's heads, and he positioned them carefully in the gallery, using stiff wire and battens. He fixed them in patterns which deviated from the vertical and horizontal planes, being made up of swirling, sloping lines. The heads were also dripping in luminous, lime green paint.

His second book was entitled, *Everything I know About Poetry.* The book was luxuriously bound, in dark, burgundy leather, and it had expensive, gold- tooling for the title and the sub-heading, *Is This What You Are Waiting for?* Inside the book, the pages were totally blank. The only way that readers could find anything to catch their imagination was to soak the book in water, whereupon the words: *Now You See It - Now You Don't* were displayed, thousands of times, in childlike writing. It was as if they had been penned by a drunken infant.

The critics went wild. They loved his "refusal to be bound by the strictures of modern inanity." There were many other such examples of critical sheep following the artistic crowd (even though his Swiss installation had utilised those wretched heads.)

His last project was entitled, *Is This the Deal Thing?* He hired the Royal Albert Hall and covered the floor with hundreds of pine trees, which were planted in hexagonal, wooden tubs. In the middle of the auditorium floor a giant gantry was erected, with a noose suspended therefrom.

He prefaced his event with samples of head-banging rock music, which were played backwards in loops, and lasers circled the arena. His beloved Hoffman Ensemble started the show proper, and then there was a short piece entitled, *A Sneeze: Kazoo*, which was played by two hundred kazoo players, sitting among the pine trees.

After that excuse for a tune, the P.A. was turned up to a deafening volume, and snatches of badly edited and poorly mixed music thundered away, with deep bass undertones. The hall was filled with red smoke. This was followed by a short period of blackness and complete silence.

When the lights went up again, Hoffman was standing on a platform just under the gantry, with the noose around his neck. He spoke sonorously, and an eerie, echo and reverb. effect distorted his voice. He was using a head mike, like those which prancing, nonentity, boy bands use, and he said, "Tonight, I will die, or I will show you that I can master escapology. That would be another feather in my artistic quiver."

A helper showed Hoffman a pair of golden handcuffs, and then manacled Gervaise's hands behind his back. The audience members had all been given wireless remote-controls, and they had been told that they would be instructed what to do with them, when the climax of the art event was reached. The music playing through the P.A. was changed to a strident piece featuring bagpipes and banjos. The awful cacophony had to be heard to be believed. To be quite honest, it would have been much better not to have heard it, even if that meant you didn't believe.

Hoffman looked round the audience and smiled.

"Take your remote controls, and switch them on, using the power button."

The crowd obeyed.

"Now press the button marked - A."

The platform on which Hoffman was standing slid out, and so did the gantry. He was still cuffed and standing on the platform, with the noose round his neck.

"Press button - B."

The platform fell away dramatically, as Beethoven's Fifth Symphony thundered its opening chords – Da, da, da, da, da, da, da, da. Hoffman was now suspended by his neck, and he was spinning wildly, as he gagged and spluttered. He tried in vain to get back on the platform. Sadly, it was too far below him to be reached. He gurgled his last words.

"I meant button - C."

His head was at a strange, crooked angle, and the music had been stopped. There was an announcement that the rest of the show had been cancelled. In the papers the next day, his art project was hailed as being "astounding, and a real testimony to a truly talented man."

Sprecher and Tinsley started to prepare a deluxe edition of both of his books, to be included in a box set, together with a D.V.D. of his fatal finale.

Chapter 38

TWO SO-CALLED SISTERS

We live together as two sisters
and have done for many years.
If either left we'd miss her.
That is one of our main fears.
For some time, we've been this way,
but we love each other well.
Since happy just meant gay,
and our secret, we'd not tell.

WE LOVE EACH OTHER WELL

Amy and Rachel Chandler had lived in the same terraced house for many years. The two sisters had never married, and they had kept each other company for all those years, after having moved to Brighton, from somewhere which was obviously in, or near, Newcastle. They had never lost their Geordie accents. They joked that they were the major influence for Ant and Dec, even though they could never tell which one was which.

Amy was tall and lean, with grey hair which was surprisingly abundant for a woman who was in her late seventies, and Rachel was her exact opposite, except for being a few years older. She was short and heavy, with sparse, follicular coverage. They didn't look like each other at all.

The old ladies were polite, quiet and lived well within their means. They always seemed to have enough of everything, without ever having plenty. They were both good cooks. They put that down to having to prepare meals properly when they were growing up, as there was not today's preponderance of ready dishes, and what they referred to as "processed muck."

They were healthy (for their age), and walked along the promenade, every morning, before returning to their house for a light lunch. In the afternoon they sometimes went to the cinema, although the ear-splitting volume of the soundtracks gave them headaches.

If they didn't go to the pictures (as they still called it), they had a look round The Lanes. Amy had visited the library to look up the history of the intriguing twists and turns of the alleyways in The Lanes, where the shops now offered antiques, jewellery, fashion items and much more.

"Rachel, I found out that The Lanes were once a popular part of Brighthelmstone. Catchy name, don't you think? No wonder they changed it to Brighton."

They sometimes listened to the buskers, and they always dropped a coin or two into their suitcases or caps, or whatever they were using to collect their money. They had noticed that when buskers first set up, they invariably put a few coins of their own into their collection vehicle, in order to encourage shoppers and browsers to dip into their pockets, to reward them for their heroic efforts to entertain passers-by.

Over the years the music played and sung by the buskers had changed. Most of them now seemed to have small amplifiers, and magic sounds played beneath their singing or guitar playing. The ladies knew nothing about backing tracks, but they could recognise an orchestra which wasn't there - if you see what I mean. The buskers came in all sorts of shapes and sizes, and some had very good voices.

Some were not so talented, but the sisters appreciated their bravery in performing for a constantly fluctuating audience, whose primary purpose in being in The Lanes was, almost always, not to listen to buskers.

One day, Amy heard some bystanders saying that Brighton was a well-known, gay place. She thought that this was right. Amy had always thought of it as being a happy and welcoming town. Rachel laughed when Amy mentioned this overheard comment. She had been elsewhere, that particular afternoon, and she had only met up with Amy, after she had finished having a check-up at the dentist.

"Amy, I fear that you aren't up to date with the current usage of the word gay. It refers to homosexuality."

"Oh, so gay doesn't mean happy any longer?"

"No dear, believe me. I'm right."

The two "sisters" were anything but, and they had been lovers from their early twenties, in another time and another place. Their secret had been discovered by a vile and nasty man, who had threatened to spread rumours about their relationship. He had spitefully and conveniently ignored the fact that they genuinely loved each other.

They didn't flaunt their love for each other. They knew that there were many people who would not be able to accept their passion. They also knew that male homosexuality was against the law, but didn't know that lesbianism was never criminalised. They were both teachers at an infants' school, in their hometown, a few miles outside of Newcastle. They loved their work, and their little charges loved them. Indeed, the small children idolised the pretty and vivacious young ladies who imparted wisdom to them.

One day, they were called in to see the headmaster, Nigel Hargreaves. He was a tartar, as most headmasters were in those days. He terrorised the pupils, as he swept down the corridors of the school, with his black gown swirling behind him. He was a huge man, with a bristling, ginger beard, even though his hair was blonde. He had a booming voice, which would have even given Brian Blessed a run for his money.

"Come in ladies, and sit down. It's come to my notice that you two are having a disgusting and unsavoury relationship, involving unnatural practices. What do you have to say to that?"

Amy rose and stoutly defended herself and Rachel.

"We live together and love together. We've never made a public declaration of our romantic entanglement, and we never will. We are good teachers and get on well with the girls and boys."

"Ha! The boys will be safe, but the girls are in danger from your dirty influence. If you move into two separate houses, and you vow never to fiddle with little girls, I'll allow you to stay on at the school. If you don't do as I say, I'll sack you both and will make sure that the local newspaper knows why."

Rachel was surprised that this narrow-minded man could even bear the thought of them staying. However, his motive was to become clear.

"In return, I think you should allow me to visit you, for research purposes only, so I can watch your love-making, in order to understand what happens. This will be an interesting academic exercise, and it will be a private arrangement."

The two ladies, then known as Amy Chandler and Rachel Osborne, were absolutely horrified. This odious person was not quite so priggish after all. He wanted to look at glamourous, young ladies when engaged in their "unnatural practices." Rachel picked up the ink-well from his desk and poured ink all over his fluffy, fair hair. He was so angry that he was unable to speak.

Amy said, "We will leave this school, this town and your stinking presence. If you ever repeat any of this to a single soul, we'll have no hesitation about reporting you to the school governors, and we think they will be interested in your desire to witness lesbianism, at first-hand."

Hargreaves knew when he was beaten.

"You win. Let me have your written notice to leave our employment by the end of school-time today, and I'll say no more. I can't afford to risk my position, so I will even give you good references."

Amy and Rachel moved to Brighton, and Rachel adopted the same surname as Amy. They became "sisters" – presumably still doing it for themselves. They found good digs, and they were lucky enough to get reasonable jobs at another school.

A few years later, Amy's aunt had died and left her enough to buy a small terraced house, which had been their home ever since. Rachel decided to find out more about Brighton's laissez-faire attitude to being Gay (with a capital letter - probably.) She explained the changes in the law about male homosexuality to her "sister" and told her all about the people who nowadays Came Out.

"But why do they need to do that, Rachel?"

"It's all about freedom and pride. The freedom to do what they want without fear and criticism, and the pride to publicly show their love for their partners."

Amy and Rachel were married at a civil ceremony, several weeks after this conversation. They spent a pleasant Norfolk weekend, at a self-catering cottage, in Blakeney. As they strolled along the quay, after a beautiful dinner with Cromer crab and a delicious salad, Amy asked Rachel, "Does this mean we have Come Out?"

Chapter 39

DELICATE ESSEN

Essen was a fragile girl.
She was a dainty lass.
She'd give a pretty twirl.
She'd shake a pretty mass
of raven coloured tresses.
She was weak, although quite bonny
and would wear nice lacy dresses.
She would flirt with her pal Johnny
but would often be so ill.
She thought she would grow better
and her mum would coat the pill.

SHE WAS A DAINTY LASS

Stacey Natasha Washburn had always been a delicate and frail child. Even when she had been born, six weeks prematurely, it had been clear that she needed to be nurtured and molly-coddled in order to survive. The doctor had been surprised by her mass of dark hair, but she had a shocking, pale complexion, which was made even more noticeable by the contrast with her hair.

The ward-sister said, "Mrs. Washburn, we have to take your baby immediately and must place her in an incubator. She's small and weak, and this will help her greatly."

As the sister picked up the baby, Keith Washburn left the room with the doctor and asked him outright what the child's chances were.

"I won't pretend. The next few hours, and even days, will be crucial. We'll do whatever we can to give her strength, but it will be touch and go. I would advise you to temper what you say to your wife, as she's had a rough time herself, and she must rest."

The next day, the doctor thought the baby was slipping away, and he advised Keith to register her birth and names, before it was too late. The sad father hurried to the registrar's office, but when he got there he realised that although he and his wife, Pippa, had talked about lots of names, they had not settled on anything firm. The registrar asked Keith what the baby was called, and he said, without really thinking, "Stacey Natasha."

"An unusual name, Stacey. Are you sure?"

"Yes, it was my mum's maiden surname, and we always said we'd like to call our first-born child after her. However, Mum's christian name was Maude, and I wouldn't want to saddle a young child with a name like that."

"I see. That's now official."

On the way back to see his wife in the maternity ward, Keith found himself wondering what he had done. He told her about the names he had registered, and his wife said she hated both of them. Pippa said she would always call her daughter S.N.

"Essen? That sounds like a good Scandinavian name. It's a deal," said Keith.

Against all expectations, little Essen rallied round, and after a few weeks she was allowed home. She was still tiny, but she was a delightful baby. Pippa was well aware of how an unfortunate name could become shortened, as she herself had always disliked being called Philippa. From an early age, she had become Pippa and soon, in a likewise manner, all of the family and their friends forgot that Essen had ever been Stacey Natasha.

Her progress through childhood was marred by many illnesses and accidents, and she was dogged by ill-health. In spite of this, she was a sunny-natured and smiling girl, who was always willing to help others. The boy next door, Johnny McCrimmon, took a shine to Essen when they were both in their early teens, and she flirted with him continually and effortlessly, in that way that all young ladies know how to do. It's as if they have a natural, coquettish nature.

Day by day, young Johnny became more and more enamoured of Essen. He often helped Pippa to look after her, when Essen was ill. Johnny was a good nurse, even at the age of thirteen or fourteen. One day Essen came downstairs early in the morning, and she complained of feeling very unwell. She was coughing badly, and on inspecting her daughter's hand-kerchief, Pippa saw that it was badly soiled with thick mucus and blood.

"Mum, I can hardly breathe, and my heart is beating so fast. I feel awful."

"Would you like something to eat or drink?"

"I just want to sit down, as I'm sweating one minute and then freezing cold. I couldn't possibly eat or drink anything. I feel sick too."

Keith had left the house at dawn that day, and Pippa was scared in case Essen should worsen, whilst she went to the phone box. (This was before today's glut of mobile phones.) She banged on the wall, so Johnny could hear that help was needed. By this means, they summonsed Johnny, when Essen was poorly, and when they wanted her dear, love-smitten boy-friend to run an errand or to mind Essen.

He came straightaway, and using the key which Keith had given to him, he opened the front door. He hurried into the parlour, where Pippa sat with her arm around Essen, whose breathing had worsened. Essen said that every breath hurt her more.

"Johnny, stay here with Essen, and I'll go to the phone box to ring the doctor."

Johnny nodded. Pippa ran out of the house, leaving the front-door ajar, in her panic. Johnny heard it banging to and fro, and he went to close it. When he came back, he noticed that Essen was wringing wet, due to her high temperature, and her eye-lids were fluttering. She was trying to speak, and he had to put his ear to her lips to hear what she was saying.

"I'm scared, Johnny. Kiss me, and tell me you love me."

Johnny did so, gently and quietly. The front door was thrown open, and Pippa ran in.

"The doctor's calling an ambulance and says he thinks Essen may have pneumonia. Johnny, please stay with her, while I get her things ready for the hospital."

Pippa was not gone long, but when she returned Johnny was cuddling Essen and kissing her, and she was crying. Pippa was not sure that Johnny should be in such close proximity to Essen, but she knew that any protests she made would not make any difference. Young love, she thought. So wonderful, so strong - and so brutal.

They heard the ambulance coming, and two burly men in uniform were admitted, after they had taken a stretcher out of the emergency vehicle. They examined Essen carefully. One of them took Pippa out of the room and warned her that Essen was very ill. Like the doctor, he thought that pneumonia was the cause. When they returned, Johnny was still kissing Essen.

"I wouldn't do that, sonny," said the ambulance man, kindly.

"But…I love her, and she loves me."

"I'm sure you do, and I'm sure she loves you too, but she's desperately ill, and you mustn't endanger your own health."

Pippa stood at the door, as Essen was stretchered out of the house. She told Johnny to lock up and promised him she would find a way to let him know how Essen was doing. Later that day, Pippa finally managed to contact Keith at work, and he rushed to the hospital. Essen was in a critical state. Pippa asked Keith to get some clothes and toiletries for Essen from their home. Keith said he would let Johnny know how Essen was.

Johnny took the news that Essen was on the danger list very badly. Keith went back to the hospital, but Johnny's parents kept him at home. Day by day, Essen made remarkable progress, and in three weeks she was back at home.

Keith and Pippa had deliberately chosen not to tell Essen that four days after Johnny had been kissing and cuddling her, he had developed the same symptoms which had been displayed by Essen. Johnny had been taken to the same hospital, and the doctors and nurses had been shocked when he died suddenly, after two weeks in a special ward.

Essen's parents now had the terrible task of telling her that her first love was no more. Essen was distraught and inconsolable. She vowed that she would never have another romance. As she grew older, she was more and more quiet. She went to St. Mary's Church and talked to the vicar regularly. She studied the requirements of becoming a nun, and the suggested steps that were involved, such as meeting nuns and talking to a mentor.

When she was just twenty, she entered a convent and adopted the new name, Sister Natasha. As Sister Natasha, she devoted herself to

God. She also studied to be a nurse, and she worked hard in third-world countries, to help the suffering and the poor.

Keith and Pippa were immensely proud of Essen in her new role. Neither of them were particularly religious, but they understood how her pain had driven her to find a real purpose in a different life, which she had vowed would always be a remembrance of her Johnny.

Sister Natasha lived to be sixty-three, before dying of malaria, in Africa. She had never forgotten Johnny, but knew that she had done something worthwhile with her life. As she died she said, "It is done," and then she sang these words.

"Johnny - Remember Me."

Chapter 40

NO FIX, NO MEND

A fault at birth had been the cause; there was no fix, no mend.
A new consultant stated, he could make him less verbose.
His Ma and Pa agreed to try, this hopeful clever plan.
It went well, but Charlie wasn't pleased, still quiet and morose.
They asked him why he was so sad, and he just cried and cried.
The operation, though thorough - he was still a weeping man.
He was not how he believed he'd be, in fact he thought they'd lied.
He'd hoped the goal - the aim would be, to make him just like Norman.

JUST LIKE NORMAN

Charlie Horne was a gentle, friendly and affectionate child. He looked angelic, with his curly, straw-coloured hair and his rosy cheeks. He had many friends, but his best pal was Norman Creasey. Norman had sandy hair and was lean, with the loping gait of a natural gymnast. Norman made many allowances for Charlie, who couldn't always understand things very well, and who also had trouble walking. Both of these disabilities were due to birth defects.

Charlie had callipers and used a crutch to help him walk. Norman didn't care about those things. All he knew was that Charlie was his top buddy. At school, there were many people who also treated Charlie well. There were just a few who tried to bully him. Norman had thumped the unruly child who seemed to be organising the vendetta against Charlie. That had stopped the trouble immediately. Charlie had said, "If it gives them some kind of fun, let them do it. I don't care. I know who my true friends are, and you're the bestest one, Norman."

Norman always helped Charlie when he fell over, and he often had to pick him up. He was definitely the bestest pal that anybody could have. Norman was a keen athlete, and Charlie loved to watch his friend competing in the events mounted by the school and the local gymnastic club for young boys and girls. At one sporting event, Norman came off the track, after having won a race, and he found Charlie crying.

"I'm so pleased to see you winning, Norman. But I wish I could be like you, and I could think quicker, and run and walk properly."

"Charlie, we're all different, and you've got qualities that other people don't have. You are kind. You love animals, and you're always joking. You make me laugh."

When Charlie and Norman were both ten, Charlie told his closest friend that his parents had been asked to take him to a special hospital, which specialised in problems caused by difficulties encountered during birth. Of course, he didn't say this in so many words; what he actually said was, "I'm going to be mended in a special place. My mum and dad are taking me to this place to see a kind man, who can fix me."

The initial appointment was promising. The consultant, Mr. Dinsdale Featherstone, was charming, persuasive and convincing. He looked the very picture of what a senior consultant should be. He was smart, and he was wearing an expensive, chalk-striped suit. He had tortoise-shell spectacles, and his hair was greying nicely at the temples. Charlie's mum thought he looked like George Clooney. Naturally, she realised this didn't automatically make him a good specialist, even though he was handsome.

She had therefore made various enquiries about Mr. Featherstone, and the feedback showed him to be a renowned expert in his field. She had Googled his name, and all of the hits shouted his praise. He was quoted in many medical papers, and he lectured frequently at conferences around the world.

The most helpful, and therefore the best website by far, was www.thankstofeatherstone.com, which had many glowing testimonials on it. All of these came from grateful parents, carers and patients.

The consultant had explained that the operation he planned, would help to make Charlie, "just like normal." He had hesitated to use this expression, but he wanted to reassure the parents that Charlie would be more like other children.

The big day came, and Charlie's parents took him to a massive hospital in Catherdale, which specialised in operations for youngsters, and which had now begun to pioneer the new process recommended by Dinsdale Featherstone.

Grant and Colleen Horne had stayed the previous evening, with Charlie, in a small hotel near the hospital. (They wanted to be in good time on the day of the operation.) On the morning of the op., Grant was wearing his usual outfit of a black shirt and black trousers, with a black coat. He had brushed his stiff, black hair, and made an effort to look smart, but Colleen wished he would sometimes jazz the wardrobe up a bit.

Colleen was wearing a turquoise dress with green, glass "emeralds" all over it. Her blonde, peroxided hair had been curled and moussed, and she wore a red, biker-chick jacket. Grant wished she would tone down her wardrobe a little.

Charlie was wearing a white T-shirt with a picture of a Spaniel on it, outlined in bold, black. The slogan underneath said, *I Am a Top Dog.* He had jeans on, and he sported a fashionable, green hoodie. He thought both his parents looked great.

Charlie had been starved and was ready for his ordeal. True to form, he was looking forward to it. Charlie usually looked forward to everything. They sat in a waiting room, after booking in at reception. A titian-haired nurse, who had strikingly pretty features, came to fetch Charlie. Grant gazed at the nurse and admired her trim form, encased in a wonderfully tight, nurse's uniform. He tried hard not to imagine what was beneath the starched dress. Colleen smacked him playfully on his cheek.

"Stop that, Grant. You should have a cold shower, and anyway I thought you didn't like red hair."

Grant grinned and said, "Why would I want to look at anybody else, when I have you, my darling?"

"Oh yes - why indeed? I think I'll take down your poster of Emma Peel, when we get home."

They both realised that this false jollity was just a defence mechanism. They were desperately worried about young Charlie. The consultant had not pulled any punches. He had told them that, as with all operations, there were unavoidable risks.

For several hours, Grant and Colleen drank awful coffee from a machine, paced up and down, read old copies of the Readers' Digest, and they also both read and re-read the daily newspaper, which was as depressing as it always is. Eventually Mr. Featherstone himself came to see them.

"The operation went very well. Charlie will be ready to see you shortly. He's hooked up to various machines, tubes and monitoring devices. None of that should alarm you. It's perfectly routine, and it gives us efficient ways of keeping a close watch on him."

When they saw him, Charlie looked small and helpless, but he gave them a cheeky smile. They talked to him only briefly because they had been warned that he was still weak from the anaesthetic, and they knew he would need to be well rested, in the next few days.

Charlie made quick progress, and soon he showed them how he could walk without his callipers - and even with no crutch. He was much abler, but he seemed subdued. After a while, Charlie admitted to his dad that he thought the consultant had said he would be, "just like Norman."

Grant asked Norman to visit his son. Norman patted his friend on the shoulder, and he said, "I'm glad you're not like me. I'm impatient, and I get angry if things don't happen on time. Dogs don't seem to like me, and as for cats – they hate me. I can't tell jokes, and my singing is awful."

Charlie had to laugh. It was true that Norman couldn't hold a tune.

"Never mind, matey. You are still my bestest pal."

Chapter 41

EDDIE DE SNAKE OIL

Eddie was a trav'lling salesman.
He sold all manner of notions.
He was a weedy and a pale man,
but he helped to ease the motions
of those constipated poor folks,
sat for hours on their thrones.
And he'd sell them herbal, hot soaks.
Which would warm their poor, cold bones.
If they needed much more hair,
He supplied a useful remedy.
If their life was hard to bear
he could cure this woeful malady.

ALL MANNER OF NOTIONS

Eddie de Snake Oil was, without doubt, one of history's least successful rogues. He had a dodgy approach to everything he did, and he always looked for a loophole, or a way round things, so he could gain the most benefit from an opportunity, with the least amount of work or effort, both of which were strangers to him.

At the crucial time in the telling of this tale, he was thirty-six, going on fifty, with greying, mutton-chop sideburns and swept-back, silver hair. He wore a pair of half-moon spectacles, which invariably perched themselves near the tip of his beaky, Roman nose. He had a most mellifluous tone of voice, and he could sell ice-creams to the Eskimos, but I suppose that would be selling ice-creams to the Inuit, nowadays. (Selling ice creams to the Inuit – Innit?)

Eddie often claimed that he had been friends with Jesse James. It is possible, but not likely, that he did cross paths with Jesse. Eddie also said he had been born in Clay County, Missouri - just like Jesse. As you couldn't ever believe anything that he said, without a pinch of salt, it may be that he never knew the famous outlaw at all.

Eddie started his life of petty crime in Miss Veronica Morley's junior class, at Margrave School for Young Gentlefolk. He had taken to stealing items from other pupil's desks and backpacks, releasing them into a life of sale and counter-sale. He could afford to sell them at reasonable prices, as he hadn't been compelled to pay a bean for the articles in question.

He often sold them to people who, knowing that they were probably pinched, couldn't complain to Old Ronnie (the term of endearment attached to Miss Morley by her protégés), when they found that their newly bought precious goods had mysteriously disappeared from their possession. Thus, the items in question often found their merry way back to the original owner, who was usually glad to be reunited with the long-lost comb, book, shoe laces or whatever had been removed by Eddie in the first place.

Ronnie was a good old girl. Well, she wasn't that old, maybe fifty-five or so, but she was the kind of woman who had looked old when she was born, and she continued to age quickly as she got older. She was, thin and bent; she had bottle-top glasses, a lace bonnet and wispy, grey hair. She was also a good sport and liked a game of cards and rye whiskey, or so I'm told.

The same little bird who cheeped the information that Ronnie loved gambling and drinking, also apprised me of the fact that she had been around the clapboard block a time or two. She was never an oil painting, and so she had always been grateful for good company and a bit of horizontal exercise. She was, by all accounts, very good at the ancient art of canoodling (and the rest of the stuff that goes with it.) Her lovers did not want their peers to know that they had been consorting with such a plain woman. This worked out fine, and Ronnie had managed to preserve the myth that her virginity was intact.

Ronnie had a near miss a few times, but when she had a welcome warning of oncoming periods, the good news was, that the game was not up. The children loved her, and she loved them. Her favourite was young Eddie, who at that time was known as Eddie Melrose.

In the end, Eddie was caught stealing things from the town store, and he was punished, reasonably lightly, by being compelled to do deliveries for Mr. Whistler, who was the proprietor. Whistler was kind enough to recognise that Eddie was basically a loveable chap, even if he wasn't all that honest.

Eddie was fascinated by the medicinal cures sold by Mr. Whistler. There was a miracle hair-restorer, which was guaranteed to promote the growth of luxuriant tresses within six days. The six-day period amused Eddie. If the user was that worried about hair loss or baldness, surely seven, eight or even nine days would have been just as acceptable?

Dr. Argus' Patent Lifter of Spirits was also popular. It claimed, a mite ambitiously, "to remove the symptoms of downheartedness and to give back jollity and mirth." The contents of the bottles both looked and tasted like cheap fire-water, and Whistler sold the remedy for about six times the price of that kind of alcohol.

Another cure was *Antoinette's Pregnancy Stopper*. This was sold, under the counter, to girls who had not been as lucky as Ronnie, and who had been knocked up, after being knocked off. The contents smelt just like *Dr. Argus' Patent Lifter of Spirits,* and Eddie was mightily amused when he saw Mr. Whistler filling rows of empty bottles, with different labels for the two medicines, out of the same large, stone jar.

He came to an arrangement with Mr. Whistler, that he would not tell the editor of the Margrave Herald about this deception, provided he could learn the tricks of the trade from him and be paid a fairly modest blackmail amount weekly. Whistler was happy with the arrangement. He now had some full time help, which would be provided by a boy who would keep his mouth shut. Eddie stayed with the shop for eight years, leaving when he was almost twenty-two, when the shop was closed.

The labels on Whistler's bottles had always been supplied by his brother, who was a printer. The brother died when he fell off a horse, after drinking a few too many bottles of *Dr. Argus' Patent Lifter of Spirits.* All of Whistler's brother's possessions had passed to Whistler himself, lock, stock and barrel.

When Whistler shut up shop, Eddie did a farewell deal, under which he arranged to take the entire medicinal stock, the dead brother's printing press and the still, off Whistler's hands. For Eddie's new venture, he printed some handouts. He was pleased with the contents of the flyers and his new name:

Professor Eddie de Snake Oil
Medicinal Cures for All Ailments
Curative notions and potions for constipation (and the opposite), pregnancy solutions, soothing hot-soaks, hair restorers and good, mood-lifting solutions.

In your town - Next Week.
Come Ye All and buy reasonably priced items for your illnesses and medical combooblements.

He was especially proud of *combooblements.* He thought it sounded most impressive. Eddie was pleased that he had taken over the still (and all the other equipment which Mr. Whistler had used to make the nasty tasting, but multi-purpose, spirit which was the base for all of his wondrous remedies.) With a little food colouring or a tiny bit of ink, Whistler had also sometimes changed the appearance of the liquid, so that it could be used with impunity, by seekers after amazing cures for unrelated ailments.

Eddie had been saving for some time, and he bought a covered wagon with some of his nest-egg. He painted a curtailed version of his handbill on each side of the wagon, and he started to travel with his medicine show.

He worked the circuit for nearly ten years, before being caught out by Lady Fate. One of his many female conquests became with child, and she tried to abort the baby by using *Antoinette's Pregnancy Stopper.* She had purloined a whole crate of the pregnancy stopper from Eddie's wagon.

After six bottles of the fire-water, she felt much happier, but she was still pregnant. She drank some more of the fake cure, after which she fell down the stairs, at the local hotel, and lost her baby. Her former condition was revealed by her massive blood loss and the sad sight of the miscarried foetus. Her father ran Eddie out of town.

After returning home, he realised that he would like to make a much more drastic, and permanent, job of dealing with Eddie. He rounded up a dozen of his friends, and they found Eddie in another town, still peddling his wares. They waited until Eddie had finished his session with seekers after new hair or less depression, and they went to where he had hitched his horses and gone to bed in his wagon.

Two of the vigilantes went inside, and they bound and gagged Eddie. The dead girl's father led a strange procession of his friends, the wagon and a few other people who had also had trouble with Eddie, to the town cemetery. A few sticks with rags wrapped round them were dowsed in some of Eddie's fire-water. They were ignited and thrown into the body of the wagon. Being full crates of cheap alcohol, it went up in flames very quickly.

Poor Eddie was incinerated, good and proper. A few years later, the town became one of the first in the West to have a crematorium, after one of the people who had set fire to the wagon realised that the cemetery was full, and that fire was the answer to the problem. He called his new project, Snake Oil Crematorium, so Eddie's name lives on.

Chapter 42

QUARRELLING

If a duckling is a youngster,
quarrelling must be a baby.
If a funny man's a punster
a little quarrelling is, just maybe,
the start of something loud and dark,
the onset of a tiff,
no jolly walking in the park,
the cause of painful rift.

THE ONSET OF A TIFF

Quarrelling is something that we all do, but few of us are really good at it. By good at it, I mean that not many of us are persuasive enough to convince our husbands or wives that they are wrong. In my humble opinion (I don't mean that at all, but who does - when they say that?), what we all want is for our opponent to realise that we are right, and that whatever specious arguments they have been using, are just plain wrong and stupid.

I'm Colin Lee, and I live in Leigh-on-Sea. I usually introduce myself as Lee - from Leigh, and to my surprise nobody ever understands that, and not one single person thinks it is funny. Can you believe that? I work as a shop assistant in an emporium which sells antiques and bric a brac. I call it an emporium, but it's really a small part of one of those popular Antiques Centres, a few miles from Leigh, and I usually travel there (and back of course), on my trusty steed. This is an old Raleigh bike from the sixties, which I have restored lovingly. I had some trouble getting exactly the right shade of paint, and the decals were difficult to find, but all the money which I spent on refurbishing the bike was well worth every penny.

Peggy is my dear wife. (I call her that because she spends so much every week on fripperies - like toilet paper and suchlike.) She thinks I'm mad. She maintains that I could have bought a good, modern bike for about half what I have spent on the original Raleigh wreck and the rebuilding exercise. She fails to understand (a frequent occurrence), that I don't want a bike built in China, and I enjoyed the hours and hours of work, which I spent on the Raleigh.

She has it easy, she does, as while I am at the emporium every day, all she has to do is to look after the house. Do you know, one day I came home and found dust on the top of the doorframes in the hall? When I mentioned this to her, she went red in the face and shouted at me.

"I'm fed up. I'm fed up with this house. I'm fed up with you prattling on about an old bike, and I'm fed up with having no money."

"My love, let's talk about this, like reasonable people. All I ask you to do, is to keep the place clean, and I come home to find thick layers of dust all over the place."

She picked up a vacuum cleaner. (It was the one which she keeps calling a Hoover even though it's made by Electrolux.) She threw it at me. I wonder that she had the strength. It's a small, cylinder model, but it hurt me - and my pride. She took the bag thing off the vacuum cleaner and emptied all of the contents over my head.

I was sitting on the settee, trying to see if my toenails needed cutting, and she stamped on my toes. She left the house in a rage. Actually, she left the house in a dark-blue coat and a furry hat, like a Cossack's, and black, leather boots. This was on Tuesday night.

By Friday, I was beginning to think I should contact the police, to see if they could find her. I'd spoken to her mum on the Thursday. (She doesn't like me.) I suppose that was my fault. The last time I saw her, she asked me if I liked her dress, and as I'm always honest, I said no. She went very icy and didn't speak to me for the rest of our visit.

I was quite pleased, as I don't usually bother with people I don't like. Anyway, her mum hadn't seen her, and she said she thought it was probable that Peggy had finally regained her senses and pushed off with a better man.

I ask you, how ridiculous is that? I work hard, and all Peggy does is push the vacuum cleaner round now and again, and she cooks terrible food. That's another thing I find annoying. She gives me dinner and then always asks me if I like it. I usually don't, so I say so. She then says something which insinuates that I am ungrateful. I'm nothing of the sort. I am pleased that she does her best with her limited, culinary skills.

I also went round to see her friend, to see if she had heard from Peggy. I think she's her only friend, as she is the one person who comes to see her. Yvonne Newbold is her name. Yvonne is O.K, I suppose. She's tall and thin, and she thinks she looks like a model, with her long, dyed-brown hair. She would probably have grey hair by now if she hadn't tinted it a peculiar, mousey colour.

Peggy says the reason that other people, besides Yvonne, don't come round is that I am a boring, old fuddy-duddy. I think that takes some beating. I can talk for hours about all sorts of subjects, and I may be old, but I'm always right. Yvonne seems to like me. She made advances to me one night. (I think that's what they are called.) Peggy was making tea, and I was forced to make conversation with Yvonne. She was probably a half-decent looking woman, before she lost too much weight, but she always wears heaps of make-up, and she stinks of that particular brand of scent which smells like rotting blackberries.

Once Peggy was out of sight, Yvonne closed the door and came over to sit next to me. She took my hand and placed it on her breast. That was quite nice; she then tried to unzip my trousers. I explained to her that trousers should always have button flies like mine, just like they always used to. She giggled.

"Oh Colin, I expect you have lots of rules which govern your life."

I was pleased that she had raised one of my favourite subjects.

"Yes, that is so. For example, pies should always have shortcrust pastry, bread and butter pudding should always be served with custard, and wives should always obey their husbands."

Yvonne looked at me with a peculiar gaze. It may have been that she was pretending to be astounded.

"Dear Colin, why don't you kiss me. You know you want to."

"I wouldn't mind. However, I had fish and chips and an onion for lunch, so I don't think that would be wise."

"Don't you ever break loose?"

I was going to reply in the negative, but Peggy came back in the nick of time. She didn't notice that my flies were undone. (Yvonne had unbuttoned them all the way down, but I'm afraid her hands had not ventured inside.) Peggy placed my favourite tea tray on a coffee table. That's always irked me. Why are they called tea trays and coffee tables? I think they should be called tea or coffee trays, and tea or coffee tables. I noticed that the tray wasn't straight. I do like my tray to be in line with the edges of the tea or coffee table, and I went to correct Peggy's error.

"Stop it, Colin. I done it right, and you're just making a silly fuss, like what you always do."

"Peggy, you meant to say, 'I did it right, and you're just making a silly fuss, like you always do.'"

She glared at me. I asked if there was anything wrong.

"No, nothing at all."

She sounded a little strained. However, as there was nothing wrong, it wasn't worth pursuing the conversation. I digress, and that's something which I always deplore in other people, so I'll get on with my tale. When I went round to see Yvonne, to find out if she had seen Peggy, she opened the door a little and stood at the entrance, effectively barring me from getting into her house.

"I'm tied up at present, Colin. How can I help you?"

"I wondered if you'd seen, or heard, from Peggy? She went out on Tuesday, and she hasn't been back ever since. I spoke to her mum, but for some unknown reason, she wasn't keen on discussing her whereabouts with me."

"I haven't seen her for a couple of weeks. You should really report it to the police."

I went home and rang 999. The operator told me that 999 calls were for emergencies only. I told her that this was an emergency, but she said plenty of people went missing for a few days and came back unharmed, and she told me to go the local police station.

I had to go to Southend police station. This is a boring, concrete building behind the Civic Centre. The Civic Centre is opposite a few tall, empty and pretty well derelict office blocks. It's like a clerical graveyard. Southend used to be a nice place, with independent shops like Keddie's and Owen Wallis in the High Street, but now it has all the usual names which you see everywhere. I swear if an alien was set down in one town centre and then another in England, it wouldn't be able to tell the difference.

The man behind the counter at the police station looked tired and bored. After I had explained what had happened, he looked even more tired and bored. He kept talking about mispers. I remonstrated with him and told him that if he was referring to missing persons, that was what he should say. He looked at his watch and muttered something like, "Pedant!"

I tackled him about that, but he just said, "Exactly."

He also said they would keep an eye out for Peggy and that other forces would also be alerted to the situation. Isn't if funny how policemen always use their own lingo? They never walk down a road, or drive down it, they always proceed. They never proceed up or down a road. They always proceed in an easterly, westerly, southerly or northerly direction. I thanked him for his courtesy, and I do believe he blushed. It was either that, or he was too hot.

Later that evening two police officers, who looked about sixteen, came to see me.

"May we come in, Mr. Lee? We believe we may have news of your wife."

One of the officers was a young man, who was cultivating a weak attempt at a moustache, and he had a shaven head. The other was a young girl who could break your heart, by just looking at you and lowering her gaze. I wondered if there were extra, special penalties for making love to black-haired, black-eyed and exceedingly trim police ladies.

After I had made them tea, and set the tray on the tea or coffee table, the officer continued, "Our enquiries have revealed that a lady matching the description of your wife (and the photo you gave the desk sergeant in Southend), was spotted boarding a plane at London Heathrow Airport, yesterday evening.

"On closer checking, we found that the passport she had with her, revealed her to be Margaret Julia Lee. She appears to reside at this address. I thought your wife was called Peggy?"

"Her given name is Margaret, and Peggy is a well-known nick-name for Margaret. Where was she going?"

"Her destination was New York, and she was in the company of a heavy-set man of about fifty, called Josiah Willis. She seemed cheerful and well, and was not under duress. We cannot be of any further use to you, but at least we can say that it seems that your wife is travelling with this man of her own free will, and she appears to have come to no harm."

I thanked them politely, as is my wont. I rang Yvonne to tell her that Peggy was safe. After I had told her the tale divulged by the police, she burst into tears. She told me that Josiah Willis and she had been involved in an affair for quite a while. In fact, when I went round to see Yvonne, to ask if she had seen Peggy, Josiah had been in the house, so I now knew why she hadn't let me in.

Yvonne came round to see me the next day. She looked as if she had been weeping, but she was comparatively attractive (under the circumstances), and I wondered if she could still master the undoing of fly buttons. I had resolved to change. I made her some instant caffeine and put the tray on the coffee table. It was too straight, so I set it at an angle. She laughed and sat on my lap.

Chapter 43

DES TINY

Des was small, and they called him tiny.
All food made him beam and glow.
It made him smile; his face was shiny.
His Pa said he was, a so and so.
Although compact and on the slight side,
Des grew large, fat and dumpy.
His tubby weight made it hard to hide.
No easy ride, for rumpy pumpy.

NO EASY RIDE

Desmond Elliot started out as a teeny, tiny thing. He was a mere scrapette of a baby. Despite his minute entry into to this world, he more than made up for it when he started piling on the pounds, in his early teens. I should make it clear, that he was wholly to blame.

He scoffed food like it was going out of fashion, and his breakfasts were in three mega-stages. At home, he had his first morning meal, usually of four Weetabix with sugar and full-fat milk, followed by three slices of toast, with a liberal covering of butter and jam.

On the way to school, he would look in on his fattest friend, Scott Marriott, and he would be fed his part two breakfast by Cindy (Scott's mum), who was the largest mother he had ever seen. Scott's dad, Maurice, was even huger. Scott was titchy by comparison, but between them they made an awesome sight for a lad who was used to being small and thin, and was only just beginning to work on his weight gain.

Cindy was a dimpled and smiling dream for Des, with her chubby cheeks and straggly, tawny locks, and she had fascinating, leonine eyes. She was the sexiest lioness, and Des had already experienced wonderful dreams in which she took him to her bed, for real love from a proper catwoman.

Maurice had the kind of ice-blue eyes that can make a person look like a psycho, but his complete baldness and his lack of eyebrows gave him a more benign (and frankly Humpty Dumpty), look. This egginess overcame the oceanic lustre of those dead, blue eyes. He used to introduce himself as Al O'Pecia - the well-known, hairless, Irish man - in order to deflect unnecessary, and sometimes unkind remarks, about his shining, hairless pate and face.

The smallest member of the Marriott household was young Scott, who was a comparative stripling at thirteen stones. It must be said though, that thirteen stones at age eleven, is not an ideal weight.

The second part of Des' breakfast was dished up by Cindy every day, with smiles and laughs and admonishments to eat every mouthful, so he would grow big and strong. It was usually comprised of three fried eggs, four rashers of bacon, heaps of beans, tomatoes and mushrooms. These were supplemented by chips, onions, and as many rounds of toast and marmalade as Des could cram in to his mouth, within the time between when he arrived at Scott's house and the hour of doom. This was the time they had to leave for the walk to school.

Part three of the breakfast, every day, was a large bag of toffees, six sticky buns, five Mars bars and a family-sized bar of milk chocolate, all of which were devoured at break-time, as a sickly brunch. Des said that the Mars bars made up for the other meals, as they helped you work, rest and play.

You get the idea. Des ate like a pig, and a ravenous pig at that. I won't even bother to list the other meals (lunches, dinners, suppers and snacks), on which Des gorged, as you wouldn't believe how much this young boy could stuff into himself.

Desmond's mum and dad, Ben and Lena, tried to make Des (who had decided to have a smaller name, even if he couldn't have a smaller body), eat less, or at least to eat sensibly. Ben was on the large side, but his wife was skinny. Ben would often say, "I'm massive, but my wife is Lena!" This wasn't a funny joke, not even the first time you heard it, but Ben always thought it was amusing.

Des gradually ballooned, and by the time he was sixteen he was twenty-seven stones of rippling flab. Ben and Lena took him to the doctor; he was totally unhelpful. He said Ben should just make his son eat less. He also said that Ben should enrol Des into some form of physical training, which might help him to shed a few pounds. Des' parents did try to do that, but their son ate in secret, and he was still encouraged to partake in pig outs by the mammoth Marriotts. He also shied away from any form of exercise.

The turning point for Des came when he met Verity Hilton. Verity would have been a catch for any young adolescent with surging testosterone issues. She was astoundingly vivacious and seductive. However, Des knew that if he was ever lucky enough to make love to her, even with gentlemanly leaning on elbows, she was likely to be squashed as flat as a pancake, by his mountainous weight.

Verity, with those pale green eyes which can melt the hardest hearts (and who also had the blondest of white-blonde hair), was a real honey. The problem was that Verity was just not interested in boys, except Des. Why this was so, is totally beyond me. It was also beyond her mum and dad, and Ben and Lena.

Both sets of parents could see no future for Des with the lovely Verity. Des sat her down one evening, and he stammered, "Verity, I know that you like me a little bit, but I'm no good for you. I'm more than three times your weight, so you must find somebody else to be with."

Verity took his hand and said, "I love you Des. I want you, and we must find a way to be with each other for the rest of our lives."

She proposed that she should put on as much weight as possible, so they could be obese together. Des was horrified and told her that this was not a good plan. Verity was adamant. She knew that Des had tried everything he could, albeit half-heartedly, to slim down, but all the lukewarm, weight-loss methods, diets, oils and exercises had failed miserably.

Over the next two years, Verity (as true as her name implied), ate and ate. Her parents, and Ben and Lena, tried to stop this anti-diet. In spite of their well-meaning advice, she porked out recklessly. She was soon looking very curvy, and then moved on to being chubby. She went through all the stages of plumpness, like tubby and jumbo, until she was getting on for thirty stones.

Des and Verity waddled around together and seemed happy. They had rented a small flat, which could just about accommodate their two whale-like tubs of lard, but they had decided not to attempt to make love until Verity was a little heavier than Des. By then, he was at his peak weight of thirty-two stones. At the weigh-in, which they did every week, they made plans for their fatty consummation.

Finally, on a fine Monday in August, Verity stepped on their special scales and was gratified to see that she was almost seven pounds heavier than Des. She skipped a heavy fandango to the bedroom, and he slom-mocked after her, in a daze. They stripped off, and she lay on her back with a come-hither look.

Des tried his best, but found it difficult to balance on those famous elbows. Verity egged Des on and soon, satisfied and erotic noises could be heard from the pair of them. The bed was making noises too, but they were neither satisfied nor erotic, and the bed legs gave way suddenly, causing Des to tumble on top of Verity, without the gentlemanly support alluded to earlier. They laughed, wheezed, tried to catch their breath and then simultaneously experienced surging pains in their gargantuan chests. Without much ado, they both shuffled off their gigantic mortal coils. Their synchronised timing was both immaculate and melodramatic.

When the doctor arrived, he was admitted by old Mrs. Sullivan, who lived upstairs in her own flat. She had phoned the surgery, in extremis, when she heard the almighty racket downstairs, as the bed died, closely followed by its occupants. The doctor had never seen two lovers die together, just by expressing their mutual adoration in this way. There was no doubt about what had caused the dual annihilation. Their fat-laden hearts just couldn't take the extra strain. Ben and Lena were mortified, but Maurice and Cindy tried to sympathise with them. Ben said, "At least they worked, rested and played together."

Chapter 44

WORD BUDS

Word buds are the perfect seed.
They make phrases, fine and sound.
They are sometimes all you really need
to build a sentence, or a paragraph round.
If you hear a repeated word,
listen with your right, or left ear.
Tell me what you felt and heard,
And I will ease your fear.
I'm The Word Bud Controller
I run the whole grand plan.
I'll tell you when it's all over
Yes, I'm the main Word Bud Man!

PHRASES, FINE AND SOUND

Celia Crawford didn't like it in the asylum. She had only been there for a week, but she hated the locked and padded room and the stern and bitter nurses. The conceited doctors were even worse. She had tried to explain that she had been brought there by accident, but they all looked at her as if she was mad.

One of the nurses had even threatened to restrain her, when Celia was trying to remove a word bud from her ear, with a pair of tweezers. The bud was trying to grow a whole sentence, in her ear wax. It said that this would not take too long and that if it were to be left undisturbed, it might even manage to cultivate a whole paragraph.

"If you leave me here, I promise that whatever I grow will be dedicated to you, wherever it is blown on the breeze. I know you are an intelligent and articulate woman, and I thought you might like to be a part of this whole word bud phenomenon.

"The Word Bud Controller says that there are 27,567,432 buds under development at present in the U.K., in hosts ranging from full humanoid status to lowly mice. The mice are mainly receptive to high frequency sounds, so the usage of word buds by them is a little limited. Human hosts produce the best results."

"Get out of my ear, you damned parasite. I'll drown you in olive oil if you don't vacate my ear immediately."

"Ah, that's good. Olive oil will help the sentence to evolve and may even bring about a decent paragraph fairly quickly. If you can manage to shut out the constant repetition of the verbal building-blocks, I might even be able to create a short story, in just a few weeks."

Celia had initially been complaining to the doctor, at her local surgery in West Bay, that she had a single word in her ear. She said this word was being repeated thousands of times a day, in a speeded up version of the repetitions, just like the annoying, Chipmunks' records from the late fifties and early sixties.

The G.P. had looked at her and was dumbfounded. Celia was well dressed and elegant. Her features were unremarkable, but they had all been put together nicely, and she seemed to be a pleasant, but schoolmarmish lady of sixty or so. She had one of those old-fashioned buns, and her hair had been too tightly gathered, but she was neat, tidy and alert, with clear eyes and long eyelashes. Nicely preserved, was how he might have described her.

The doctor told her that tinnitus was probably the cause of her problem, and he suggested all the usual remedies, such as sound therapy, counselling and getting hearing aids. Celia was unconvinced that tinnitus was the reason for the never-ending words.

"Tell me, Mrs. Crawford, what are the words, which you are hearing today?"

"This morning, it was stilton."

"Do you mean that you had stilton for breakfast?"

"No, I mean that it was going, stilton, stilton, stilton. This was from about seven thirty until eleven. Then it changed to steak, stilton, steak, stilton – over and over again - until fiveish. The words changed again, and they became, steak and stilton, steak and stilton, steak and stilton.

"This was until just before I came into the surgery this evening. I was glad I'd made an appointment the day before, as I knew that I had to get something done, before it drove me completely bonkers. When I sat down opposite you, it changed to steak and stilton pie, steak and stilton pie, steak and stilton pie, steak and stilton pie."

"Are you eating properly? You look a little thin."

"I eat as well as I can, but this nagging by the word bud is getting even worse than I ever thought was possible."

"Where did you get the term word bud from Mrs. Crawford?"

"It told me that it was a word bud, and it wanted to use my humid, warm ears to create sentences, then paragraphs and maybe even a short story."

The doctor was flummoxed. He had never had a patient with such an unusual, fictitious illness. He asked Celia if she had ever had an imaginary friend at school.

"Of course I did. Most kids go through that phase, but even when they have such a hazy pal, they usually know, deep-down, that it's just make believe."

The word bud now started to change tack, and the word being repeated was now - people. People, people, people.

"It's just changed. The word being repeated in that awful squeaky voice is people - like this: people, pcople, people. Oh – now it's, people see, people see, people see, people see."

"Let me take a look in your ear."

Dr. Finnegan selected a shining, medical instrument, placed a headband on his forehead, with a sort of miner's lamp attached to it, and he peered down one ear and then the other.

"Interesting, but all I can see is some wax. I can't see a word bud - or whatever you think it's called."

"Did you hear anything when you were near my ears?"

"Not a sausage."

At that moment, the patient stood up and she said, "It's now people see us, people see us, people see us, people see us."

"Aha, let me know what the next word that you hear is, please Mrs. Crawford."

Celia sat down and closed her eyes. She found that if she did this, the word bud often had more success in creating a phrase or a sentence. It had never managed a paragraph, let alone a short story, but it had been quite successful with sentences.

"O.K. Now the word bud has created - people see us everywhere, people see us everywhere, people see us everywhere, people see us everywhere."

The doctor decided to make up an illness which he could pretend to cure, as he thought that this might well get rid of the problem.

"I believe that you have a rare malady called Conwaytwittyitis."

"Oh, and what is that?"

"The brain is over-reacting to external stimuli and creating words in your head, which you think are caused by a word bud. These stimuli could be extreme temperature changes, strong aromas, overheard conversations, radio frequencies and many other types of natural or man-made triggers.

"I'm going to refer you to Mr. Marvin Cranham. He is a renowned expert in C.B.T., or Cognitive Behavioural Therapy. C.B.T is often used to retrain the way patients think. This may change your behaviour, to enable you to cope with this perceived problem. I'll write to Mr. Cranham today, and I promise to contact you soon, to let you know what he proposes."

"I'm so grateful Dr. Finnegan. The words now are - people see us everywhere, they think you really care, people see us everywhere, they think you really care, people see us everywhere, they think you really care, people see us everywhere, they think you really care."

The good doctor was even more convinced that there was no such thing as a word bud, and that the words were merely caused by half-forgotten memories. After Celia had left his room, he made some notes on his pad.

Once the surgery hours were over, he wrote a polite note to Mr. Cranham.

Dear Marvin

It is such a long time since we have met, that I wonder if I am pushing the boundaries of our old friendship when I ask you to help me with a slight subterfuge. I believe this may well help a patient of mine, who thinks that she has a "word bud" in her ear, that is trying to create phrases, sentences, paragraphs, and maybe even short stories in the warm wax.

I can find no physical abnormalities on a superficial inspection, but I should be grateful if you could firstly, do whatever you can to see if there is actually a physical cause, and then if there is not, adopt a little ruse which you may find amusing…

The letter continued in a rambling kind of way and Dr. Finnegan explained about his made-up disease, Conwaytwittyitis. Cranham laughed at this glorious invention, but he wrote back this short, appropriate, missive.

Dear Phineas
I remember you well, old boy. We had great fun at medical school, and I often wondered what had become of you. I would be delighted to help you, and your patient.

It is important that we rule out a normal cause, before plumping for treatment for Conwaytwittyitis. I will see Mrs. Crawford in my consulting rooms in Wimpole Street, and all you have to do, is to phone Oriana Prigg, my personal assistant, on the number at the head of this paper, to make an appointment.

In the meantime, I attach a list of preliminary tests, which you should run before she comes to see me.
Yours sincerely
Marvin Cranham

Upon receipt of this helpful letter, Dr. Finnegan telephoned Celia Crawford and asked her to visit him again. Celia duly sat in front of Dr. Finnegan's desk and looked round the untidy, but efficient looking, office. There were many framed certificates on one wall and some medical books in a heavy, mahogany case on the opposite wall. The examination couch was shrouded from view by thick, white curtains, and there were heaps of different coloured files and assorted papers on the desk itself.

"Mrs. Crawford, I've had a reply from Mr. Cranham. He wants you to have some tests, before we can firmly plump for Conwaytwittyitis as the cause of the malady. Most of these tests can be done here, or in the local clinic.

"I want to take your blood pressure, and I'll also take a little blood for some tests. I will arrange a hearing test at the audiology clinic at the hospital in Stanport. We'll also do some scans to see if there are any physical signs, which we might investigate.

"Once we have all the results, we can send you to see Mr. Cranham. I have the contact details of his personal assistant, and she can arrange that appointment, once Cranham has reviewed the results of these preliminary tests."

Dr. Finnegan followed up these procedures, exactly as he had promised. All of the results were completely normal. He telephoned Oriana Prigg himself, and she answered in a husky, sensual voice. He was almost overcome with curiosity to see what she looked like.

"Miss Prigg…"

"*Ms.* Prigg - if you don't mind!"

"I'm so sorry Ms Prigg, we older gentleman are not always as alive to today's changing standards as we should be. I'm Dr. Finnegan. My patient, a Mrs. Celia Crawford, would like an appointment with Mr. Cranham as soon as possible, please. I've already exchanged pleasant letters with him. We studied together at medical school."

"Yes, I saw those letters. Thank you for following them up with the tests. The results which you forwarded arrived a few days ago, and we've been looking forward to your call."

This woman sounds like dynamite, thought Finnegan. I wonder if she is as attractive as she looks?

"I would like to accompany Mrs. Crawford to the meeting with Marvin. I'm most interested in this very unusual case."

"I'll consult his diary. Let me see - he is free on the morning of April 24th. Would that be to your liking?"

Dr. Finnegan nodded, but then he realised that this didn't work on a telephone. He had to clear his throat two or three times, before he said, "That would be fine. I haven't seen old Marvin for many moons. Perhaps he and yourself would like to go to lunch at The Blue Oyster, in The Strand, with me - after Mrs. Crawford is sent on her way home?"

Oriana Prigg chuckled, and she oozed, "That would be most acceptable. Shall we say eleven thirty a.m. for the appointment with Mr. Cranham - and lunch at one p.m.? If you would like me to, I can book a table."

"Yes please."

Oh yes, oh yes, oh yes please, thought Dr. Finnegan, almost mimicking a word bud.

On the day of the consultation, Mrs. Crawford and Dr. Finnegan arrived in good time, and a frumpy, matronly and greying lady, with huge Deirdre Barlow spectacles, opened the door for them.

"Good morning, I'm Oriana Prigg. You must be Dr. Finnegan."

Finnegan smiled to himself. He knew that he was an old fool. After a few minutes, they were ushered into Marvin Cranham's consulting rooms. They were black and white, and white and black. There was nary a hint of any colour. Even the books on the white shelves, were bound in black leather, and the chairs, examination couch and desk were all unapologetically black.

Mr. Cranham wore a black suit, with a white shirt and a black and white striped tie. He wore black rimmed spectacles. He had black eyebrows and a black goatee beard. His hair was black (tinted like the goatee?), and he had an affable, but professional, manner. His manner was neither black nor white.

"Good morning, Mrs. Crawford and to you my old friend, Phineas Finnegan. I'm most happy to welcome you both to my humble rooms."

Humble, no – thought Finnegan. Expensive – yes.

"Mrs. Crawford, I've studied the papers sent to me by Dr. Finnegan, and I believe that an intensive course of C.B.T. may well assist you with this problem. I will now explain exactly what will happen, and over how long this treatment will last."

Dr. Finnegan was fidgeting and said, "Perhaps I should leave you to cover the details with Mrs. Crawford?"

"Yes, that would be fine. Oh, and by the way, I'm unable to come to lunch with you and Ms. Prigg, but I'm sure she will entertain you."

Finnegan left the room, and Oriana Prigg smiled at him. She stood up, and she fetched her coat from the hat stand at the side of her desk. She said in that wonderful, but seriously misleading, voice "Come on! Let's spend your money at The Blue Oyster. They won't mind if we turn up early."

Dr. Finnegan and Oriana had an extravagant, but exquisite, three course lunch, with far too much wine, followed by far too much cognac. Finnegan was most surprised to find that, beneath that imposing façade, Oriana was funny and affectionate. She was also uncommonly tactile. However, he soon realised that he was inordinately pleased, every time she reached over and stroked his cheek, or lightly brushed his hand.

By the time they had finished their extended lunch, he was head over heels in love with this tempting Jezebel. They ended up in her bed for the rest of the afternoon, and they were married within three months. They lived a long and happy life together, and Oriana often reminded him that he had fallen in love with her voice.

Marvin Cranham did his best with Celia Crawford and the C.B.T. course. As Dr. Finnegan had thought, it didn't help. At the end of the unsuccessful treatment he sat Mrs. Crawford down, and he said, "We can now definitely say that the problem is Conwaytwittyitis. You've also mentioned that the words have changed; sometimes the words are, since my baby left me, since my baby left me, since my baby left me, since my baby left me. This indicates to me that you may also have Heatbreakhotelophobia."

Mr. Cranham suggested some hypnotherapy, and Celia agreed to try a short course of sessions with a specialised practitioner, who had been recommended by the consultant. The hypnosis did not banish the word bud. At a follow up meeting with Marvin Cranham, he told her, "There's nothing else I can do for you." He continued, "I suggest that you try all of the well-known tinnitus remedies. Varying your diet may help."

Celia tried not to cry. She had pinned her hopes on C.B.T., and then on hypnosis. She left the office, before she started weeping, and she went home. Over the next six weeks, she started drinking heavily and mixed the alcohol with prescription drugs, in a wilful and irresponsible way.

The word bud kept talking to her. It manufactured clumsy phrases, long sentences, badly constructed paragraphs, and finally made a short story. Her word bud told her it was now going to create a novella. Celia knew she could not stand the constant reiteration of words, and worse than that – having to listen to something possibly in excess of twenty thousand words.

She finally took a Stanley knife out of her tool case, and she hacked off both of her ears. That made no difference to the word bud. She was bleeding badly, and she was in severe pain, when she phoned for an ambulance. At the hospital, they contacted Dr. Finnegan, and between them, they decided that she would have to be sectioned. Within a short space of time, she was discharged into the care of St. Barnabas' Home for the Bemused.

This is pretty much where we started our story. Celia Crawford didn't like it in the asylum. She had only been there for a week, but she hated the locked and padded room and the stern and bitter nurses. The conceited doctors were even worse. She had tried to explain that she had been brought there by accident, but they all looked at her as if she was mad. Inside her head, the Chipmunk voice sang, "It's only make believe," over and over again.

Chapter 45

THE DOOR TO HAPPINESS

A portal faint and hard to find,
can lead to joy and gladness.
If you just hunt and never mind,
the fleeting temporary sadness.
Once through the door and on the run,
you'll stay, and never leave.
The air is clean, warm is the sun,
an ecstasy you will believe.

THE AIR IS CLEAN, WARM IS THE SUN

Theo Addiscott had always been searching for joy, peace and happiness. In spite of this, his whole life had been a catastrophe, and his friends couldn't believe how many disasters had befallen him. He had been a sickly child, with constant diseases and medical complaints; accidents seemed to hunt him out. By the time he was a teenager, he had broken both arms, his left leg and his right wrist.

Despite his tendency to attract bad luck, he was an adventurous child, and many of his breaks, bumps and bruises were as a result of his dare-devil deeds on scooters, bikes and soap-box carts. He had contracted mumps, measles, scarlet fever, whooping cough and chicken pox, and he was always catching colds. He was well-known for his throat infections and nose bleeds, and his file at the local surgery, and its companion at the hospital, were dog-eared and bulging.

His parents both died when he was fifteen. They were walking in the Gower peninsula, and they were admiring the beautiful views, when their dog, Sheba (a fine Afghan Hound), ventured too close to the edge of the cliff, a little way from Worm's Head.

Sheba slipped over the edge of the cliff, in a moment of canine abandon. She forgot to put her brakes on, before she reached the divide between mud and air. She sailed downwards, but luckily her fall was broken by a grassy ledge. She lay still for a few moments, as she was a little stunned, but then she raised a pitiful, howling request for help.

Theo was not a witness to this calamity as he had been left with his uncle and aunt in Swansea, who lived near The Mumbles. The uncle and aunt do not feature in this story very much, although they showed their true colours later that day, as you will shortly discover. Brad and Louise (Theo's parents), were desperate to rescue dear Sheba, who was still yelping and barking for succour. Brad looked over the dangerous threshold and tried to reassure Louise.

"I can see her, Lulu, and she's only about ten feet down. I can easily get to her, and if you can hang on to my scarf, I'll tie that to my belt. Once I'm down there, you can steady me with the scarf and belt contraption, and I'll hold her in my arms, until we get back to the top. It will be a doddle."

He unwrapped his long, grey scarf, unzipped his anorak and extracted his belt from the loops on his newly acquired walking trousers. He tied the scarf securely to the belt, and he gave the other end of the scarf to Louise.

"Hang on to that, and it will help me to climb down. We'll have Sheba back up here in a jiffy."

"Oh Brad, what if I can't hold you? I'm frightened that you'll trip or slide off the cliff face."

Brad looked at his terrified wife. She was short and stout, with a black parka and badly-dyed blonde hair. There the resemblance to a refreshing pint of Guinness ended, as she had a finely proportioned face with clear, green eyes, a small, retroussé nose and cupid's bow lips. Oh, how he loved her!

"Watch me, pet. Trust me, it will be so simple, and we'll have lunch at a pub in Rhossili, once we've been reunited with Sheba."

He manoeuvred himself over the point where the Afghan Hound had come a cropper, and he started to pick his way carefully down the steep, rocky gradient. By sheer bad luck, a wasp settled on a small, retroussé resting place, and Louise panicked. She had a mortal fear of wasps, as she was allergic to the poison in their stings, so she shook her head to dislodge her enemy.

The insect was having none of that, and it promptly stung her on the lower lip. She shouted, and Brad looked up. He missed his footing, and his entire weight was transferred to the scarf and belt contraption, which he had mistakenly said would be a great help. As he fell, Louise was pulled over the cliff, and the husband and wife both hurtled to the rocky shore, at the bottom of the cliff.

They were killed instantly, and even though paramedics were called quickly by some passing strangers, these other walkers feared the worst. The paramedics rang for help from a local climbing club, and they sent a specialised team down to Brad and Louise. The men from the climbing team used their mobile phones to tell the paramedics that nothing could be done. They all waited until the tide went out, so that they could get to the bodies more easily, but that was the end of Theo's parents.

In the meantime, Sheba had discovered a way to get back to the top. The paramedics, who were still at the bottom of the cliff, found Brad's smart phone, zipped securely into his inner, chest pocket. One of the men also found a note in the dead man's wallet, with the address of Theo's uncle and aunt (and their surname), written in Brad's large and untidy hand.

They were soon talking to Theo's baby-sitters. The uncle and aunt said they were going on holiday the next day, to Tenerife. They told the paramedics that Theo had to be collected that evening. They said they couldn't possibly look after him, as they had to get to the airport, early in the morning. They also refused to have the dog, or even to find a place for it to be looked after. They were unhelpful, making the angry paramedics swear, sotto voce, with understandable frustration. One of the climbers said he would take the dog home, and the paramedics said that they would have to leave Theo with the Social Services people in Swansea, once he had been picked up.

Theo lived with various foster-parents until he was eighteen, and a few days after his birthday, he took on a job at an hotel, so that he could get some (but not much), money each week. He decided to live in, so he could save on day to day expenses. He made a reasonable living as a waiter, but he had what he thought was a stroke of luck, when an ageing lady guest took a fancy to him and asked him to go back to Dorset with her, to live in her house as a gardener and general companion. Cynthia Granville meant well, but unfortunately she meant more than Theo thought she did.

She had probably been a good-looking lady in her day, but her day was a good few years ago. She was in her late sixties, and Theo was forty-something years younger than she was. She was smart enough, and had a good complexion, but she stooped, and she walked with stick. Nonetheless, she was friendly with Theo, and he couldn't see trouble on the horizon, so he decamped from the hotel, and he travelled back to Chideock, in Dorset, with his new friend.

For a few weeks, things went quite well. Theo had his own room, and they shared all their meals together in her dining room. The cottage was small but comfortable, and she gave Theo a modest wage, which was ample for his purposes, as he wasn't having to buy food, nor to pay any other bills.

She loved a Bacardi and Coke (or two, or maybe even three), of an evening, and she encouraged Theo to join her. One night, they both had far too many of these, and Theo ended up in bed with his lady friend. At the time, he was too drunk to mind, and he had actually enjoyed the fumbling playfulness which Cynthia displayed, but when he awoke, in the cold light of day, things were different. She turned over and smiled at him. Her lipstick was smeared, and she was a terrible sight, without her dentures.

"My little angel. You were such a saucy boy last night. What am I going to do with you?"

Theo got out of the bed and ran to his room. He dragged his clothes on and packed his bag quickly. Cynthia followed him and looked on in sadness.

"Theo, I gave you a home. I let you eat here at my table, and I welcomed you into my heart, my arms and my bed. We have before us the door to happiness. You've had a hard life, but I wanted to show you joy and gladness. Please stay with me and never leave."

Theo shook his head.

"Cynthia, you're a kind and loving person, but you're old enough to be my grandmother. We should never have done what we did last night."

Cynthia cried, and she wiped her eyes before saying, "Let's just have a couple of Bacardis and Coke before you go. I know you're right, but please will you just do that for me?"

Theo had the good grace to feel sorry for her, and he agreed. He picked up the bag which he had packed and told her that he would see her in the sitting room.

Cynthia went to the bathroom and took out a bottle of sleeping pills, and she shook them all out onto the edge of the wash-basin. She crushed the pills and wrapped the powder in a tissue. Once she was in her little dining room, she took out two tall glasses and poured stiff drinks.

The crushed pills went into one glass, and she picked up that one for herself, and the other, unadulterated one, for Theo. They were placed on a silver tray, and she put it on a coffee table, in the middle of the sitting room. As she did so, she heard the phone ring and went to answer it, in the hall.

Theo saw the drinks on the tray, and picked up one of them. By golly, he needed this! He was so shaken that he drank it down in one fell swoop. When Cynthia came back only a few minutes later, she saw that he was in a deep sleep. Poor little lamb, she thought, I wore him out last night. As she looked at Theo, she smiled. He started to breathe very deeply and began to choke. Cynthia belatedly realised that he had drunk the wrong Bacardi and Coke. She cleaned him up, after he died, and she dragged him into her bedroom.

"My darling, you can now stay with me for ever."

Twelve years later, Cynthia passed away naturally, in her sleep. Some days after her death, the police were called to break down her front door, as the milkman had noticed that his bottles were mounting up, and he could see that various letters and circulars were protruding from the letter box. They found Cynthia in bed (freezing cold and stone-dead), with her arms around a hideously mummified body.

She and Theo were now together forever, where the air is clean and the sun is always warm. They couldn't quite believe it, and they felt an ecstasy which was beyond compare. As they watched the police, making arrangements for the pathologist to come to Cynthia's house, they smiled at each other and floated upwards, towards the door to perpetual happiness, where age doesn't matter.

Chapter 46

JUAN SUMMER

Open your mouth, the doctor said.
I want to inspect your red tonsils.
A deep breath now, not short instead;
no huffing or gasps, or chance'll
squeeze those lungs, constricting and tight.
I want to use a special tool.
It will shine a very special light.
Swallow and make it powerful,
and do it now before it's too late.
The day is here and not too soon.
It will prove to be your last ill fate.
I said do it now or remember,
Juan Summer don't make a swallow.

IT WILL SHINE A VERY SPECIAL LIGHT

Juan Summer had never questioned his robust, good health, when he was growing up. However, in his youth he had done all those things that young men tend to do, in order to prove their macho status. He had smoked cigarettes. He had also tried Jazz Woodbines, which never seemed to generate the desired effect. Like a lot of young men, he had drunk too much. His favourite tipple was light and bitter. This was chased down by a whiskey or three, and he loved red wine. He ate too much, and he also preferred the kind of food beloved by teenagers - such as burgers, chips and too many cakes.

When he was twenty, he met Karen Fenton. The world stopped spinning for several seconds. He was transfixed by Karen, a long-legged blonde with azure eyes and perfect, film star features. She also had a golden tan, and he wondered if it went all over. He had been introduced to Karen by his oldest friend, Wayne Shuler.

Wayne had previously told Juan all about her, after meeting her in the local dance hall, at the back of the dumpy pub, on the corner of the High Street and Nelson Road. This pub was where Juan and Wayne had started to drink light and bitter, after being weaned off light and lime by Juan's dad, Alfonso.

Alfonso, a swarthy gentleman of Spanish origin, had really been looking forward to having a daughter, before Juan entered this world. He had insisted that if the baby was a daughter she would be called Sangria, and any son would be named Juan.

Some way back, his family's surname, on the male side, had been Verano, but this had been anglicised when a distant, male relative had been thrown out of Spain by a more muscular rival in love, with whom Senor Verano had been involved in a little smuggling and gun-running. The alternatives offered to Senor Verano had been to leave Spain, or to be dragged by the castanets to the top of the edge of the gorge in Ronda. From there, he would be accidentally nudged over the edge. Unsurprisingly, he decided to leave his home land.

The Verano line carried on in England as the Summers, and they became more and more fascinated with the English way of life. Alfonso loved darts, cards, village-cricket, pubs, seaside piers and beer. He had told Juan and Wayne that light and lime was a tart's drink, and he refused to buy it for them; instead he came back with two pints of light and bitter. The two lads had looked suspiciously at this flat, and frankly puzzling, mixture. In order to please Alfonso, they had started to drink the alcoholic drink with a nonsense name, but they found that it was more than acceptable.

The pub, The Nag's Head, had become their favourite place. This was in the early sixties, and pubs in those days were generally spartan. The range of food was limited; pickled eggs, crisps, ham sandwiches and cheese biscuits were pretty much the norm. On one of their many visits, Wayne had been to the bar and bought their usual, two light and bitters, which he carried back to the small, round and chipped, Formica table, at which sat Juan.

Wayne started to hunt for the tiny, blue bag of salt which was supposed to be in every bag of crisps, two packets of which had been transported from the bar to the table, stuffed in his jacket pockets.

"Ah! We're in luck. I've got three bags of salt. My record is seven, but last week I had three packets with none at all."

"Wayne, Wane, Wayne, my interest in salt is waning. Why have you got such a daft name anyway?"

"My dad loves John Wayne. He thought John was too common, so he chose Wayne. And anyway, Juan is not that different from Wayne."

"I'm called that because Dad wanted a Spanish name, and I'm 'a gift from God.' I bet you don't even know what Wayne means."

"I do too, it's an Old English name for a wagon maker. Listen carefully, for I have news of momentous importance."

"Oh no, you've been reading Thomas Hardy again!"

"Have you seen the girl I told you about yet - Karen Fenton? She goes to the dances sometimes, in the back hall. I saw her for the first time last Friday, and she's the most beautiful girl in the world. Hey - that'd be a good name for a song."

"What - she goes to dances?"

"No you dummy, 'The most beautiful girl in the world.'"

"Ha, that's rich. You'd have to be a right Charlie to sing that."

"She also has terrific, shapely breasts. I'm telling you she's a really booby-dazzler! But shut up for a minute, here she comes; Karen - over here, what do you want to drink?"

Karen looked over at the lads, and she realised that she had met Wayne in the dance hall recently. She sashayed over to their table. The reaction of the two pals was marked, and she knew it too.

"Hallo, it's Wayne isn't it? I'm Karen," she said as she offered a languid hand to Juan, who was huffing and puffing, like a stupefied goldfish.

"I'd love a Babycham, Wayne. I hope that's not too much trouble?"

Wayne would have been happy to travel to the ends of the Earth, on any mission, for Karen. His face reddened, and Karen pretended not to notice. She was nineteen, and she had been aware of the effect that she had on men of almost any age, for some time.

She sat on the bench next to Juan, behind the table, and placed a warm hand on his knee. Juan almost hit the roof. For those of you who are not youngsters anymore, do try to remember how you felt when you first met the love of your life.

Karen started chatting with Juan and later, when he got home, he tried to remember what she had said. He was unable to remember anything, except those huge, pale blue eyes, her animal smell and her luscious curves. When I say animal smell, please understand that I refer to that, almost undetectable, femaleness, enhanced by some delicately-scented perfume or cream, which smells even better than light and bitter.

Shortly after Wayne came back with the Babycham, he had realised that his friend (and the delectable Karen), were waiting for him to leave.

He stood up manfully, with a sigh of regret, and he told them that he had agreed to walk the family dog, Chalky, and he wanted to do so before it got dark.

"Oh Wayne, I don't think Chalky will get dark, even if you stay awhile."

Karen's tiny attempt at mirth was accorded a hooting, laughing and giggling reception by her entranced admirers. After Wayne left, everything went swimmingly. Juan and Karen had a few more drinks, and when they left the pub, they bought a couple of sodden and cereal-laden burgers from an old van, where a fat, greasy and unattractive man cooked fat, greasy and unattractive burgers.

Wayne was agog when he heard that Juan had walked Karen home and kissed her before he left her. Juan had felt on top of the world.

"Good name for a song," said Wayne.

Juan was working in a Dolcis shoe shop at the time, and although he didn't mind the job, he wanted to do better. The manager was an old (or so it seemed to Juan), military man, and he had asked Juan to put some beautiful, chestnut leather Oxfords on a stand outside the shop, with a sign that said, *Half-price - Seconds*. Juan spent some considerable time looking for tiny flaws and came to the conclusion that there were none. The manager explained that people would buy these perfect shoes quite happily at the reduced price, especially if they couldn't find anything wrong with them.

Karen had been asking Juan if he would give up smoking, as he was always chesty and coughed incessantly. She said, as he was not a heavy smoker it should be easy. Juan was not that attached to his Senior Service fags, so he agreed. He also started to do more exercise, in the forms of walking and cycling, and he felt better quickly.

They danced in the hall behind The Nag's Head, several times a week. The resident band was a rock and roll outfit, with a pianist, a bass guitarist, a drummer and a great, lead guitarist who could outplay

Chuck Berry. The pianist stopped sometimes, after a few songs, and he went to the back of the old, upright piano, to re-stick the contact mike to the back of the piano, as it kept falling off.

Juan and Karen's favourite song, by far, was *Breathless* – a Jerry Lee Lewis number. They loved all the material which the band played. They were called The Rocking Robins, after an old Bobby Day song. They played everything from Don Gibson to The Coasters and sprinkled in some blues specialities by the likes of Slim Harpo and Muddy Waters.

One thing led to another with Juan and Karen, and Juan was often breathless for a different, although most acceptable, reason. The trouble was that they became careless, and Karen became pregnant. Juan had to face her dad, Kevin Fenton. He wasn't looking forward to explaining that his little tootsie (as Kevin called her), was pregnant. To Juan's surprise, Kevin took the news comparatively well.

"If you're telling me that you want to marry her, that's great news. If you're telling me that you won't stand by her, that's bad news - for you!"

Juan knew that Kevin had once been a well-known wrestler. He had seen a quote from Kent Walton, who did the commentary for the wrestling on T.V. every Saturday afternoon, in The Radio Times. He had referred to The Masked Muscleman (Kevin), as "The strongest, toughest wrestler that England has ever produced."

Luckily for Juan, he did want to marry Karen, and they were spliced soon after Juan's talk with Kevin. The best man was Wayne. The band was The Rocking Robins, and the venue they used was the dance hall at the rear of The Nag's Head.

They had a week in Butlin's at Clacton for their honeymoon, and Juan started a new job at an insurance broking firm, whose head office was in London. Their marriage was incredibly happy. They loved each other immensely and had shared and separate interests. They both loved walking, dogs and the cinema. Juan had taken up classical guitar, and he was talented. He also liked cycling. Karen made dresses. She loved cooking and swimming, and all in all they were an ideal couple.

Their daughter, Lana, (the cause of the sudden wedding), was a bonny baby, and as she grew up she became just like a miniature Karen. The fly in the ointment, was that Juan started to become out of breath regularly, and sometimes this was only due to drying himself after a bath, or even just from walking upstairs in their small, pebble-dashed house, in Rosemount Road, a few streets away from The Nag's Head.

Juan shrugged off his illness, until he collapsed in a heap, after trying to cycle up the gentle hill from The Nag's Head to their home. He managed to get to see their doctor fairly quickly, and the G.P. arranged various tests at the hospital, after performing a cursory initial examination.

Juan was sent to see a specialist, who was much more thorough. The test results revealed that Juan was suffering from emphysema.

"Why should I have that?"

"Are you a smoker?"

"Not now. I gave up fifteen years ago, or perhaps more. I was probably twenty-five when I stopped smoking."

"Well, that's the cause."

The specialist arranged for Juan to be given various puffers, and that was that. He had told Juan that his airways were restricted and that he would never again be able to breathe the way he could, before he smoked. He explained that Juan had a long-term, progressive disease. He was cold and unsympathetic. He knew that if Juan had never smoked, he would probably never have contracted emphysema.

Juan and Karen were understandably worried, but they soon accepted that he now had to take things a little easier. Lana asked her dad why he wheezed and had trouble breathing. Juan didn't pull any punches.

"Darling, I've got a disease which makes it very difficult to breathe. It will probably get worse, but I can put up with it at present."

Lana was upset but tried not to show it. Juan's health started to deteriorate more markedly, at around the time of his fiftieth birthday. One evening, Karen came in from a shopping trip, and she heard Juan coughing, hacking and trying to catch his breath. He was clutching at his chest, and he seemed to be suffocating. With a sudden gasp, he took his last breath, and then he was still.

Karen wrapped her arms around him. She knew that her beloved husband was no more. The doctor came, after she rang an emergency number for the practice, but he seemed unsurprised that Juan had died. Lana helped Karen to call the undertaker and to make all the arrangements for the wake. They had decided to use the hall at The Nag's Head.

They rummaged round in the drawers of the old, roll-top desk that Juan had used for his letter writing, sorting out bills and attending to personal papers. Lana found an envelope addressed to Karen, in her father's tiny handwriting. Underneath the name, Karen Summer, it said,

Only to be opened in the event of my death.

My dear Karen

Since the day we met, in our favourite pub, you have been the light of my life. I have never, ever loved anybody the way that I have loved you. You have made me so happy.

The best thing that we ever did together was to make Lana. If she is reading this now, I want her to know how special she was to me. My two girls – my beautiful family.

Please ask my old mate Wayne to help you with everything. My will is with our solicitors, Collier and Walters, and Wayne is my executor. I know that he will do a good job and that he will be a source of great comfort for you, Karen.

You already know that Wayne never married. The reason is that he has always loved you, and he felt that he would never find

someone to match those qualities that you have. Please be kind to him. He will be upset too, as he and I were friends since we were eight.

I would like to be cremated. Please have the following songs played at my service.

Abide with Me

Smoke Gets in Your Eyes (when the coffin disappears behind the curtain)

Breathless, by Jerry Lee Lewis.

You made me breathless, in an unbelievably wonderful way. Cigarettes made me breathless, and they did for me in the end.

My lovely Lana will be your best support and comforter within our family, but if you need a really good pal, choose Wayne.

I love you.

Your breathless husband
Juan.

Chapter 47

OLDE TIME DANCING

When Father Time went dancing
the quick step, stepped up in speed.
The girls were all a-prancing,
and they followed his steely lead.
The rumba and the cha-cha,
Latino dances for lovers.
All laughing and a Ha-Ha,
they have their favourite numbers.
The song was hardily finished,
when the next began to play.
As the dancers' breath diminished,
and their partners decided to stay.

LATINO DANCES FOR LOVERS

Tia and Clive Baxter had been married for twenty-two years, and their relationship was stale and boring. They were frequently quite tetchy during matrimonial rows, and even though they invariably felt guilty about snapping at each other, they knew that the magic had gone out of the marriage. It is, I suppose, inevitable that once the honeymoon is over, there is a gradual lessening in the excitement which couples feel for each other, and as time goes by, they come to realise that a kiss is just a kiss, but a curry and a few bottles of lager are something else.

Clive's friend, Stewart Groves, had even tackled him about the lukewarm nature of his own marriage to his wife, Melissa. She had generally been reckoned to be hotter than hot by Stewart, Clive and their other chums, when they had first seen her dancing in The Club de Palais, in the slightly seedy lower half of Brompton Street, in their native town of Mude.

Melissa was a statuesque red-head, in the mould of Sophia Loren, and the boys used to egg her on, when she was stripping at the club. She was built exceedingly well, and her main attractions were plain to see. She wore tight tops, before revealing all, and had earned the nickname Melissa Melons, which became her stage name for her exotic dancing.

We don't need to dwell that much on her top half, although that was the best part of her, and it also enabled clever, tassel-twirling, which made the young men laugh with embarrassment. Her lower half was not slightly seedy (like the lower half of Brompton Street.) Yes - you could say that the attractions continued all the way from her saucy derrière, extending smoothly down her superb pair of pins.

Melissa was now not as hot as she used to be, although she was still a more than acceptably good looking woman. Stewart had explained to Clive, that he wanted to rekindle the warmth he and Melissa had in their relationship, when he had been a mere whippersnapper of twenty-three, at a time when he and Melissa just had to look at each other to start a fire.

Clive and Stewart went to the Mude Working Man's Club every Wednesday, and it had become their habit to sink three pints each, to moan about the government, to talk about the weather and to have a laugh about old times, before strolling home with Clive turning left as he exited from the club, and Stewart turning right.

On the night that Stewart raised the subject of his flagging marital environment, Clive had just had a minor tiff with Tia. She had remarked on his tie, which she thought was too wide. He had raised his voice and given her a glacial stare.

"If that's all you have to worry about, I'm sorry for you. Stewart won't even care if I'm wearing a tie or not, let alone how wide the ruddy thing is. Tia is a great name for you – Aunt by name and aunt by nature."

At one time, they would have laughed this off, but as he stalked out of the front door and banged it shut, Tia had burst into tears. She had cheered up a little when she had poured herself a glass of white wine, and she spent the evening watching soap operas and quiz shows.

Meanwhile, back at the working man's club, Stewart had just finished complaining about the tedium which had set in at home. He also bemoaned the fact that he and Melissa made love only infrequently.

"I think she would rather watch Coronation Street than have sex. I've tried to make things more interesting, and I even surprised her one night by laying lots of rose petals on the bed and lighting smelly candles. She said she would have to hoover all the petals up, before we went to bed, and she snuffed out all the candles, as she thought the stink would give her a headache. That's her favourite excuse now, and I thought women could multi-task!"

"But Stewart, be fair, none of us are spring chickens. I was talking to another pal the other day, and he said he would rather have a cuppa than make love to his wife. I guess we just get too used to our spouses. Tia and I rub along O.K., but we aren't exactly Anthony and Cleopatra. What you need to do, is to try to find a hobby which will energise you both, and maybe that would bring back that je ne sais quoi."

As they went to leave the club, they looked at the notice board. The events were usually tame, as nowadays the club mostly booked singers with backing tracks, had karaoke or quiz nights, or even just a D.J. Every now and then, they had a live band, and that certainly brought back fond memories because most of them only played music up to the early seventies. This suited the club members as they were mostly elderly. One notice caught their interest.

Sasha Blackmore's Dance Nights
Every Monday in the Back Hall
Are you lacking in lustre? Let me polish up your life by showing you how dancing used to be. Learn to quick-step, fox-trot, tango and cha-cha. For those of you who are more adventurous, we can look at salsa and other Latino routines.
No experience necessary. If you can come with a partner, that would be a help.
£7 per night per person, or £12 per couple. The dancing will be accompanied by Syd and his wonderful organ.

Clive and Stewart resisted the temptation to make obvious jokes about Syd's wonderful organ, and they both wrote down the telephone number of Sasha Blackmore.

"Nothing ventured, Clive!"

"Good night, Stewart."

Both of the discontented men went home and tackled their wives about Sasha's Dance Nights. Tia and Melissa both thought it would be a good idea to sally forth and to sample the delights of these lessons, particularly the more adventurous salsa and suchlike.

The first lesson was sheer torture. Sasha was a dumpy, brassy kind of girl, but she did seem to know what she was doing. Her little husband, Job, was definitely the underdog, and he had to be at her beck and call, for every minute of the four-hour sessions. Job looked like a lesser canine too. He had bulging eyes, like a pug, and he wore a corduroy waistcoat, which had seen better days. His black trousers, which he kept hitching up, looked as if they were several sizes too large for him.

Sasha was dressed in a clinging top, which emphasised the ample rolls of fat which rippled down her body, and she wore tight, yellow trousers, which didn't fall down. The two men noticed that she had amazingly good legs "for an old bird" (as Clive put it.)

The organ wheezed into life, and Sasha and Job began to dance gracefully and with dextrous skill. After that demonstration, Clive, Tia, Melissa and Stewart decided that they had underestimated the potential quality of the lessons.

Week by week, the four of them went to the Dance Night and they mastered quite a few dance types. Well, I say they, but I mean all of them except for Clive. He was clumsy and ungainly; he lacked coordination and frequently stood on the toes of the ladies. Sasha had encouraged them to mix with the other dancers, but Clive soon found that when he asked ladies to dance, they remembered that they had to make a phone call, or they needed to visit the loo.

He became discouraged, and he tried to worm his way out of the Dance Nights. The final fiasco was a dismal attempt at jiving. Clive had seen some of the club members doing really fast dancing to one of the infrequent bands, Sylvia Sky and the Jive Clouds.

He thought they were great, and the club members made an earnest attempt to look like fifties dance-goers, with flouncy skirts and drape jackets being well represented. He asked Sasha if she would show them how to jive, and she beamed. She was always pleased when one of the less successful trainees showed a special interest in a dance.

Clive was led onto the floor by Sasha, and she showed him the basic steps. He said he wanted to speed everything up, and she asked Syd to play *Jitterbug Boogie* on his wonderful organ. At first, Clive did well, but as Sasha kept asking Syd to quicken the tempo, he missed his footing badly, and he tripped Sasha up. She fell, but worse than that, Clive went down, like a sixteen stone sack of potatoes, on top of her, and there was a loud and ominous crack.

Sasha was quite calm and gracious about her broken leg. She knew that at her age, the bones were not as strong as they once were, and she said she had misjudged how well Clive would cope with the fast dancing. She was taken to hospital by Stewart and Melissa.

Clive and Tia made their way sorrowfully, to their home. As they went in their front door, Tia said, "I know how badly you feel about this darling, so why don't we go straight to bed, and you can try some of those new tricks which you wanted to introduce, when we are alone in our room."

"Tia, I love you dearly and I know you are just trying to cheer me up. Do you mind if we just have a cup of tea and a couple of gingernuts?"

"Of course not, my little lover - there will be other nights."

She secretly hoped that they could cut down on the love-making and eat more biscuits.

Chapter 48

ON TENDER HOOKS

When love is new with vibrant quality,
a wretched absence is a searing pain.
The juveniles all have this, I do want (for me),
fair young swainesses, and their hunky swains.
The girls and boys can't wait to see their loves,
and everlasting minutes seem like hours.
They cuddle up close, like young turtle doves.
In acts of love, they lose their vocal powers.

I DO WANT (FOR ME)

Joanna Turnbull had wanted to fall in love, for as long as she could remember. She read slushy magazines and romantic novels. She fancied herself as a strange cross between Cathy from Wuthering Heights and Kylie Minogue. She also watched dopey, American rom-coms, with the greatest degree of satisfaction. Sighing sorrowfully became such a habit, that her mother threatened to take her to the doctor, as she feared that she was developing asthma.

Joanna (who refused to answer to Jo), started to wear all black, from the age of eleven, and imagined herself swooning in the arms of a brooding, Heathcliff type of character. Failing that, she would have liked to become a world-famous, pop singer, like Kylie. She didn't seem to see that these two ambitions were polarised. Her dad said, "If you want to be like Kylie Minogue, you'll have to throw away all those mourning garments and invest in a pair of gold hot-pants. And you'll need a much squeakier voice."

Vanessa (Joanna's fearsome, matriarchal relative), directed an ice-cold dagger of a glare at her husband, and she said pointedly, "Dylan, surely you can't be serious about Joanna wearing gold hot-pants?"

"Oh no my love, that would never do. I myself have always tried not to look at Miss Minogue when she prances around, wearing skimpy clothes. I'm far too respectable. I never want to stare at her tight, little rump."

Vanessa was walking past Dylan when he delivered this bit of fatuous nonsense, and she swiped a rolled up newspaper round his grinning face. Let him have his fun, she thought. I know that he still likes to look at pretty girls, but I also know that he would never stray. He loves me too much, and besides he is far too scared of losing me. No, she thought. He is stuck with me, and I'm stuck with him.

Joanna had come home with a letter from her school, asking for permission to go on a holiday in the West Yorkshire Moors. The pupils would be staying in converted barns near the Bronte Falls, and the location was a hop, skip and a jump away from Haworth.

Her mum knew that the old part of the town, with its famous cobbled hill and the Bronte Parsonage Museum, would feed Joanna's Cathy and Heathcliff fantasy, but she decided that this would be preferable to encouraging any notion that she might have, of being the next Kylie Minogue. Not that she had anything in particular against Kylie, she seemed to be a very grounded woman, and at least she did wear a bit more than Rhianna, and she didn't swear all the time - like effing Adele.

Vanessa signed the consent form and wrote a cheque for the deposit. She took Joanna to a shop specialising in outdoor wear, and together they chose rugged, water-proof gear, so that she would be well protected, when she was walking on the moors. The school had also asked if any parents would be prepared to accompany the party, "to have fun, and to ensure the safety of your loved ones." Vanessa had confirmed on the return slip, that she and Dylan would be happy to go with the teachers and the pupils.

Dylan was a well-respected solicitor in the town of Larchwood, and she herself was a leading light in many clubs and societies, having first started to join them, in rebellion, when Dylan spent too much time with the Freemasons. She loved her knitting circle, her yoga and the book club. She was also a governor at Joanna's school, and she had joined the Labour Party. Dylan was a keen snooker player, a Masonic stalwart, a local history expert and a member of the Conservative Party.

Vanessa went to church every week and was on the Church Council. Dylan went to church only for baptisms, weddings and funerals. In the last few months, he said he had been forced to go to too many funerals. They had agreed not to discuss religion or politics at home.

They had originally been dewy-eyed over each other, but now they carried on in an atmosphere of genial tolerance, except for when Vanessa tried to exercise her authority as Supreme Control Freak. This was how

Dylan thought of her when she became angry or forceful. Luckily for him, he hadn't told her of her new title.

The arrangements for the trip to Yorkshire went smoothly. Vanessa had expected Dylan to carp about taking time off work, but he said he would be delighted to go with the school party, as he had never been to West Yorkshire. His only stipulation was that he would drive the family car there and back, as he was blowed if he wanted to spend a million years crawling along in a clapped out, school bus.

He delivered Vanessa and Joanna, with their luggage, to the school gate, and he looked at the swanky double-decker Mercedes bus, in which his wife and daughter would be travelling, with some regret. If not exactly rueful, there was certainly a little rue in existence. He watched Joanna and her mum playing with the reclining seats on the coach and experimenting with the individual D.V.D. players in the seat backs, and he sighed.

Despite that minor annoyance, Dylan got back into his car and set off for Yorkshire. He selected a C.D. by his idol, Bob Dylan. As he sat back, he relished the whole of *Blonde on Blonde,* and he looked forward to enhancing the five-hour journey, by playing many other offerings from Robert Zimmerman. Not many people knew he had been named after the rabbit from The Magic Roundabout. He was happy for people to assume that his favourite singer had inspired his mum and dad, rather than a spaced out, cartoon character.

About halfway to the moors, his car started stalling, and finally it muttered to itself as it gave up completely, a little way from a small town called Brinkley. Dylan got out of the car and looked at his mobile. Recognising that there was no signal, he started to walk towards the town. This took him longer than he thought, and it was getting on for closing time at Brinkley Motors, when he opened the door and explained his situation to the owner, Brandon Hobbs, who was also the only mechanic. Hobbs was enterprising and helpful.

"Well sir, it seems to me that you are in a bit of a pickle. If you leave your car keys here, I'll pick up your motor in the morning and will fix it for you, so that you can collect it on your way back home. We can collect your bits and pieces and that now, and you can hire my old jalopy for a pittance, and that'll be done and dusted."

Dylan could see that this was a good plan. He was surprised by two things. Brandon's "old jalopy" was an almost new Audi Q7, and the pittance was a stinging and large amount to pay. He swallowed hard and agreed.

Once he was on his way, he relaxed in Brandon's beautiful car. He made fairly good time, and he pulled into the parking lot outside the converted barns at about six thirty p.m. He had phoned Vanessa when he found a place to stop, which fortunately had a mobile signal, and she came running out of the barn which had been allocated to the Turnbulls, and she threw her arms around him.

"I've been so worried. These roads are pitch black, and it's getting icy too."

Dylan gave her a peck on each cheek and slapped her backside. A nice feature it was too, he thought, although not in the Kylie league.

"Put the kettle on, Mother!"

As he was sitting down to a welcome brew, there was a frantic knocking on the door. Dylan opened it, to find a shivering and crying, young girl of twenty or so, on his door step.

"I'm Josie Wilde. Please, please help me. I've been walking on the moors and I can't find my friend. She's quite large and not very fit, and she has difficulty breathing."

"Oh please Dad, do go with her. What would you want somebody to do if that was me, who had lost her friend?"

Vanessa interjected, "Be careful Dylan, but you must do whatever you can."

Dylan wasn't that keen, but he pulled on his boots, donned a shower-proof coat and ushered the young lady towards the Q7.

"There's a little lane just opposite the entrance to the barns. We need to go up that track, right up to where I think I last saw her."

Dylan drove out of the barn entrance (or I suppose, to be correct, he drove out of the barn exit.) He could see the track, and he noted that the Q7 could only go up the track with just a few inches' clearance on each side. After that, on both the left and the right, there were low, rambling bushes, and the track itself was muddy and slippery.

He turned on the car's main-beam and drove slowly, for what seemed like an eternity. They saw a black Land Rover coming towards them, and fortunately the driver switched to his side lights, so he wouldn't dazzle Dylan. The Q7 went through some open gates and over a metal cattle-grid. The Land Rover and the Q7 stopped a few feet from each other. Josie got out of the Audi.

"I'm going to find out if this man has seen my fat friend, Kirstie."

Dylan thought that it was sensible to ask the driver, but that it wasn't kind to refer to her friend in that way. Josie chatted to the other driver, and she came running back with a *very* fat friend in tow. They both got in the car, and Dylan started to try to find a place to turn round. As he was trying to manoeuvre the Q7 (a terrific car, but a bit on the huge side), the farmer who had been driving the Land Rover came rushing up.

"No sir, don't do that. There are bogs on each side of the track. Once you get in them, you ain't never coming out."

The reluctant Dylan had to reverse about a mile and a half, before getting back on the road. There were two vehicles, a police car and a van, outside the entrance (or the exit) to the barns. (Kirstie had told Dylan that the farmer had phoned the police.) She went to see the policeman in the van, and Josie went over to sit in the police car. To do her credit, the over-upholstered girl had apologised to the policeman in the van.

"Now listen here, missy. Do you pay taxes?"

"Yes, of course."

"Then you've paid for this little exercise. I'd rather come out on a wild-goose chase than anything worse. And those moors are dangerous at night."

Dylan spoke to the coppers and thanked them. The two girls also told Dylan they were grateful for his help. He decided to drive into Haworth to get some fish and chips, as he was starving. By the time he got back to his holiday barn, Joanna and her mum were frantic with worry.

"Where have you been? We kept thinking that you might have had an accident. And then Joanna began to wonder if the girl you were helping was a psychopath with a dagger, or in partnership with thieves who would steal that nice Q7."

"Oh no girls, Josie was quite posh. She spoke nicely and was polite and very grateful. I was never in any danger, except for the boggy ground at the sides of the track."

Joanna looked at her mum and said, tearfully, "I think my days of wanting to be Heathcliff's Cathy are over. I wonder if you can still buy gold hot-pants?"

Chapter 49

BARE BEAR DISPLAY

The Peeping Tom was very shocked
to see the bears all naked.
His world was shaken, really rocked.
The bareness was quite hated.
The bears had joined a nudist club,
promenaded in the buff.
When they came home, that was the rub
Bare, bear display - quite furry 'nuff!

QUITE FURRY 'NUFF

Daddy Bear had suggested to Mummy Bear that they should strip off and sunbathe naked, on more than one occasion. Whilst she could see the attraction of lying in the sun, with no covering, she was shy and worried, in case she would be seen by prying eyes.

Daddy Bear saw an advert in The Ursine Courier saying that new members were always wanted for The Furview Society.

Do you love the sun?

Our naturist society is open to bears of all kinds, whether they are adults, teenagers or little cubs. Since we have all been commanded to wear clothes (following the Public Edict of 2045), we have lost our natural love of being free and easy in our fur.

Our club has private premises, which are not overlooked, and we also have a large swimming pool, which we stock with tasty salmon at the appropriate times in the year. You will enjoy catching your own supper.

The Teddy Bar is open all day, and we play tennis, badminton and football in our extensive grounds.

The only stipulation is that all clothes should be left in reception. The lockers are just off the welcome area, and you will have your own key, so you can leave your garments and any valuables in safety.

Club membership fees are reasonable, and at present we are offering a ninety-day trial period which will cost you nothing at all, except for modest charges in The Teddy Bar and the Honey Restaurant.

Apply in person, or telephone the number below and ask to speak to Goodbear Hodges.

Daddy was excited about the family joining The Furview Society, and he looked forward to feeling the warmth of the sun on his fur again. The government's edict had forced all animals to wear clothes.

Some of them, like little Chihuahuas, had already been togged out with daft hats and coats. However, bears didn't usually wear clothes, and it had seemed strange to do so, in the headlong rush to clothe all and sundry, which even included a prudish return to Victorian feelings about naked piano legs.

Two weeks later, the Bear family arrived at the Furview premises, and when they had signed in, Daddy went into the Boar changing rooms to the right of the reception desk, whereas Mummy and Baby were sent to the left, towards the Sow area.

Daddy took off his detested clothes, rolled them into a tight bundle, shoved them into his personal locker and shut the door. He looked for a place to put his key, realising that he now had no readily available pockets. The key was on a silicone band, and he saw other bears putting the bands round their wrists, so he followed suit.

Mummy and Baby were a little shy about taking off their togs. They did it piece by piece, in a sort of secretive striptease. They all met up at the back of the changing rooms, and they were impressed with the swimming pool, even though it was at present salmonless, as this was apparently the wrong time of year to source free-range salmon. Daddy saw three sun-loungers with no bears on them. These were the only ones that were empty, so he put his towel on one, and he told Mummy to do likewise with her towel and Baby's small one.

A Furview official approached them.

"You do realise that you aren't allowed to reserve sun-loungers don't you? If you're going to use them now, that's fine, but if you were going to go to lunch in The Honey Restaurant, or you wanted Bear Snacks in the Teddy Bar, you would need to select loungers when you returned.

"Confidentially, we've had a lot of trouble with Prussian bears who leave their towels on these sun-beds over-night, and that's not very fur!"

He laughed at his well-practiced joke. Mummy and Baby gave a pained groan. They spent the afternoon lazing around by the pool, punctuated by brief dips in the heated water. Daddy had found out that Bear Snacks were available from the Pool Bar. He came back with the menu. Some wag had changed the heading at the top to Bearu, but the list of snacks was extensive.

"Listen Mummy and Baby, we could have leaves, flowers, grass, mushrooms, berries or roots. Or they also have nuts, honey and grubs. I think I'll have grubs and honey."

Mummy and Baby chorused their agreement, and Daddy went off to buy the snacks. Having realised that his money was in his locker, he asked if he could put the meals on his tab. The bear tender said that this was common practice. Ten minutes later Daddy returned with three plates of grubs and honey.

"Grubs up!"

In the afternoon they played tennis and looked at the notice board. On the following Tuesday, the club was giving bear back, horse riding lessons. Daddy was looking forward to doing this, until he saw that the weight restrictions would mean that only Baby would be eligible.

The club had some rooms which could be rented by the night, and Daddy decided to book a family room for their next visit. The club called this accommodation, The Sloth Room. Daddy was a little offended, as he thought he was quite speedy for his age. Mummy told him that sloth was an old name for a group of bears.

At the end of the day, Daddy asked his family what they thought of the club. They were united in saying that it was wonderful. The next week they returned and left their clothes, and other bits and pieces, in the Sloth Room, which had been booked by Daddy during their first visit. The day started off hot, and it went from hot to very hot, and then to exceedingly hot. Daddy said, "I just need to go back to the room for something."

"O.K. Pa, I'll stay here with Mummy. Don't be long."

Time went by, and then it went by again. After an hour, Daddy did come back. He was wearing a fluffy robe, and his face looked different. He had left the pool as just a normal, but bare, bear. He had now shaved all his fur off his head, including his face.

He still looked handsome, but he was pink. He peeled off his robe, and there were gasps of shock from his own family and the other bears who were round the pool. Daddy had continued his shave – all over.

"I am a true naturist now. Look how pink I am."

He lay down and started to sun-bathe. He cooked himself for two and a half hours, and he dipped his baking body into the pool periodically. By the evening, he was suffering badly with sunburn, and although Mummy had found some after-sun lotion in the Pool Kiosk, it had done little to soothe his red, raw skin.

The management of the Furview Society had never seen a totally shaved bear before, and the manager told Daddy not to come back, until he had regrown his fur. After a few days, Daddy's skin started to peel. Baby looked at him and giggled.

"Daddy, you took off your clothes. You then took off your fur. And now you're taking off your skin."

Chapter 50

FIDO FIDELITY

I love my man and that is that.
He is my moon and stars.
I am a dog, not a mere cat,
and I chase, all of the cars.
He strokes my nose, and hugs me.
I just love his silly ways.
He never ever bugs me,
and I hope he always stays.
I follow him from room to room,
He puts me on his lap,
He goes away but comes back soon,
to let me out to crap.

I AM A DOG, NOT A MERE CAT

I've been told by my alpha male that I'm a dog. He actually calls me Fido or Good Dog, even when I crap on his lawn. That surprises me because he goes round picking up my poo in plastic bags. I mean – if I'm a good dog for doing my business, isn't that ungrateful of him to throw it into the big dustbin?

I live in a nice, warm house with my alpha male, who I think must be called Edmund. His bitch calls him many names, such as honey, silly bugger and darling. She uses these and lots of other names interchangeably, and I've noticed that some of them have to be said in an angry voice, whilst others can be whispered in a sort of gooey, soft tone. Silly bugger can apparently be used in both ways.

I do love him, but he does strange things. Sometimes he spills my water. That's funny. When his bitch (who I think may be called Hayley), is around, he wipes the water up carefully. If she's out, I've noticed that he just treads on the water with one of my towels and throws it into the box with the others. Hayley is also called honeybunch and my lover. When he's angry, Edmund calls her a bitch. I don't know why, because I thought that a bitch was just a female.

They let me get on the thing they call a bed, but Edmund won't let me get under the covers. If he's away, Hayley lets me snuggle up to her, and she strokes me in the bed. Sometimes, Edmund goes out before Hayley gets up, and I sneak under the covers, once I hear him close the front door.

I was young once, but now I'm quite old. I heard Edmund say that I was twelve years old, but that doesn't seem much to me. A small, human pup sometimes comes to visit, and Edmund loves her. She comes round with a slightly larger human, whom the pup calls Mum.

Edmund also calls the small human "my special grand-daughter." I don't think she sounds all that grand. She loves me too, and so does the mum human. What confuses me most though, is that the larger human, who is called Megan, also calls Hayley, Mum. Isn't it daft to call two people in the same pack, Mum?

The other day they took me to the vet's. I saw a picture on the wall there, and Hayley said to Edmund, "Look at that lovely picture of a Labrador. He's just like Fido."

She squeezed me and looked very sad. The vet was a jolly girl, who smelt of lots of animals. I thought she was fabulous, and I licked her face and her paws. I heard her say, "There's nothing more that we can do for Fido. You'll know when the time comes. Just ring me, and I will do what is necessary."

Edmund and Hayley started to do that thing which humans do, called crying. It involves howling and screwing up their faces, and it produces snot and water. I don't know why they cried. If there was nothing more that could be done, surely that meant I was perfect? That night, we all smuggled up in the bed. Edmund even let me go under the covers, and he cuddled me all night. I heard them talking about the difference between cats and dogs.

Hayley said, "Dogs need us, but cats don't."

Edmund just nodded and held me tightly. In the night I felt strange, and then I was looking down at me, from outside my body. I somehow knew that it was finished with.

They don't know it yet, but I'll be with them every day, until they join me. Another dog watched over me, and he told me that I was now their guardian angel dog. They couldn't see me, and they were also unaware of the other dog. I tried to lick Hayley, and she shivered. I floated over to Edmund and put my paw on his chest.

"Do you know, Hayley, I have the strangest feeling that, one day, we will see good old Fido again."

I wagged my tail, and a slight breeze seemed to push through the barriers between where I am now and the old place. Hayley felt the air move and smiled.

"I hope he's warm and comfortable, and his aches and pains are gone."

My new friend, the other dog in this pink-tinged and warm field, put his head against mine and said, "Look after them Fido."

ABOUT THE AUTHOR

John Bobin describes himself as an accidental author. His father, paternal grandfather and maternal great-grandfather were all writers. He is a veteran bass-guitarist, having started playing in 1960. He is a keen cyclist and loves his dogs. He lives in Rayleigh, Essex in England.